D0317084

DEBI ALPER

TRADING TATIANA

Weidenfeld & Nicolson

LONDON

First published in Great Britain in 2004
by Weidenfeld & Nicolson

© Debi Alper 2004

All rights reserved. No part of this publication may be
reproduced, stored in a retrieval system, or transmitted,
in any form or by any means, electronic, mechanical,
photocopying, recording or otherwise, without the
prior permission of both the copyright owner and
the above publisher.

The right of Debi Alper to be identified as the author
of this work has been asserted by her in accordance
with the Copyright, Designs and Patents Act 1988.

A CIP catalogue record for this book
is available from the British Library.

ISBN 0 297 82991 2

Typeset at the Spartan Press Ltd,
Lymington, Hants

Printed in Great Britain by
Clays Ltd, St Ives plc

Weidenfeld & Nicolson
An imprint of the Orion Publishing Group
Orion House, 5 Upper St Martin's Lane,
London WC2H 9EA

This one's for Greg.

Acknowledgements

Nothing happens in a vacuum. Without the constructive and loving input of many people, you wouldn't be reading this now. I would like to thank the following: my partner, Greg Kat, for his indefatigable efforts on my behalf; my father, Morris Alper, for unquestioningly celebrating everything I do; Angie Lee, my email critic and confidence booster; the East Dulwich Writers' Group, source of so much inspiration, for their continuing support; NK, for help with research; all those at Weidenfeld & Nicolson who have been involved with the book; all my other family members and friends who have shared my dreams; and finally, my children, Joe and Jacob, who do so much more for me than simply going to bed and giving me space.

Prologue

Tatiana's bare feet thudded on the pier's wooden planks. A chill wind whipped her hair into her face. Her red crop top and micro skirt provided little protection. But she was running too fast to notice.

She pushed her way through the milling crowds, her ears assailed by the cacophony of noise blasting from arcade games, speakers and amusement rides, and by the screams of terror and delight from people experiencing the gravity-death combination that exemplifies a good funfair. Voices clamoured in a dozen different languages and seagulls screeched in their own. Yet louder than all these to Tatiana were the sounds of her own ragged breathing and pounding heart.

She didn't know. She didn't know that the only way off the pier was the way she had come on to it. Forward planning was a luxury she couldn't afford. She reached the end of the pier with a despairing wail. Fighting her way through the mass of people, she did a u-turn round the trampolines. And almost collided with Viktor. The brothers had split up and would trap her like an eyebrow hair in tweezers.

Tatiana wheeled round, heading back the way she had come. She could see Georgi advancing on her. She waited until there were only half a dozen people between them, knowing Viktor would be closing in from behind. She was close enough to see the triumphant smile on Georgi's face when, without warning, she turned sharp right, ran straight up some shallow steps and across the dodgems' arena. Darting between the hurtling bumper cars, she avoided collisions by a hair's breadth. The men inside the ticket booth yelled out and raced to join the pack already hunting her. Tatiana was too fast for them, but they had enough time to prevent Georgi and Viktor from taking the same route, buying her a few precious seconds. But she was tiring now. It had been a long time since she had run anywhere. Her legs had turned rubbery, and she staggered forwards under her own momentum.

A low black and white building loomed in front of her. Thanks to Georgi's insistence that she learn English, she could read the sign outside. 'Ladies'.

They were close behind her again. She lurched round the side of the building and in through the door. See? No forward planning.

A dead end on a dead end.

1

I WAS USED to things that went bump in the night. I lived in Boddington Heights. A crumbling, stinking slice of hell in the heart of the beast that is the Old Kent Road. Violent arguments between so-called lovers, parents and children, dealers and dealt-to were daily occurrences. Police busts were regular.

My strategy for blocking out other people's dramas was well-established. In order to prevent myself hearing something I would find impossible to ignore, I would turn the TV or stereo to full volume if I was still up. Bury my head deeper into the pillow if I wasn't.

But the commotion I heard in the early hours of that particular damp May night evaded my usual tactics.

For starters, I'd just switched off the TV, so the clanking of the ascending lift's gears sounded louder in the sudden silence. As did the assorted bumps, thumps and curses that followed the opening of the lift doors on my floor. I brushed my teeth to the accompaniment of footsteps clattering on the iron staircase on the other side of my bathroom wall. I gazed at the dolphin transfers on the wall tiles, studiously ignoring what could only be the sound of someone forcing the padlock on the trapdoor to the roof. The metallic crashing of something bouncing down the stairs made me jump, but I didn't allow it to interrupt my flossing routine.

I hummed loudly and covered my ears with my hands as I wandered round the flat switching off lights and checking that the front door was secured by both bolt and chain.

But I still couldn't drown out the thuds, groans and grunts of exertion as something heavy was dragged up the stairs to the roof.

Merciful silence resumed as I went over to my bedroom window and closed out the darkness and the drizzle behind plum-coloured velvet curtains. I snuggled under the duvet. Something was happening on the roof. But it was none of my business. And now it no longer intruded on my senses, it was easy to ignore.

The lull didn't last long. Just long enough to allow me to drift towards sleep. A shriek pierced the darkness, followed by a fearsome clanking that sounded like a ship weighing anchor. I shot upright as something thudded against my window. The shoddy double glazing (one of the council's much vaunted 'improvements') shuddered in protest, but by a miracle it withstood the force. A panic-stricken voice gibbered in terror three paces from where I sat, naked and trembling in my bed.

Given what I've said about Boddington Heights, you might be forgiven for thinking such an occurrence would not be unique. Except that I lived on the top floor. Of a twenty-storey block.

I leapt from my bed and crossed to the window. Steeling myself, I pulled the curtains about a foot apart. And almost immediately yanked them shut again. I staggered back into the room, shaking my head in disbelief and wheezing for breath. This wasn't possible. It couldn't be happening. It had to be some weird kind of delayed hallucination. A throwback to my smackhead days. The wilderness years.

I was shivering uncontrollably. I pulled on a baggy sweatshirt from the chair at the end of the bed and forced my unwilling feet back to the window.

This time I only opened the curtains a chink. Enough to confirm that it wasn't me who was insane. Just the situation. So that was OK then. I suppose most people would be more terrified knowing that what they were seeing was really happening. But not me. My big fear is insanity. Everything else comes a long way behind.

A man, wearing something black and shiny, glistened in the rain outside the window. He was suspended by one ankle, hanging upside down and face out. The view over the sleeping city, even on cloudy nights, is spectacular. But I doubted if my companion out there appreciated it.

A pair of white buttocks, protruding from a cut-away section in his skintight suit, was pressed against the glass, like a child's face squashed against a toy-shop window. Red stripes crisscrossed their compressed surface. I gazed at them, fascinated.

His voice, muffled by the double glazing, was clear in intent if not content. This was one seriously scared bare-botty man.

So what should I have done? Call the cops? No way. I don't have the kind of relationship with the police where you actively initiate contact. Anyway, for all I knew, Mr Dangly Stripe Bum might be a serial killer. Or a paedophile. Perhaps what I was witnessing was a version of rough justice. But not necessarily less just than that meted out by the legal institutions in this country.

I cocked my head on one side and contemplated the buttocks pressed against my window one last time, before flicking the curtains shut with a decisive swish and returning to bed.

Sleep was impossible knowing that if it wasn't for the glass in my windows I could have reached over, parted the curtains and dabbed Savlon on the sore arse of a man suspended upside down, 250 feet above ground level. I sat up and smoked a fag, using the inhalations to keep my breathing deep and even. I recited song lyrics in my head to phase out the gibbering outside. This wasn't my crisis. I didn't have to allow it to affect me.

Interminable minutes later I heard the screeching of metal on metal, accompanied by a squelching noise as the buttocks slid up my window. Not long after, I heard footsteps on the iron stairs coming back down from the roof.

I tiptoed to my front door and pressed my eye to the spy hole. Two people swam into my fisheye view. One of them stabbed the lift button. The doors shuddered open and they stepped in and turned round to face me. Their distorted faces shone sickly green in the fluorescent light: a woman, slightly built with spiky hair, wearing a mini skirt and corset under a tight leather jacket, and a good-looking Asian guy. The woman seemed to be bruised down one side of her face. I ground my eye into the spy hole. The lift doors were shutting, but I could see something on the man's forehead. At first I assumed it was a scar or a birthmark. But then my wobbly vision made it out just as the doors slammed shut. It was an A inside a circle. An Anarchist symbol.

My curiosity was piqued. They weren't what I was expecting. Whatever that was. And what had happened to Mr Dangly Man? I gave myself a mental slap and repeated my mantra. Not my business . . . Not my business . . .

I carried on repeating it as I pulled on jeans, trainers and cagoule. What is it about me? Why can't I learn not to interfere? No one in the other three flats on my floor felt the urge. The couple who lived opposite would probably have been indulging in their only obvious pastime – extreme S&M sex. Unless of course one or the other of them had been recently sectioned, as was frequently the case. The newly arrived Somali couple would be too scared. They only ever opened their door to pass in or out and infrequently at that. A bunch of lads lived in the fourth flat. I'd never been able to work out their scene, but they were out until the early hours most nights.

I unbolted, unchained and unlocked my front door. All the time refusing to ask the obvious question: What was the point of all this security if I walked straight through it and into the exact unknown danger it was supposed to protect me from? I clicked open the latch, and pulled the door towards me by the letter box so that it would appear to be shut unless it was pushed. By me. In a hurry.

My heart thudded louder than my footsteps as I climbed the iron staircase. The trapdoor leading to the roof was open. Drizzle slanted down from the square of black sky on to my upturned face. I emerged on to the roof – a square of flat concrete framing the lift motor housing in the centre. Massive arc lights at each corner warned low-flying aircraft and illuminated the desolate gloom.

A dark rain-sodden bundle lay by the roof edge, huddled in a foetal heap. At first I thought he was dead. Fighting the urge to run back down the stairs, I crept over to him. A distant siren floated upwards. I heard shouts and running feet. Car doors slamming. Drunken singing. Other people's lives. Mine was frozen on this roof. With this man.

A tiny sob and a groan issued from the heap. Not dead then, I thought. That's good. I suppose. There was a strong acidic smell. As I came closer, I realised my partner in this surreal tableau was lying in a pool of his own vomit. This was not a problem in itself. People with direct experience of Class A drugs get used to taking evacuated body fluids in their stride. What *was* a problem was what to do next. I'd got this far. I'd got dressed. I'd come up on the roof. I'd seen what was there. Now what?

'Um. Do you need help?'

It sounded lame. No, worse. It sounded really stupid. But it was the best I could do. In response, the bundle gibbered and curled up tighter.

'Please. Don't hurt me,' he whimpered.

'I'm not. I won't. I just . . .'

Well? What was I just . . . ? Just checking? Just being nosey? Just enjoying the night air?

'. . . I just wondered if you were OK . . .'

The bundle shifted and turned over to face me. The white face, ghostly pale in the unforgiving arc light, looked up at me with surprise. Or maybe it was disbelief at the stupidity of the question I had just asked. He was middle-aged with dark, floppy hair. Close up I could see that the suit he was wearing was made of skintight black leather. He was lying on his arse, which was probably just as well. I'd seen as much of it as I could handle for one night. He was staring at me with an intensity I found uncomfortable. What had I got myself into this time?

His voice, when it came, was surprisingly even and calm.

'Can you get me down from here?'

'Are you injured? Can't you walk?'

'Not with this on my ankle I can't,' he grunted.

I looked down and for the first time realised his foot was secured to the railing on the roof edge by a length of heavy chain. I squatted to get a closer look. The chain was attached to the railing by a device like a giant key ring. The other end was slotted through a pair of handcuffs attached to the man's ankle. There was no way I could undo the handcuffs, but the clamp device looked straightforward enough. My fingers fumbled with the wet metal.

'There you go,' I said, holding the chain aloft in triumph.

I wished he would stop staring at me. I was relieved when he heaved himself up into a sitting position and rubbed his ankle around the cuff. But then he swivelled his head again and resumed his appraising gaze.

I felt a flash of irritation. He was the one sitting there with a striped bare arse, handcuffs on his ankle and puke on his chin. I didn't have to be there at all. I turned back to the stairs.

'Please,' he urged. 'Please. You've got to help me.'

I stopped in my tracks.'

'Got to?'

'Please. I'll make it worth your while. Why did you come up here if not to help me?'

He had a good point there. I turned round.

'How can you make it worth my while? It doesn't look to me like you've got pockets in that outfit . . .'

'If you help me get out of here, I'll see you right. I swear.'

I hesitated. But then the same demon who had persuaded me to come up to the roof in the first place against my better judgement whispered in my ear. Why not? Well, actually I could think of a thousand reasons why not. But I ignored them all.

'Come on then. You'd better come down to my flat.'

2

THE STRANGER ON the roof hauled himself up on the low wall, grimacing with pain. He hobbled after me, side-stepping down the stairs, holding the chain attached to his ankle in one hand. Pushing open the door to my flat, I pointed him at the bathroom. Meanwhile, in true *EastEnders* style, I put the kettle on for a nice cup of tea. I splashed water over the teabags as my guest splashed water over himself. He emerged a few minutes later, wrapped in my towelling bathrobe. His skinny legs protruded from beneath the tattered hem. I stared at the handcuffs clamped to his ankle. It would have helped if I could've at least detached the chain . . .

'We need a hacksaw,' I murmured. 'I haven't got one. Sorry.'

He lowered himself, wincing, onto my threadbare settee and took the mug of steaming tea from me.

'I've put sugar in. It's good for shock . . .'

He acknowledged my combined canteen and first-aid skills with a nod.

I wasn't keen on the silence, broken only by the sounds of slurping and the jangling of the chain as his foot juddered on the floor with a nervous tic. I made an attempt at jaunty good humour, on the basis that sounding like a prat was better than making no sound at all.

'So. This is my home. Be it ever so humble. Welcome. My name's Jo, by the way. Jo Cooper.'

He nodded again and fixed me with his unsettling gaze.

'I think it would be best if you didn't know my name,' he said.

That was a bit of a conversation-stopper. We sipped our tea in silence, his eyes appraising me over the rim of his mug.

'If you don't mind me saying so, you don't sound like someone who would live here.'

He looked round my standard-issue local authority living room.

'By the way, where is "here"?'

I hate that. I hate it when people do that pigeonholing thing. And then get suspicious if you don't fit in with their narrow idea of how you're supposed to look or sound.

'Gor blimey, guv. Wot was you finkin?' I spat out. 'People wot live on council estates gotta speak like Dick Bloody Van Dyke in *Mary Poppins*? As it goes,' I said, resorting to my normal far-from-posh tones, 'my mother was an artist. Very middle-class. I had what you would probably call a "good education". You shouldn't go making assumptions about people based solely on where they live, you know. And by the way, where we are is Boddington Heights. That big road you were dangling over is the Old Kent Road.'

I was babbling and I knew it. He was supposed to act like the grateful recipient of my Good Samaritan routine. He wasn't playing his role right.

'Can I make a phone call?'

I tossed him my mobile. I don't have a land line any more. I have a horror of bills, so pay-as-you-go suits me down to the ground.

I took the mugs back into the kitchen and pretended not to listen. Not that there was anything interesting to hear.

'Hi. It's me. I've had a spot of trouble. Can you come and get me? I'm at some place called Boddington Heights. It's some hellish high rise off the Old Kent Road.'

Pause.

'Yeah.'

Pause.

'I'll tell you when I see you. How long before you get here? OK . . . Yeah . . . I'll give you this number. You can ring me when you're downstairs.'

I called out the number, thereby ruining any pretence that I hadn't been eavesdropping.

My guest spent the next twenty minutes gazing at my goldfish as they drifted in their bowl on the window sill.

'They're called Moby and Dick,' I volunteered.

'People say goldfish have no memory,' he mused.

I wasn't sure if he was talking to himself or to me. Or to the fish.

'But there's no way to know for sure. Maybe people just want to believe that so they can justify keeping them in bowls with a few coloured stones as their only entertainment.'

I took this as an implicit criticism. I didn't like this man. And I didn't like the way he made me feel. I was relieved when the phone rang. And then irritated when he picked it up. It was my phone after all. Even if it was two in the morning. There was no guarantee the call would be for him.

It was, of course. I told him he could keep the bathrobe. I couldn't face the idea of watching his stripy buttocks walking out my front door. I gave him a carrier bag for his own gear. He didn't even say goodbye.

The next day a package was delivered addressed to Ms J. Cooper. Inside was the softest, fluffiest bathrobe I'd ever laid eyes on. In the pocket was £500 in £20 notes.

3

THERE WAS A time when, if I'd had that much cash in my hands, I'd have been round Solo's to score enough smack to be wasted for weeks. Two years down the line and five hundred quid in cash in my no longer trembling hand, the choices were mercifully wider.

I suppose I ought to go back a bit and explain how this well-educated daughter of a middle-class artist came to have a serious drugs habit and be living in Boddington Heights in the first place. Well, I lied about the 'good education' bit. Unless you count University of Life stuff. My mother may have spent her formative years in Dulwich. But I spent mine in Peckham. Which illustrates what a difference a few streets and a different postcode can make.

Mum was a hippy chick. A flower child of the sixties. Except I never called her Mum. She was always Des. Short for Desiree. I never met her (and therefore my) family, who disowned her when she took to the road in a psychedelic camper van with some fellow travellers she met at Glastonbury. They spent a couple of acid-fuelled years going round the free festivals selling the weird sculptures Des created from natural materials.

She ended up in a commune squatting in a rhododendron forest in Cornwall, living off the land and the dream. That's where I was conceived and born when the dropout sixties had rolled into the radical seventies. I've no idea who my father was. If Des knew, she never told me.

When they were driven off the land, the commune fragmented. Some went straight – or sold out, as Des would say when she was feeling bitter. Others couldn't hack the transition and ended up homeless and/or crazy. I suppose I was the reason Des didn't go down that road. She arrived back in London and went straight to Southwark Council's Homeless Persons' Unit. The Happy Families Unit, she used to call it. In spite of their many attempts to force her to find her own solution to her crisis, she used the confident assertiveness that comes from a middle-class upbringing and refused to budge. We slept on a friend's floor at night and spent every weekday at the unit until they were sick of the sight of us.

I was four at the time. I have vague memories of the numbing hours spent in that soulless place filled with tears, stress and suitcases.

They told Des that as someone who was homeless, she was deemed to be desperate, and would be made only one offer of housing. She couldn't turn it down for any but the most extreme reasons. They gave her a printed list of what these reasons might be. Damp and infestation were not included.

We ended up on the Aylesbury Estate. As far a cry from Cornish rhododendron forests as you can get. And then the Thatcherite eighties did for Des. She couldn't get over the elevation of greed to the status of a virtue, and a predominant mindset that equated altruism with stupidity. She made few friends on the estate, where her accent and flowing Bohemian clothes were viewed with suspicion. She became mired in depression, punctuated with manic highs, during which she would try to become the Bestest Mother in the World to make up for her emotional absence the rest of the time.

I treasured those highs, when I would catch glimpses of the young, idealistic Des, and could recognise for a moment the woman captured in the black and white photos framed on the mantelpiece. Her intuitive creativity would come to the fore and she would make wonderful games and construct surreal models out of toilet rolls, egg boxes and cartons. Taking up all our limited floor space, they made the childish attempts of *Blue Peter* presenters look unimaginative and bland by comparison. I wrung every last drop of pleasure out of these times, knowing they would end all too soon.

I learned to survive. I'd make excuses for Des when she failed to turn up for parents' evenings or prize-givings. I developed a fantasy life that was the scourge of my teachers, who were unable to convince me that the truth was not negotiable. Until I was old enough to meet friends outside school, I never went to other kids' homes, knowing that I wouldn't be able to reciprocate.

Des died when I was eighteen. She fell on the tube tracks at Elephant and Castle. Or jumped. The inquest recorded an open verdict. I'm not sure how much difference it makes. Either way, she left me.

The council repossessed the flat. I was told I no longer needed two bedrooms and was rehoused in Boddington Heights. They made me feel like they were doing me a favour. If I had heard of someone else being treated in this callous manner, I would have been beating down the council's door in protest. Boddington Heights was a notorious dumping ground. Housing a distressed and vulnerable teenager there was tantamount to manslaughter.

But it didn't happen to someone else. It happened to me. So I just accepted it. I've always been better at championing other people's causes.

The downward spiral into addiction was inevitable.

4

I STARED AT the money. I knew exactly what I was going to do with it. I counted out five twenties and put them to one side. That was for fun. The rest of it I could put towards an idea that had been growing in the back of my mind for some time.

When I came off the smack I decided to go the whole hog and come off the equally addictive Social at the same time. I had a regular cleaning and gardening job in leafy Dulwich – where they can afford to pay someone else to do the work they don't want to. I also ran a weekend stall called Wax Lyrical in Greenwich Market for Smokey Pete. That was where my investment opportunity lay.

Pete made candles. No, Pete *created* candles. He lived in a two-bedroom flat in New Cross, where he slaved over vats of hot wax ten hours a day. The flat was paid for by a trust fund set up by his wealthy parents, who had died when Pete was in his late teens. The candles were his life's work and its purpose. Pete was agoraphobic. Since the external world was denied to him, he devoted his substantial energies to his internal one. The candles were exquisite creations of swirling colour and shape. He'd advertised in *Time Out* a couple of years earlier, just when I was looking for new directions: '*Practical help needed by agoraphobic candle maker looking to expand his horizons.*'

I'd gone round and been mesmerised by the multi-coloured curtains in his room, formed by candles suspended by their wicks from string that criss-crossed the ceiling like a web made by a spider on acid. You had to negotiate routes through them every time you moved, but that didn't bother me. They radiated beauty and soul and so much that was missing on the streets outside. If I could have created candles like that, I think I might have quite liked to be agoraphobic too. Pete and I clicked straight off. He was a bit weird, I suppose. But who am I to talk? Since that first meeting, I had become his link with the outside world, doing his shopping and running the market stall.

Anyway, I had creative instincts too. I was my mother's daughter, after all. I would use my unexpected windfall to buy wire, beads, clasps and tools. For ages I'd imagined making jewellery and I had loads of ideas for designs. I could sell them on the stall. I was sure Pete wouldn't mind. There would still be enough money left over to pay the rent and stock up on depleted essentials. Potential was lurking in the near future. Amazing what a difference a few hundred quid could make.

I stashed the cash and prepared to embark on organising the fun factor. I grabbed my mobile and keys and ran down the needle-bottle-and-condom-strewn stairs to a flat five floors below. Maureen opened the door looking every bit as glamorous as usual. She must be well into her fifties, but she's a living bonking advert for hormone replacement therapy. She oozes sex from every pore. I've never seen her without full make-up. I reckon she must sleep in the stuff. She was dressed in her standard everyday attire of tight lycra top with plunging neck-line, miniscule skirt, high heels and rubber gloves. Her glossy blonde hair teased at her perma-tanned shoulders as she leaned over in a Givenchy cloud to peck me on the cheek.

'Oh hi, love. C'mon in. I'm just doin' the bathroom.'

Maureen was always 'just doing' something in the heavy-duty cleaning line. She could seek out dirt in corners no one else would have known existed. Then she'd blast it to a grime afterlife with noxious quantities of ozone-depleting products. I suspected she was single-handedly responsible for inflicting more environmental damage on our beleaguered planet than all the chemical corporations in America put together.

It seemed her granddaughter, Kirsty, agreed with me on that point. Kirsty, aged twelve, and her younger sister, Delilah, lived with Maureen. Their mother, Lisa, lived with several hundred other women in a large building in Holloway.

'Bloody 'ell,' Maureen was saying, 'I only asked 'er to go and buy me some bleach. Anyone would think I sent 'er out for nuclear warheads.'

'Shit, Mo! What's that?' I gasped as we walked into her front room. It was a carbon copy of my own except that it was furnished in fifties suburban (flock wallpaper and lots of chintz) and much, much cleaner.

It also contained the biggest bunch of flowers I've ever seen. They engulfed the polished wood table and filled the room with a smell so pungent you could taste it.

Maureen beamed.

'They're from 'im. Me new bloke. Calvin.'

'The one from the minicab office?'

' 'E's not just *from* the minicab office, love. 'E *owns* it,' Maureen boasted. ' 'Ere. Take a look at this.'

She peeled back the Marigold from her left wrist to expose a classy-looking watch. I peered at the tiny writing on its face.

'Cartier? Blimey, Mo. Where'd he knock that off?'

'Oooh, you're just jealous, you bitch,' Maureen teased. 'Calvin is straight as a ruler.' She snorted. 'And nearly as long, which is more important if you ask me.'

'How old is he?'

'Thirty-seven. Older than what I'm used to, but I thought a more mature man might be good for me.'

'Mature? Christ, he's still young enough to be your . . .'

'Shut it, Jo! Don't say it. I'm warning you . . .'

Maureen wagged an admonishing finger in my face. I pretended to bite it and we both burst out laughing.

I told Mo about my rooftop encounter and my surprise windfall. She had a laugh at the stripy buttocks, a go at me for getting involved in a potentially dangerous situation and then made me an offer of a cup of tea to celebrate. In turn, I told her about my plans for the hundred pounds I'd put aside for a celebration a bit more stimulating than one that would fit in a cup with some skimmed milk.

'Brighton?'

'Yeah. We can all go on the train. Fish and chips on the pier and enough goes on the dodgems to inflict permanent damage on our spinal columns.'

Mo thought it was a great idea. With one small alteration. She stared at her tea for longer than was necessary and gave me a sly look from the corner of her eye.

'If you was to go with the girls on your own . . . next week, say, when they're on half term . . . And then maybe they could stop the night with you . . . that would leave me free to . . .' She gave a coquettish tweak to her eyebrows and lips.

'. . . shag Calvin's brains out,' I finished for her.

'Exactly. So that's settled then, yeah?'

Of course it was.

5

THE TRAIN JOURNEY from Victoria to Brighton passed pre-dictably enough. Delilah never stopped chattering. Kirsty communicated – if you can call it that – in monosyllabic grunts pushed out from between stiff lips.

Don't ask me what Delilah talked about. I tend to screen it out. But it doesn't matter, as she seems not to expect – or need – any response. Delilah gets by on sheer charm and being stunningly pretty. She'd managed fine in her ten years so far, though I some-times wondered how she'd cope in a situation that might demand more practical skills. Her father, Dwayne, is a gym instructor at Peckham Pulse Leisure Centre and Delilah has inherited his athletic prowess, infectious good humour and laid-back attitude to life. Unfortunately, Dwayne's laid-backness also extends to the parenting department. But then Delilah did have to share him with his three other children in three different parts of the borough.

Still, at least Dwayne was on the scene and in his daughter's life. Which was more than could be said for Kirsty's father. Poor Kirsty is a different kettle of hormones altogether. She was conceived in a real-life behind-the-bikesheds encounter when Lisa was fifteen. It's impossible to say who her dad was, beyond the certainty that he was one of a small army of spotty youths who had coughed up fifty pence for the fumbled pleasure of offloading their adolescent spunk.

Kirsty had been bypassed in the charm stakes. And she hadn't even been in the queue when cute and pretty were distributed. Puberty had not improved matters. Always doughy and ungainly, she now had to contend with a growth spurt that had seen her overtake me by two inches in height and two shoe sizes, as well as introducing her to the delights of spots and lank, greasy hair. As if this wasn't enough, a baleful deity had landed her with teeth that required more metal to straighten them than you'd get in the average-sized family car.

I loved Kirsty. I loved them both, of course, but I saved my special affection for Kirsty. I loved the way she wore her plainness with defiant pride. And I also loved her for not hating Delilah. She had no great intellect to balance her lack of other attributes. No creativity, sharp wit, vivid imagination or other obvious skills that might oil the wheels of her life. But she was solid, loyal and loving. And she had a laugh – more precious for its rarity – that was like music.

We piled off the train at Brighton and made our way straight to the pier. We waded through crowds of day trippers and tourists to the amusement arcade, where we were bombarded by the noise of hundreds of machines choking on thousands of coins. Kirsty and Delilah took turns on simulated racetracks, motorbikes, snow boards and fighter planes, and indulged in every type of armed combat imaginable. I held back on the pacifist lectures. They knew how I felt. Kirsty had given me a questioning look before settling into the seat of a spaceship and blasting legions of unsuspecting Martians into techno oblivion. But I'd smiled encouragement at her. And even congratulated her on her 'kill' score. That's how bloody nice I can be.

We headed for the caff before they eliminated any more species. The girls were amazed that we were going to eat inside at real tables, off real plates with real forks.

'Yep,' I told them. 'No styrofoam containers and wooden stabbers today, guys. Just go easy on the fizzy drinks. We'll check out the funfair after. We don't want any messy accidents.'

As we left the café, Delilah skipped ahead and Kirsty rewarded me with a laugh and an arm linked through mine.

'Thanks, Jo,' she mumbled through her mouthful of metal. 'This is brill.' I glowed with satisfaction. It doesn't take much to make kids happy. Love will do it. But a few quid helps a lot too.

It may seem unwise to hit the funfair with stomachs filled with overloaded platefuls of saturated fat, but that's what we did next. I kept my feet firmly planted on the pier's wooden planks while Kirsty and Delilah looped the loop on the roller coaster, swooped over the sea in seats attached to the narrowest of chains, defied death in flimsy inverted bucket contraptions, bounced on trampolines and shrieked their way round the ghost train. I joined in when we got to the dodgems, where we created metal mayhem in every conceivable combination. Kirsty and I rammed Delilah. Delilah and Kirsty took revenge in a savage broadside on me. Delilah and I chased Kirsty. Then we took three separate cars and went for an all out demolition derby.

We staggered out of the arena on wobbly legs, having inflicted enough damage on our skeletons to keep an osteopath in business for a year. My throat was sore from yelling and my head was throbbing from the maelstrom of noise raging around us and the buffeting of the omnipresent wind of Brighton's seafront. Twenty different types of music pounded from assorted rides and speakers, punters shouted in thirty different languages. Screams of terror, whoops of delight and the shrieks of seagulls assaulted my ears. The frying onions from the hot dog stand combined with the burning flesh from the hog roast and the syrup sweetness of the crepes to create an olfactory stew seasoned with sea salt. I felt nauseous and giddy from the sensory overload.

I felt a tugging at the sleeve of my denim jacket.

'You OK?' yelled Kirsty into my ear. I nodded assent and attempted a smile. There was a tug on my other sleeve.

'I need a pee,' Delilah shouted. I turned to Kirsty.

'Me too,' she giggled.

We headed off to the toilets. I can't speak for the gents', but the ladies' loos on Brighton pier are a wonder to behold and a haven of noise- and wind-free tranquility. Victorian confections of dark wood and gleaming tilework set off sparkly surfaces that would have even impressed Maureen.

The girls went straight into the cubicles, while I splashed water on my face at sinks so white they hurt my eyes. I leaned on the edge of the basin and gazed at my reflection. A bit pale but not too bad. I'd seen far worse in mirrors. I ran my fingers through my hair and tied it with an elastic band, creating a semblance of order. As my equilibrium gradually returned, I became aware of the other women reflected in the mirror: hustling children, washing hands, blasting them under dryers before giving up and wiping them on their legs.

One woman in particular drew my attention. Mainly because she was doing none of the above. She stood in the corner by the door, her back against the wall. I assumed she was waiting for someone. The longer I looked, the more she intrigued me. I'd thought at first glance she was in her late twenties or early thirties. But as I looked closer I could see she was younger. Much younger. The illusion had been created by a layer of thick make-up applied with an unskilled hand. She wore a micro skirt and a red crop top. Her shoulder-length blonde curls were another illusion – her natural hair colour was evidenced by dark roots and eyebrows. Her feet were bare and she was waif thin. And she was scared.

Once I registered what I was seeing, I couldn't take my eyes off her reflection in the mirror. Her bird-like chest rose and fell with rapid breaths. She was wringing her hands so hard it must have hurt. Every so often, she closed her eyes and leaned her head back against the tiles, her lips moving in what looked like silent prayer.

I couldn't help it. By the time Kirsty and Delilah came out of their cubicles, I was already in front of the girl.

'Are you OK?' I asked in a low voice.

Her head jerked forward and she fixed me with eyes so full of terror I felt a stab of pain in my chest. I clasped my hands around hers.

'What is it? It's OK. What's wrong?'

I was dimly aware of other women passing us, looking at us with undisguised curiosity and in some cases suspicion.

'Oh, please,' she breathed, her eyes pleading. 'I have to get away.' She spoke with a strong accent I couldn't place.

'Away? Where to?' I queried, confused. I could sense Kirsty and Delilah fidgeting behind me, but they would have to wait.

'Away,' was the not very illuminating reply. 'Away from men . . .'

This wasn't easy, but I couldn't abandon her now.

'Men in general? Or some in particular?'

'Men,' she repeated. 'Out there.' She cocked her head towards the exit. 'Very bad. Very dangerous.'

Oh, great. Wouldn't you know it?

OK. Jo Cooper to the rescue. Again. This was getting to be a habit. Maybe it's like some kind of chain reaction. You help one person. And that puts you in a position to decide if you're prepared to help another. And another. Perhaps I was being tested. Perhaps I was trying to restore the balance against all those people who had turned away and pretended not to see when I'd needed help. One thing was definite, I'd gone into those toilets to wash the sweat and grime from my hands. But I couldn't wash my hands of this vulnerable young woman by walking away.

'Can you tell me how many men? And what they look like?'

In response she dug her hand into an embroidered bag slung over one shoulder and rummaged until she found a small plastic wallet. She pulled out a tiny square photo taken in one of those booths and held it out with trembling fingers that ended in savagely bitten nails. Two faces gazed out at me from the photo. One was hers. She was looking directly at the camera and smiling. Her arm was round the shoulder of a man whose lap she was sitting on. He was older – late thirties, I guessed – with short, dark hair, high cheekbones and penetrating eyes. He was not smiling.

'He is one,' she whispered. 'The other is his brother. They look a little same.'

I didn't have to think too hard about whose side I was on. No matter what she might have done or what the story was. One terrified young girl and two heavy-looking blokes. No contest. I took the photo from her and showed it to the girls.

'Right. Listen carefully. I want one of you to go out and walk round the toilets and back in again from the other side. See if you can spot these guys, but don't draw any attention to yourself. I just want to know where they are.'

Delilah jumped up and down, pulling at my hand.

'Me. Me. Oh, please, Jo. Let me do it. Please.'

Not drawing attention to herself was not Delilah's style. Kirsty was far better suited to the job.

'Can you do it, babe?' I asked.

Kirsty gave a confident nod.

'Sure. Back in a mo.'

She straightened her shoulders, took a deep breath and walked out of the door.

I handed the photo back and the girl replaced it with studious care. I noticed she never looked at it, though.

What was this girl's story? Where was she from? And what was she so afraid of? I wanted to ask, but felt it wouldn't be fair to put pressure on her. It would look as though I was demanding something in return. I didn't want her to feel my help was conditional: I save your life, you satisfy my curiosity.

I could feel Delilah's suppressed excitement beside me.

'It's OK, Dee. Don't worry. You'll get your chance to perform,' I reassured her.

We didn't have long to wait. Kirsty returned, a little flushed and breathless.

'Saw 'em straight off,' she said. 'On the corner there, by the quad bikes. They're a bit creepy. Just standin' there, starin' at the door. I don't think they noticed me,' she added with pride at a job well done.

I gave her an encouraging squeeze and outlined my plan to the three of them. Nothing elaborate. The best plans are the simplest. I made sure the girl understood. She gave a little moan, but nodded.

Just as we were going out of the door, she grabbed my hand. She had a tight grip for someone who looked so frail.

'You are good person,' she breathed.

Which was all the thanks I needed.

As soon as we turned the corner from the door, I saw them. They were standing, nonchalant yet alert, in the right angle formed by the edge of the pier and the fence overlooking the quad bikes. The sea stretched, choppy and grey, behind them. Their eyes were trained on the toilet entrance, but they looked straight through us as we walked towards them. The shorter one I recognised from the photo. He was wearing a navy tracksuit and smoking a cigarette. Next to him was his brother, older and chunkier and sporting a mullet imported direct from the seventies. He was wearing a worn leather jacket and jeans.

I only had half a dozen steps to take this in before we drew level with them in the narrow space between the pier rail and the toilet block. I heard a nervous giggle from Delilah behind me over the roar of the quad bikes.

My heart pounding, I barged into Junior, knocking him off balance.

'Oi!' I yelled. 'What d'you think you're doing? You thieving bastard. Get your fucking hand out of my pocket.' My voice was cracking with a cocktail of fear and nerves, but it probably did no harm.

Junior recovered his balance and spat some words at me in fury. It was no doubt just as well that I didn't understand any of them. Both brothers began shouting together at each other and at me. All the while they were jostling and hopping to maintain sight of the toilet door. Behind me, Delilah set up a melodramatic wail to add to the bedlam. Behind *her*, I knew Kirsty would be taking up her position. Doing her best to use her substantial bulk to block their view.

Delilah was totally over the top. Her acting was so appalling she could have got a job on *EastEnders*.

'No! No!' she screamed. 'Don't take our money. It's all we have. Oh, what'll we do? What'll we do-o-o-o?'

I was still yelling too, but I risked a glance back and saw the girl duck out of the toilet and run in the opposite direction.

Little and Large must have seen her too. Now we were more than just an annoyance. The stakes had been upped. Junior gave me a shove that threw me against the toilet wall. The brothers made to run away from us, round the other side of the building to cut her off.

They were too quick. They would catch her. I used the ricochet from the wall to throw myself forward in an attempt to block them, with the certain knowledge that I had no chance. We'd failed.

I waited for the blow that would knock me aside, but it didn't come. Instead, a massive hand shot over my shoulder and slammed into Junior's chest, pinning him against the rail and trapping his brother in the corner. The hand seemed impossibly huge and was attached to a matching arm, smothered in tattoos blurred under a forest of ginger hair. Three gold rings, the size of babies' heads, decorated the fingers. A gold link bracelet that would have done me as a belt hung from the wrist.

The brothers had both paled.

'No. No. Is mistake,' Junior blathered.

I looked over my shoulder. The arm was attached to an awesome body. The man was stripped to the waist. His trousers hung low to accommodate a pendulous paunch. Most of his visible body surface was covered in tattoos. And as he was over six foot with a massive girth, that's an awful lot of skin. In spite of the wind whipping in from the sea, sweat glistened on the top of his shaved head. A cross the size of an anchor hung round his neck. His blue eyes were paler than the late spring sky.

He turned them to me.

'These blokes givin' you trouble, love?' he growled.

An unlikely saviour, but I had to think fast. I had to buy time, but I also couldn't let this escalate too far.

Delilah launched her bid for centre stage with a banshee wail, but I silenced her with a hiss.

'Let me handle this, Dee.' I turned back to the Incredible Bulk. 'I think he tried to nick my wallet . . .'

'No! Is not true!' gibbered Junior, his brother miming shocked denial beside him.

'We no thief. We no want your money. Look,' he said by way of explanation. 'We no need money. We have.' He pulled a thick wad of notes from his pocket and waved them at us. Big mistake. I could have told him.

Bulk eased me to one side. I flattened myself against the toilet wall to allow him access to his quarry. He grabbed Junior by the elastic waistband of his trackie bottoms and performed a simultaneous twist and lift, raising him, squealing, to his toes.

'Where'd you get all that then? Eh? How many fuckin' pockets you pick to get that lot? Don't worry, love.' He turned his face to me, while keeping those impossibly blue eyes trained on his squirming victims. 'We know how to take care of their sort.'

Far enough. Back off. I didn't know what Little and Large had done to terrify that girl so badly. But I wasn't about to be a party to them being pulverised on the flimsy grounds that they were foreign and therefore shouldn't have any money. More importantly, I reckoned enough time had passed for the girl to get off the pier and disappear to wherever she was headed.

'Oh shit! No!' I injected horror into my voice. It wasn't hard. 'I can't believe it. Look!' I pulled my wallet out from the pocket furthest away from the men and held it up with the flourish of a conjurer producing a rabbit. 'It was in my other pocket. Oh, I'm so sorry. I thought he'd nicked it. What an idiot I am. I'm really sorry . . .' Then, when Bulk showed no sign of backing down, 'Um – you can let him go now . . .'

The Brothers Grim rolled their eyes in confusion and fear. And in Junior's case, pain. Bulk looked suspicious. Or maybe just disappointed.

'Yeah. But hang on, love,' he interjected. 'He still tried to dip you. He wasn't to know it was in the other pocket . . .'

'No, look. Really. It's OK. Thanks for your help. But I've got my money. No harm done. I'd rather just drop it . . .'

Bulk sighed. He gave one last twist to Junior's waistband before reluctantly releasing him.

'Sorry to put you to the trouble,' I simpered, still attempting a convincing conversion from Damsel in Distress to Embarrassed Prat.

'No trouble, love. No trouble at all. My pleasure.' I didn't doubt that for a moment.

He stood back to allow the brothers to scuttle past. I thanked him again and we moved off. Amazingly, even Delilah was silent. Shock, I think. It wouldn't last long. We sat on striped deck-chairs, next to three generations of an Asian family munching on samosas and pakora, to take stock and recover. The girls were aided by ice cream. I smoked three fags, one after the other.

After that, we agreed that we'd had enough of the pier for one day and decided to explore the Lanes. Just as we reached the concourse at the front of the pier, Junior appeared from behind a billboard where he must have been waiting.

'If I see you again,' he hissed in my ear, 'I kill you.'

That kind of took the shine off things. I hated to think I'd ruined the girls' day. I tried to sell it to them as part of the adventure, but they weren't fooled. Kids are not stupid, just because they've stacked up less experience. They still know danger when it leaps out at them from behind a billboard. We decided we'd seen enough of Brighton after all and headed straight for the station, with promises of popcorn and videos back home.

Once on the train, it didn't take Delilah long to recover. She resumed her normal incessant chatter. And the day had given her plenty of material. Somehow I didn't find it as easy as usual to screen her out. Kirsty looked pale, but said she was fine. It occurred to me I never had used the toilets on the pier for their usual function. I hate toilets on trains. It's like being locked in a claustrophobic cupboard. But I welcomed the opportunity to escape Delilah's high-volume monologue.

It was not to be. I swayed along the carriage, only to find the toilet door locked. Which was odd, as I was sure no one had gone in there since the train had started. Wasn't there some rule about not using the toilets when trains are in a station? I sat down in an empty seat, closest to the cubicle.

Minutes passed. There were only a couple of other people visible from where I sat. One was asleep and the other was immersed in a thick novel. I could still hear Delilah's voice, even though I was half a carriage away. Maybe the door was stuck. I strode over and tried the handle. The little bar stubbornly maintained its engaged status. I checked my watch. The train had left Brighton twenty minutes ago. I rapped on the flimsy door.

'Are you all right in there?'

People are notoriously circumspect about what happens when they pull their pants down. As if anyone does anything different to anyone else. The English are especially reserved and I was aware I was probably embarrassing whoever was inside.

On the other hand, I remember jacking up in a toilet once and passing out. Hours later, I found I'd been locked in. For the weekend. When I worked that little one out and decided it wasn't an option, I'd had to climb through a tiny cobwebby window and came crashing down into an open drain. Not pleasant.

As it turned out, the person inside the train toilet was

neither English nor a junkie. The handle turned. The door opened.

'You!' I gasped. And then watched in horror as the toilet's occupant burst into tears.

It seemed we were destined to meet in toilets. And once again I was destined not to avail myself of their facilities. I put my arm round her shoulders and guided her back to where Kirsty and Delilah sat watching open-mouthed as we lurched up the carriage towards them.

I gave the girls a fiver and told them to go off and find the trolley guy and buy whatever they wanted. I knew whatever it was would be guaranteed to rot teeth faster than heroin rots brains. But I reasoned that Kirsty's were protected by a suit of armour that would deter the most determined glucose molecule and Delilah could handle a little imperfection.

The girl's voice was so quiet and her accent so unfamiliar, I had to concentrate to hear her. And what I heard sent shivers down my spine. I was no stranger to sordid stories, but hers was unlike any I'd heard before.

She told me her name was Tatiana. She was seventeen. From the Ukraine. Her parents were both dead, killed in a car crash a couple of years before. The man in the photo was a friend of her father.

'He look after me,' she said.

He had been so kind. And not out of a sense of duty alone. Oh, no. He loved her, she assured me with defiant pride. He really did.

He loved her so much, he had smuggled her out of the Ukraine to England. They would have a good life together, he told her. Full of beautiful dresses and all the things a young girl like her could wish for. She was so pretty. So sweet. He would take care of her.

The long journey by truck scared her. She was from a small town. She'd never been further than Kiev before. But she was not afraid with Georgi by her side. Dealing with the authorities. Showing papers. Greasing palms. Protecting her. Guiding her. Loving her.

In London, they stayed with Georgi's brother, Viktor. She didn't go out much. The brothers would go off to do their business. She would stay in and watch TV and listen to the English language tapes Georgi brought her. So kind he was. So solicitous.

She didn't know what business they were in. She never asked. And they never said. Then one day Georgi came home. Very serious. Very sad. He sat her down and took her by the hands. Restricted by language, Tatiana acted out the voices for me, as though she was taking both parts in a stage play.

'Tatiana,' she said in a deep voice, impersonating Georgi. 'My dear sweet little bird. We have a problem. Viktor and I owe some money to people. They are bad people. Impatient. They will not wait. If they do not get their money they will hurt Georgi and Viktor very badly. Maybe they will even kill them. Tatiana will be left alone. The police will come. They will arrest her. Send her back to the Ukraine.'

Tatiana's voice and body language changed as she switched to the response she had given.

'Oh, Georgi. My love. My heart. This cannot happen. There must be some way we can find the money. I will work. There must be some job I could do.'

'Oh, Tatiana. Dearest child. You would do that for me? You would do that for your Georgi? I knew. I told Viktor we can rely on Tatiana. She is a good girl. So good. She will repay our kindness. She will show her love for us and by so doing she will save our lives.'

'Tell me, Georgi. Only tell me. What is it I have to do?'

Tatiana demonstrated Georgi caressing her hands. Stroking her cheek. Smoothing her hair from her brow. Then he told her what she had to do.

She recoiled in horror as she must have done at the time.

'Oh, no, my love. Not that. Please. There must be something else I can do to get the money. I will work hard. I am not afraid of hard work. But please do not ask me to do that.'

Tatiana mimed Georgi shaking his head sadly. No. There is nothing else. Just for a short time she will have to do this thing. Then she can stop. And they will be happy together again.

She told him she didn't know if she could do it. He shrugged. He understands, he said. He would hate her to have to do it. He only asked because he could think of no other way. But it is a hard thing to do. A hard thing for a woman to do for her man. He will try to persuade these men not to kill him. Maybe they will only beat him. Maybe scar him to teach him a lesson.

Tears trickled down Tatiana's cheeks as she told me what her fateful response had been:

'Oh, my darling Georgi. I cannot allow that to happen. I will do as you ask.'

And she did. Tatiana's voice dropped to a whisper. She was no longer acting out the parts. With shoulders slumped, she told me about the savage turn her life had taken from then on. Georgi and Viktor would bring men to the flat. One or two a week at first. Then one or two a night. Until Tatiana was servicing up to five men a night, seven nights a week.

Her pleas for an end to this existence were met with sadness and reproach at first. He still loved her. Even more than ever. Why could she not do this thing for him? Had he not always looked after her? She had a place to live, nice clothes, food – was this such a big thing to ask in exchange?

She never saw any money. She rarely went out of the flat. Further complaints were met with anger. She was selfish. She was rejecting him. After all he had done for her. She knew no one else in London. The thought of Georgi turning against her was more than she could bear. If she was lonely and terrified in the flat, how much more would she be if he threw her out to fend for herself?

I was riveted to my seat, barely aware of our surroundings. She was little more than a child, yet she'd experienced horrors no adult should have to bear. She carried on talking in a monotone, her eyes cast down.

Every day she cried and begged, she told me. She was so

unhappy. There must be another way. Then one day he hit her. Her incessant whining was getting him down, he said. It was only a slap on the cheek. But it changed everything. She lay in the bath and thought about her life. She still loved Georgi, in spite of everything. But she could see now, he didn't love her.

'My mother tell me once,' she said, 'that if a man hits you and gets away with it, he will hit you again. And again.'

When she came out of the bath, Georgi kissed her and stroked her reddened cheek. She was a good girl, he said. She had been working too hard. She needed a break. They would drive down to Brighton, themselves and Viktor. See the English seaside. Relax and have a day out. It would do them all good.

Tatiana, survival teaching her cunning now, agreed. And planned her escape. But her plans did not go beyond escaping. She had no money. She had nowhere to go. Knew no one. Had no one to turn to.

So there you have it. Tatiana's story. Would you turn your back on that?

6

DELILAH ACCEPTED THE new arrangements without a murmur. Well, that's not true of course. Murmuring is not in Delilah's oral repertoire. What I mean is, far from objecting, she adopted Tatiana with enthusiasm, snuggling up to her on my settee and engulfing her with her charms. Tatiana was the ideal recipient, compliant and mute, seemingly exhausted by her flight and subsequent emotional offloading. I didn't attempt to dampen Dee's attentions. Tatiana probably only understood a fraction of the verbal bombardment, but she seemed open to it. I had to remind myself she was closer in age to the girls than she was to me. And had been starved of company that wasn't male, older than her and naked.

I wasn't so sure about Kirsty. She was quiet, even by her own standards. I tried talking to her, but she refused to acknowledge there was anything wrong. I figured she might not be sure herself, so I left her space to experience whatever it was. Maybe Tatiana was just one pretty person too many in the room.

Sleeping arrangements were a bit of a problem. I didn't have the heart to interrupt the bonkfest Maureen would no doubt be engaged in downstairs. So Kirsty and Delilah had my bed, Tatiana slept on the settee and I . . . Well, I probably had more experience of crashing on floors than the others.

I didn't sleep, but it wasn't just the discomfort of the bedroom floor. I couldn't get Tatiana's story out of my head. The limitations of her English grammar and vocabulary made the awful facts seem even more stark and ugly. Yet there was something oddly romantic about her tale, in spite of the sordid nature of the details. Something that didn't quite ring true. But not for one moment did I doubt that she had been abused and exploited. And there was still the problem of what to do next.

Wouldn't you know it? I didn't have to worry after all. Which is to say, I did still worry, but there was nothing I could do about it. It was just before dawn when I got up. But it was still too late. She was gone.

I lay on the vacated settee, breathing in the lingering scent of cheap perfume, and watched the sun rise over the sleeping city. My mind strayed to the bedroom windows in the next room that had framed those memorable buttocks. If it wasn't for those buttocks, there would have been no money, no trip to Brighton and no me there to help Tatiana in two toilets in succession. Where had she gone? I had a sudden thought and jumped up to check the pockets of my denim jacket hanging in the hall. My wallet was there, but the £25 I had left from the fun fund was gone. The irony wasn't lost on me.

I didn't resent Tatiana. She was welcome to the money. I would have given her more anyway. I was sad that she didn't trust me. But I could understand it. Anyway, I've known desperation of a different kind myself. Or the same kind but from a different source. There's quite a few people around who I've ripped off in my time. Some have forgiven me – like Maureen. Others never will.

I was still worried, though. Twenty-five pounds wouldn't get her far. I could worry . . . but it was out of my hands now. At least she knew where I was. I was a bit more pissed off when I realised my mobile was missing too.

I felt stiff and sore from dodgem damage, tension and a sleepless night on the floor. I don't often get to see the dawn. It inspired me to do some stretching. My own unique combination of yoga, t'ai chi and light torture. Once I started, I got really into it. I'm not a great one for exercise. It requires too much discipline. And I'm not big on discipline. Pounding the streets seems like madness to me. And the idea of going to a gym or exercise class fills me with horror. I like swimming, but hate pools. Maureen works out at the gym regularly and looks fabulous on it. Each to their own.

But I do like my stretchy stuff. It keeps me supple, honed and the meditative quality keeps me on a relatively even mental keel. An hour later, I got the urge for something more energetic. The girls were still spark out. Which was fair enough since it was still only seven o'clock. I put on my Walkman, slotted in an Ibiza tape and let rip.

The dance bliss-out lasted just the one track. I'd been strutting my stuff with my eyes closed. I leaped several feet into the air as I felt a tap on my shoulder. I opened my eyes to see Kirsty standing in front of me wearing an oversized T-shirt with a picture of some boy band on the front. She was bleary, her face swollen with interrupted sleep. I pulled the headphones off.

'What?' I demanded.

'Someone's at the door,' she mumbled, before shuffling back to bed.

I could hear it now. Not knocking. Thumping. Someone hammering on the door with their fist. It was familiar. It never occurred to me it might be anything to fear.

I toyed with the idea of ignoring it. But decided against it when I realised that if the noise had awoken Kirsty, Delilah wouldn't be too far behind. And it was still too early to be dealing with her. I dragged my unwilling feet to the door. Looking through the spyhole was a formality. I knew what I would see. And it wasn't a pretty sight. I opened the door a crack. I knew nothing I could do would make this any less painful. Let alone short and sweet. Maybe I could just hope for short.

He was wearing a wine-coloured dressing gown, tightly belted over striped pyjamas, and tartan slippers with little zips on the front. His cadaverous head balanced on the end of a skinny wrinkled neck giving the impression of a belligerent tortoise. There was only one consolation. His wife wasn't with him. The Miserable Gits lived in the flat below mine. They hated me. I didn't take it personally. They hated most people. But especially Young People.

He launched into a standard tirade. I couldn't work out why it didn't bore him as much as it did me.

'Do you have any idea what time . . . *blah, blah, blah* . . . what day it is . . . *drone, drone, drone* . . . selfish . . . *whinge* . . . thoughtless . . . *moan* . . . thumping . . . *bleat* . . . no carpets . . . *grumble* . . .' To which I rolled out my standard response. 'Sorry . . . *mumble, mumble, mumble* . . . understand . . . *mutter, mutter, mutter* . . . can't afford . . . *grunt* . . . hope . . . *shuffle* . . . try . . . *groan* . . .'

Maybe you think he had a point. After all, I had been jumping up and down on a floor ten feet above his head at seven in the morning. But the trouble with the Gits is, they're so programmed into expecting the worst of others that you find yourself some-how delivering it. Their general pain-in-the-arseness exempts people (well, OK, me) from the usual niceties and considerations they might have received if they hadn't been so relentlessly . . . Miserable and Gitty.

We were locked into playing roles in some ghastly social intercourse. But there was a more serious consideration. People like the Gits could cause a lot of trouble. They had lived in Boddington Heights for over forty years, since the block went up in the sixties. Since then it had become the last-chance saloon for people the council were forced to house after they'd been evicted from elsewhere. If you were labelled as a nuisance neighbour here, it was the end of the road. There was nowhere else to go. I reckoned the Gits were probably as hated down the Neighbourhood Housing Office as they were by their co-tenants. But I couldn't afford to give them too much fuel. So I always ended up giving them grovelling apologies and despising myself as much as they did.

You couldn't predict when Mr Miserable Git would decide he'd made his point and punished me sufficiently. It never came soon enough. After an interminable lecture he finally walked away, shaking his skeletal head on its stalk neck and still muttering. Leaving me free to go and splash cold water on my face. Not just because it was morning. It was my usual reaction to any encounter with the Miserable Gits.

I stared at my reflection in the mirror. It's a strange thing to have no idea of who your father is. What he looked like, his mannerisms, his character. I often wondered how much of the 'me' that was in me was in actual fact him. My physical appearance gave few clues. He wasn't black or Asian, that much was obvious. But that was about it. I was Des's daughter, all right. Same above-average height, supple androgynous (OK then, skinny) body, long straight brown (under the henna) hair. My eyes were a little larger and wider-spaced than hers, my nose a trifle longer and my cheekbones more prominent. (Though that was mostly a result of the inevitable hollowed cheeks you get after a couple of years on the smack.) Not a lot to go on, if you're trying to build up a picture of an unseen parent.

The upside is that having no hard facts I could give my imagination full rein and let it gallop off to whatever fantasy father figure I wished to create at that particular time. Never mind that the real person who provided the sperm which entered the egg which produced the me was statistically most likely to be dead or an investment banker. My fantasy fathers were never less than heroic free spirits, carrying the ideals of the sixties and the rhetoric of the seventies into the savage new century.

In short, they'd never lost the plot like Des. And if they had known I existed, they would have moved heaven and earth to track me down and claim me as their own.

Such is the stuff of fantasies. The last resort of those who have trouble accepting their realities.

Remembering when I had first seen Tatiana's reflection over my shoulder in another mirror, I forced my mind back to the present and made a mental note to buy more henna as I coiled my hair into plaits.

I spent an hour cleaning the kitchen, scrubbing tiles and diminutive work surfaces. After that, I even defrosted the fridge, using a hairdryer to speed up the polar ice-cap melt and warping the freezer box door in the process. By nine o'clock I'd expended more energy than I sometimes do in a week, but I still couldn't get Tatiana out of my mind.

I wasn't worried about the guy who threatened me. I live in south-east London and the encounter happened in south-east Brighton. But if everything she had told me was true – and my instincts told me the crucial bits were – she didn't know anyone else in London. The flat the brothers had her holed up in was in Whitechapel. Could she have gone back there? Maybe she'd convinced herself they would treat her with more respect now she had shown herself to be not entirely passive. She wouldn't be the first woman to escape from an abusive relationship only to walk straight back into it.

I sat down at the tiny table with a cup of tea and gazed down at a city engulfed by the morning rush hour. I wondered how many people there were in the area I could see. In houses, offices, shops. On buses, trains and planes. Walking, driving, running. Eating, sleeping, working. How many people would die in the time I was sitting there? How many be born? Who would be crying, who would be laughing? Who would be just plain bored?

She was out there somewhere.

I turned as Kirsty walked into the room.

'Hi, K. Y'all right?'

Kirsty grunted as she slid onto the vacant chair, where she sat

slumped, her hair hanging like curtains through which a reddened nose peeped. Even her nose looked disconsolate. I poured
her a glass of orange juice and made some toast.

'Where's Tittiana then?' she eventually managed through a
mouthful of toast and stainless steel.

'It's *Tatiana*, K. You know that. She's gone. I don't know
where.'

Kirsty raised her head and gave me a metal smile.

'You didn't like her, did you?'

'Dunno. S'pose not.'

'Why not? What's the problem?'

Kirsty shrugged.

'I dunno, Jo. She just seemed – like – hard or something. Like
she was out for what she could get. I think she could be trouble.'

I smiled. Kirsty was at that age where she could go from
sounding like a kid to an adult in the same breath.

'You sound just like your nan,' I said. 'But I don't think you're
being quite fair, babe. Tatiana was frightened. Anyway, I approached her. It's not like she came up to me asking for help.
What would you have done? Said sorry, can't help because I
don't really trust you but I'm not sure why?'

Kirsty wriggled in discomfort.

'Well, no. But I'm not sorry she's gone,' she said with a defiant
tilt to her chin. 'Sometimes you're just too nice, Jo. Some people
take the piss, y'know?'

I leaned over and kissed her on the cheek.

'I think you're just being protective of me, K. Which is really
sweet. But I don't think it's necessary. I'm big enough and ugly
enough to look after myself.'

Kirsty blushed.

'You're not ugly,' she expostulated. 'I think you're really
beautiful.'

I wrapped my arms round her in a grateful hug.

'Thanks, babe,' I smiled. 'We're all rainbows.'

We spent a comfortable half hour together and I even got her giggly at the memory of the Man Mountain who had come to our aid on the pier. Delilah joined us and we all nibbled toast watching morning TV in the front room. A news programme was showing footage of a traffic-stopping demonstration.

'Look,' squeaked Delilah. 'It's Bermondsey. Just down the road.'

And it was. A noisy crowd thronged the street which I recognised as Southwark Park Road. The newsreader told us the object of their attention was a shop selling tropical fish which, according to the demonstrators, was a front for a fascist operation.

I sat forward on my seat, fascinated. London's so vast, it's rare for major news stories to be that local. I remember thinking it made the report seem personal. As if we were somehow involved. Talk about premonitions . . . A crustie-looking guy with greasy hair in a long plait was being interviewed. I squinted at the screen as I stared at the determined face of the woman towering behind him. She was an enormous black woman with short dreads. And she was utterly familiar to me. The last time I'd seen her, her head had been shaved, but there was no mistaking her. There couldn't be two women who looked like Mags, my support worker at the drugs project I used to go to. I didn't share my revelation with the girls, but it gave me a warm feeling seeing Mags's face again. Even if it was on a screen.

The report ended and was replaced by a piece about a dog who answered phones. By this time, I judged enough time had passed for Maureen to get herself together sufficiently to welcome us back.

I phoned first, to make sure we wouldn't be interrupting anything. Mo answered, sounding predictably knackered. A fact which I took vicious pleasure in pointing out.

'Yeah,' she replied in a flat voice. 'Well, I been up all night, ain't I?' I gave a dutiful snigger. 'No. Not what you're thinkin', you dirty cow. Come down and I'll explain.'

7

I EXPECTED DARK circles under her eyes. But I could only see one. The other was invisible behind a thick wad of gauze, secured by white tape.

'Nan!' shrieked Kirsty and Delilah in unison, flinging themselves into her arms.

''Salright, girls. I'm OK. It's only a scratch. Don't worry,' Mo reassured. 'Go on. Go in the front room. B 'n' B are here. You mind them for me while I chat to their mum and Jo in the kitchen.'

Delilah attempted a launch into a dramatised version of our trip to Brighton, but beat a reluctant retreat when Mo and I chorused a warning. Kirsty clung on to Mo's arm for another moment.

'Go on, darlin',' Mo encouraged. 'I'm fine. I'll talk to you later. Promise.'

I followed her into the kitchen, where a stocky woman with an intricate cane row was sitting on a stool, building a spliff. Mo bent and picked a tiny piece of tobacco off the floor, invisible to anyone with two functioning eyes. I greeted Claudette, then turned my attention to Maureen.

'What happened, Mo? Not Calvin . . .'

'No!' Mo expostulated. 'Not bloody Calvin. He wouldn't hurt a fly. Course, he'd rip the head off a dodgy punter, but he'd never lay a finger on me. No, girl. I poked my eye out on a bloody narcissist, didn't I?'

Surreal images flickered through my brain, comic book style. None of them seemed likely. Surely shome mishundershtanding. I decided to play it safe by extracting further information.

'Blimey, Mo. How did you do that then?' The strategy worked.

'They was dropping pollen stuff on me table. I thought I'd use an old toothbrush to knock it off the stalky bits in the middle and I only went and stabbed one of them in me eye. It swelled up and it wouldn't stop watering. So Cal took me down casualty at Kings.' Mo shuddered at the memory. 'Seven hours. *Seven fucking hours,*' she exploded. 'Seven fucking hours with no fucking fucking!' Claudette and I shook our heads in sympathy. Maureen was on a roll now. 'And I'll tell you another thing. Whoever designed that waiting room was one sadistic bastard. The chairs go this way, right?' She indicated rows with her hands. 'And the telly – the telly goes *this* way.' She traced a right-angle to the rows. 'So if you want to watch it, you've got to screw your head sideways and pray you don't have to get treated for a dislocated neck while you're at it.'

Claudette offered the spliff to Maureen, who refused.

'Bit early for me, thanks. I ain't slept all night, remember?'

'I don't remember the last time I got a full night's sleep,' Claudette complained. 'Out of them two, there's always got to be one sure to wake me. Like they work shifts or something.'

'Them two' were B 'n' B. Not bed and breakfast, bread and butter or bacon and beans. B 'n' B were Bliss and Blythe, Claudette's four-year-old twins. They lived next door to Maureen.

'I didn't sleep too well myself,' I confessed.

I told them about Tatiana. They both had a go at me at first for getting involved. Then they competed with each other to come up with an account of the worst consequences I'd incurred in the past for not minding my own business. Claudette remembered the time I'd intervened when a guy was beating his woman in the car park. And then had to leg it when they found something in common after all and united to turn on me. But Mo won hands down with her rendition of me bringing home a stray cat – even though I have a hideous allergy that had me clawing at my skin for days until I had to admit defeat and turf him back out. I didn't tell them I still put bowls of food out for him by the bins.

When I told them Tatiana's story, though, they both backed down. I didn't know anyone, and wouldn't want to, who would have reacted differently on that train. Claudette said there was a kid who was a refugee in B 'n' B's class. He'd arrived a couple of months before, not speaking a word of English. But at that age, kids learn fast and, children often being less judgemental and more sorted than adults, he'd been accepted and liked by his classmates.

Adults are not so clever. Claudette said she felt really sorry for the kid's mother, who always stood silent and alone when she came to pick up her son.

'No one talks to her,' Claudette explained. 'She must be really lonely. Stranger in a strange land and that.'

'Have *you* tried talking to her?' I asked.

She grimaced as I passed the spliff back.

'Well, no . . . but she wouldn't understand, would she?'

'How do you know if you don't try?'

'OK, Ms Bloody Do Gooder. I'll tell you what. You pick the kids up next week. You talk to her . . .'

'I think I will,' I nodded. 'Monday OK?'

'I don't believe it,' Maureen interrupted. 'Don't bloody encourage her . . . Here, give me that.' She grabbed the spliff from Claudette and took a deep drag. 'My vision's already whacky with one eye. Might as well make it worthwhile.'

'I can't believe you did that dusting flowers, Mo,' I giggled. 'Who in the world cleans out the inside of flowers with a tooth-brush?'

'Yeah,' drawled Claudette. 'Good thing she ain't got a garden. She'd be out there cleaning every blade of grass with wet wipes every morning.'

Maureen snorted. 'I can tell you this though. If I had a garden, I wouldn't have any bloody narcissists in it.'

Quite right, Mo. Quite right.

I spent the rest of the day shopping. A replacement mobile, fuse wire, pliers and other DIY bits I got locally. Leather thongs, beads, clasps, feathers and shells required a trip to Covent Garden. I didn't hang about. I was on a mission. I couldn't wait to get back home and start transforming my purchases. Yet wherever I went I was aware of the number of Middle and East Europeans on the streets. I knew many of them would be from the former Yugoslavia – Bosnians, Kosovans, Albanians – and others from the former Soviet Union. Men were the most visible, hanging round in pairs or small groups. I'd never really registered them before. I don't give a toss where people are from and can't see why some people believe in tighter immigration controls. I presumed that most of them had suffered to one extent or another, or they wouldn't be here. Who knows what sights they had seen, what horrors they had endured? I suppose some of them might have been perpetrators rather than victims, but I didn't believe the tabloid hype. They weren't all pimps, extortionists and criminals. Yet obviously, out of all of them, there would be some who would fit the bill. Des used to tell me, where there is poverty and suffering, there will always be some ready to exploit it for their own power and enrichment. All I know is, life where they came from must be pretty hellish if they chose to live here instead. And for some, choice didn't come into it.

Claudette didn't know where Yaroslav, the boy in B 'n' B's class, came from. But she told me that in the strict pecking order of the school playground, asylum seekers and refugees were the bottom of the heap among the older kids. 'The skinniest, poorest little straggly no-hoper still thinks he's better than the asylum seekers,' she said. I don't suppose Yaroslav's mother had 'chosen' that for her child. Any more than Tatiana had chosen her life.

After I got home, I spent hours coiling, clipping, twisting and threading, sitting cross-legged on my front-room floor. The thing about working with your hands is it leaves your head free for thinking. Sometimes that's a good thing. Sometimes it's an absolute pain in the arse. I made good progress on the manual front, finishing several pieces that I liked enough to regret having to sell. But the thinking part of my brain was not providing the same satisfaction. I still couldn't get Tatiana out of my head. And I had the strongest feeling that my encounter with her hadn't ended when she'd left with my cash and my mobile.

8

AS PREDICTED, SMOKEY Pete had no problems with me selling my jewellery on the stall. He was even kind enough to like the stuff. I felt a buzz of adrenalin as I laid the pieces out on the black cloth, arranging them round the candles. I only had a dozen to sell – three chokers and a pendant, some bangles, earrings and a couple of rings. There would have been more, but I had given a pair of earrings each to Mo and Claudette and bracelets to the girls. I refused to take any money for them. They told me I'd never get rich that way. But I told them if I experienced cash-flow problems I'd just have to find myself another bare-botty man to rescue.

Modani, on the next stall, was predictably sniffy. 'Mmmm. Quite sweet in a retro kind of way. Some people might quite like them,' was her comment. It didn't bother me. She can't help it. Modani is a gen-u-ine Upper Class Person. There's a few of those around at Greenwich Market, but most of them have someone else to do the long hours in all weathers flogging their stuff. Modani has these deb friends who pop along to see her and oooh over the floaty silky things she makes and sells. They're all called things like Tiggy, Tarka and Santa and have incredibly loud, braying voices. What amazes me is the way they radiate good health. Even though it sounds like they abuse their bodies as much as the rest of us. It's just that their substances of choice are champagne, Pimm's and cocaine. I reckon they have extra-robust immune systems as a result of being the products of generations of people at the top of the social pile.

Other stall holders were more positive. Merlin, who runs the occult stall, Tina, who sells hats, and Gino from the deli were all supportive. More importantly, over the course of the weekend I sold all bar two of the pieces. Mind you, I calculated that at the prices I charged I'd valued my labour and creativity at a tad below nineteen pence an hour, leading me to conclude I needed to either radically review my pricing structure or work a great deal faster. Luckily, Pete's candles made enough for him to live on and to pay me.

The following Monday, I went to the school to pick up B 'n' B as promised, after my gardening job. They were in the nursery section of a red-brick school, which finished at 11.30. The adults hanging round outside as they waited for the door to open were in distinct groups. There were two posses of mums with one token dad (divided strictly along class lines), a huddle of child-minders with double pushchairs and an earnest pair of grandmothers. Yaroslav's mother was easy to spot. She stood apart from the others, looking a little uncertain but with a defiant tilt to her head. She was a large-boned woman with prominent cheekbones and deep-set blue eyes. I headed straight for her.

'Excuse me – do you know if Bliss and Blythe are in this class?'

She looked surprised and shook her head.

'I sorry. I don't . . .'

I was dimly aware of the conversations around us drying up. I could feel several pairs of eyes watching us. With curiosity, I think. But I can imagine if you were prone to paranoia – or simply isolated and culture shocked – it could have felt like hostility.

'Bliss and Blythe,' I persisted. 'They're twins. Two.' I held up two fingers. 'Brother and sister.'

'Oh yes.' She nodded with relief at understanding *and* knowing the answer. 'Is here.'

'Thanks,' I grinned. 'You have a child here?'

'Yes. Yes. My son, Yaroslav.' Her voice was soft and throaty. From the little I'd heard so far, her accent sounded very similar to Tatiana's.

I held out my hand.

'My name's Jo.'

She hesitated for a moment, as though unsure of how to react to this unexpected show of friendliness, then shook my hand. Her grip was loose and fleeting.

'I am Nadia.'

The door to the nursery opened and the waiting adults moved forward in a wave. The teacher called each child's name as she identified their matching carer. Claudette had told her I would be picking up B 'n' B, who ran to me clutching what would have been heralded as intuitive and groundbreaking art if they had been a couple of decades older.

Yaroslav, a pale, skinny boy with cropped blond hair, gave his handiwork to his mother. She spoke softly to him as she helped him into a worn blue anorak. Neither of them smiled much, but her movements with him were tender.

'We're going to the park now,' I told her. 'Why don't you and Yaroslav come?' She looked mystified and shrugged. The child spoke rapidly to her. I realised he was translating. It must be strange to have to rely on your four-year-old child to communicate for you. She shook her head. They held a whispered conversation, the pleading note audible in his voice.

At last, a smile.

'We go home,' she said. 'Then we come.'

'Meet you in the playground, Slavi,' Blythe yelled.

The skinny child beamed at us as he grabbed his mother's hand and towed her to the gate.

Burgess Park is long and narrow, along the site of a former canal. It stretches from the Old Kent Road westward to Camberwell New Road, with a kids' playground in the middle, which we headed straight for. Nadia and Yaroslav arrived an hour later, just when I'd nearly given up on them. Yaroslav ran to join the twins on the climbing frame. His mother hesitated for a moment before sitting opposite me on the bench at the picnic table.

She had a huge striped canvas shopping bag, which she placed on the bench next to her.

'My mother send,' she said, and with great solemnity began pulling packages from the bag. As she produced each item, she recited their names in English as if it was a test or a quizshow. 'Bread.'

It was good she told me. It was unlike any loaf I had ever seen. Dense and black and heavy as a breezeblock. 'Cheese.' This I recognised. 'Meat.'

Some kind of dry-looking salami. 'Fish baby.' Fish baby? It was a little pot filled with bright orange glutinous balls. It took a moment before the penny dropped. Caviar. Not the super-expensive black kind, but some cheaper version. 'Tea.' In a flask. 'Lemon. Sugar. Cups. Plates. Knives.'

The bag was a cornucopia of strange delicacies. Some more appetising to my Western palate than others, it has to be said.

She zipped the empty bag closed with a flourish, folded it, set it on the ground at her feet and looked up expectantly. I gave an embarrassed grunt and pulled some limp Marmite sandwiches, a bag of apples, cartons of juice and packets of crisps from my rucksack and laid them on the table next to her feast, where they sat looking forlorn and inadequate.

We called the children over. I felt slightly redeemed when B 'n' B turned their noses up at the unfamiliar food and hit the sandwiches and crisps with gusto. Nadia insisted I try everything, though I drew the line at the salami. Des was a strict vegan and would never eat anything with a face. I eat fish but have never touched meat. I tried to explain this to Nadia, but it was clear she found the concept bizarre.

After lunch, the kids ran off again, leaving us to clear up the debris. We sipped the strong black tea, with its conflicting tastes of lemon and sugar. And Nadia told me her story. The tea was bitter-sweet. Nadia's story was just bitter.

They were from the Ukraine. Weird. To my knowledge I'd never met anyone from Eastern Europe before. And now here I was, apparently forging some kind of relationship with two Ukrainian women in as many weeks. I wanted to tell her about Tatiana, but I didn't want to feel I was gossiping. And anyway, this was Nadia's turn . . .

Her English was slow and halting – even less proficient than Tatiana's. Every so often she would look up a word in a battered dictionary. It must have been so hard for her. Not just a strange language, but also a whole new alphabet.

Yet her story had a rehearsed quality to it. As though she'd had to repeat it many times. Her husband, Yuri, had worked in a chemical plant. He had spearheaded a campaign for compensation when several workers were injured in an industrial accident. But the factory owner was the local mayor. She said he was a member of something I didn't understand. She flicked through the dictionary.

'Fascist,' she said, closing the book with a snap.

The harassment had started in a small way. Threatening letters and phone calls. Graffiti on the door to their apartment. A brick through their window. Then Yuri got the sack and the real pressure began. Their electricity, water and phone were cut off without explanation. Yaroslav's teacher refused to allow him in the classroom – he was forced to stand outside the door. Petrol-soaked rags were pushed through their letter box, scorching the walls. Even when they could barely find water for cooking and washing, they kept a full bucket by the door. For emergencies.

One day, Nadia was walking along the street with Yaroslav when a car mounted the pavement and headed straight for them. They ducked into a doorway. It missed them by inches. Terrified, the family made secret plans to leave. Both of their parents gave them their tiny savings to buy air tickets. A contact gave them the name of an English solicitor and told them the procedure for applying for asylum. This piece of information alone cost them the equivalent of several weeks' wages. They knew they were being exploited, but had no choice.

Then, a week before they were due to leave, Yuri was arrested. The police wouldn't even tell her what the charges were. She had a choice now, but it was a hideous one. To stay – in the hope that Yuri would be released and they could make good their escape together. Or to leave without him and pray he would be able to follow at some point.

Throughout the telling of her story to me, she was stoical rather than frustrated, talking in a flat, almost emotionless voice. Sometimes her English would fail her, the events and their attendant sentiments beyond the help of the dictionary. But although I knew I was missing some of the detail, the gist was always clear.

After a while, I realised why she never looked at me as she spoke. I had been concentrating so hard on following her words, I'd completely forgotten about the children. But apart from when she was looking something up in the dictionary, she never took her eyes off Yaroslav. At one point he shouted something to her and she called back in an encouraging tone. I could see why she would be proud of him, as well as protective. He was independent and daring, bordering on reckless. One of those kids who seem to have no sense of fear and, against the odds, their confidence pays off. I hoped that confidence would continue to be justified in the future.

I also hoped the solicitor whose name she had paid so much

for was a good one. I could imagine how hard it would be to convince the Home Office bureaucrats. Too many restrictions. Limits and targets. Too much power and too little compassion. And a predilection for assuming everyone was lying.

Nadia pulled some papers from her shoulder bag and handed them to me. They were submissions to the Home Office for asylum status filled in by the solicitor on her behalf. I'm far from being an expert, but even I could see they had been completed in a slapdash manner, with no real attempt to present a reasoned case. The Home Office must have agreed. Her claim was turned down. Details of her right to appeal against the decision were contained in a terse letter.

So Nadia had been betrayed by everyone – the people she had paid for the solicitor's name, the solicitor himself and now by the system, which didn't give a damn. It seemed there was no shortage of people looking for a way to exploit the predicament she was in and enrich themselves in the process. I felt impotent rage at the injustice and inhumanity she had experienced.

'What will you do now?' I breathed. She shrugged. 'You need a new solicitor.'

'I know,' she said. 'This not good advocate.'

'There are groups – organisations – who might help.'

She nodded, waiting for more. But my resources in the area were few. Beyond looking up 'Refugees' in the Yellow Pages, I had no idea where she could go for advice.

I asked if the staff where she lived could help. It was an old church that had been converted into a refugee hostel.

'It is bad there. Very bad. Too many people. Very small room. Workers are . . .' flick in the dictionary '. . . kind, but very much work to do. No time to help one person. All people there have big problem.'

I could imagine. I trawled my mental address book for contacts who might help. Or at least be able to point me in the right direction. One image floated to the surface. That of a mountainous black woman with short dreads. I hadn't seen her in person for over two years. But I'd seen her face on the TV more recently.

I'd felt a strong connection to Mags the first time we'd met, when I'd stumbled into the local drugs project in search of a route away from heroin a few years earlier. How and why I came to the decision is another story. Suffice to say, I found the route. It led through a twisted nightmare of self-loathing, savage sweats and ripping pain. And a knowledge that you never really leave the road. Mags credits my success (so far – being in recovery is a permanent state) to my own determination. I know I couldn't have done it without her support. I still phoned her occasionally, even though I was no longer a client, and she was good-hearted enough to always sound pleased to hear from me. I knew she wouldn't blink an eye at me contacting her for information about where Nadia could go for advice. And I had blind faith that her resources were such that she would have answers.

'Look,' I said. 'I know someone I can ask. She might be able to tell me where you can get help.' She nodded again. There didn't seem to be much optimism in the gesture. I couldn't help but agree. If I was the only hope she had, she might as well start packing. 'I'll try now,' I said, pathetic in my eagerness.

I pulled my mobile from the rucksack and called the familiar number.

'New Dawn Project,' a voice sang at me.

'Hi. Could I speak to Maggie Jackson please?'

'Sorry. Mags isn't in today. Can anyone else help you?'

'Um, no. Thanks. I'll try again tomorrow.'

Damn. It had been a slender thread. And it turned out to have nothing attached to it. At least, not before tomorrow.

We called the children over and started to walk back along the old tow path.

'Nadia,' I said. 'Could I ask you something? Is there a big problem with prostitution in the Ukraine?'

She frowned. I took the dictionary from her and found the word. I pointed out the Ukrainian translation. She snatched the book back and glared at me as she rattled off an angry response in her own language.

'No. No,' I protested, horrified. 'Not *you*. I'm not asking if *you* are a prostitute.' I was grateful the children had run ahead and were out of earshot.

'In the *Ukraine*. Is it a problem in the *Ukraine*?'

'We are not all this – this – *thing*,' she replied in glacial tones.

I tripped over myself to apologise for the misunderstanding. Eventually she relented and relaxed a little.

'Is big problem. Is true,' she shrugged. 'But not only in Ukraine. Is big problem here too.'

I tried phoning Mags again the next day, but if I'd been hoping for a nice warm glow of satisfaction, I was destined for disappointment. It seemed that if anything was going to sort out Nadia's problems, it was going to take more than me making a phone call.

This time the voice on the other end told me Mags was on compassionate leave and wouldn't be in for the rest of the week.

'Can anyone else help?' the solicitous voice asked.

No. I didn't think they could, thank you very much. It's not common practice to phone a drugs project for advice about asylum seekers.

Compassionate leave. I realised with a guilty lurch that I knew almost nothing about Mags's personal life, while mine was an open book to her. I sent her a silent wish for strength to cope with whatever loss she was enduring. Best I could do.

The thought made me feel depressed and inadequate. I stood at the window and gazed down at the smoky city, thinking about the waves of immigration and the diverse ethnic mix that gave it its character. I thought it was probably the best thing the city had to offer. Compensation for the noise, the dirt, the stress.

It's a strange business, living so high above the ground on which everything else operates. You feel disconnected, forced to spectate from afar but prevented from participating. Life is something that goes on *out there*, separated from your own existence not just by bricks and mortar but also by distance and height. I felt a need to connect at ground level and grabbed my mobile and denim jacket. I ran down the stairs, rather than wait for the lift, and hit the streets.

I strode down the traffic-clogged road to Elephant and Castle. The open area at the front of the shopping centre was a hotch-potch of market stalls selling clothes, household goods and CDs. There was a tatty, down-at-heel feel to it all, which did nothing to lighten my mood. One whole area was dominated by South Americans, the music, cafés and stalls all run by and frequented by Spanish speakers transplanted from another continent. Elsewhere, small groups of men from countries off the tourist map but on the warmongers' stood huddled, smoking. At least they had a community of sorts. Women like Tatiana and Nadia had no such support.

I bought a paper and went into a greasy spoon for a cup of vile tea in a chipped mug and a two-day-old doughnut. The caff was called Café Archimedes, but most of the regulars referred to it as Ancient Grease. I sat at the Formica table and scraped the caramelised sugar from the doughnut. It hit the plate like old scabs. As I flicked through the paper, a face leaped out at me. I felt a jolt of recognition. It was him. There was no doubt about it. He was trying to turn away from the camera, one hand defensively in front of him. He was wearing a sharp suit, with a shirt and tie. Very different attire to when I had encountered him.

So this was the everyday persona of Mr Dangly Stripe Bum, then. I read the article. His name was Stanley Highshore and it seemed he had a lot more to hide than a stripy arse. You could almost hear the journalists smacking their lips when they'd uncovered this one. Top BBC producer – sado-masochistic rituals – husband of Tory MP – fascist plot – torture, grizzly murder and betrayal. This one had the lot. A positive jackpot of sleaze.

I read on. Wheels within wheels, as Des would say. Everything's connected. The fascist plot had prompted that huge demonstration in Bermondsey I'd seen Mags at on the TV. Some guy, Nicholas Heath, had been murdered in Peckham the following day. He had been decapitated by a train and his head had ended up in the jaws of a Rottweiler. And this was somehow connected to Highshore's former lover. Weirder and weirder. The details were sketchy. Much of this was old news now and so referred to in passing. I cursed myself for not having followed the story as it was unfolding.

I wondered where Mags's compassionate leave fitted in, or if it had nothing to do with any of this. Some other drama, maybe. I was even more determined to speak to her now. And glad of the excuse. It wasn't just curiosity . . . Well, OK, it was mostly . . . Sorry Nadia. But if Mags could help, it wouldn't matter that my motives had been less than pure. I would try to contact her first thing next Monday.

9

I SHOULDN'T HAVE made such a definite plan. Plans, in my experience, never work out the way you intend. And the more definite the plan, the more likely that events will conspire to prevent you carrying it out. That's the way it's always been for me anyway, though I recognise that my childhood may have had more than the average share of unpredictability.

The plan lasted all week. It lasted through the gardening and cleaning job, the jewellery making, numerous chats with Mo (her eye having emerged bleary and bloodshot from its bed of lint none the worse for her narcissist attack) and another trip to B 'n' B's school.

This time, Nadia invited us back to the hostel she and Yaroslav called home. From the outside, it still looked like a church. Except the small groups of people hanging round sitting on the low wall and steps, standing on the corner smoking, talking earnestly into mobiles, didn't look like your average congregants. Nadia explained that a mobile is essential if you're a refugee. The only way to contact solicitors, supporters (if you were lucky enough to have any) and family and friends back home.

There were also a couple of flash cars parked outside in the driveway. A Merc and a Jag, their owners, a couple of beer-bellied white guys, leaning against the sides smoking. They looked incongruous and I wondered what they were doing there. They looked suspiciously like men who knew how to make a buck – or several thousand – from the misery of others.

I followed Nadia into the cool, shadow-filled interior. On the left was a small office. A tired-looking woman, about my age, sat behind a glass screen, tapping on a computer keyboard while talking on a phone.

'No.' She shook her head. 'We have no spaces at all, I'm afraid. We're expecting some relocations in the next week or so, but right now we're chocca. Have you tried Lewisham?' She looked up from the computer screen and nodded at us. 'Hang on a sec . . .' she said into the phone. She reached above her head to a wooden board, pierced with rows of numbered hooks with keys hanging from them. She lifted one down and handed it to Nadia.

'There you go, Mrs Nobotkin,' she smiled, before turning back to her phone call and computer screen.

We walked down a dimly lit corridor punctuated every few feet by cheap hardboard doors. We passed knots of adults and children representing the victims of all the conflicts I knew only from TV and newspapers. Afghanistan, Somalia, Kurdistan . . . people from Middle Europe, the Middle East, Eastern Europe . . . from Africa, Asia, South America . . . The only thing they had in common with each other was a shared experience of hatred, horror and oppression. But what experience did a man from Azerbaijan have of a woman from Ethiopia? Or a family from Romania of an elderly couple from Rwanda?

The alienation and mutual distrust was palpable even in the short walk down the corridor. Probably only exceeded by their alienation and distrust of the world outside the hostel walls. The children seemed to provide the only bridge across the cultural divide. Adults reached down to ruffle their hair and murmur shy greetings as we passed. One woman pressed a sweet into each of their hands. I smiled thanks at her, deciding now wasn't the time to deliver a lecture to B 'n' B about the dangers of accepting treats from strangers.

Nadia stopped in front of one of the anonymous doors and inserted her key. She stood back and I walked into her 'home'. It was a tiny square room, with two cheap single beds covered with pale blue candlewick bedspreads, a chest of drawers and a small sink with an unframed mirror screwed to the wall above it. There was a square Formica-topped table with two upright chairs below a barred window that looked onto the bins in the side alley.

Yaroslav pulled a cardboard box from under the table and began producing toys. A few battered cars, a one-legged Action Man, some marbles, a yo-yo . . . Within minutes he and B 'n' B had occupied every inch of the available floor space with some complex fantasy game that I suspected had strong militaristic overtones.

Kids are amazing. The less they have, the more effortless it seems for them to entertain themselves. At home, B 'n' B seem to have just about every toy Argos and Woolies have to offer. Yet their attention span there seems so minimal it's almost non-existent, and they constantly complain of being bored. They flit from toy to game to video with the abandon of a pair of hyper-active butterflies on speed. Yet given the minimal content of Yaroslav's toy box and the incredible breadth of their own underused imaginations, they looked like they could play happily for hours. For Yaroslav himself, I suspected the novelty of having friends round would have been enough.

The room was stuffy. Nadia opened the window and invited me to sit on one of the wooden chairs. A faint smell of rotting vegetables wafted in from the bins.

'I make tea,' she said. 'I have . . . (flick in the omnipresent dictionary) '. . . kettle.'

She told me she hated the kitchens and rarely cooked hot food.

I could imagine the problems. The different languages preventing communication. The different cultures providing confusion. The different foods creating suspicion and distaste.

She showed me photos. Nadia and Yuri on their wedding day. Yaroslav as a baby. Her parents. She handed them to me one by one, first devouring them herself as though willing them to come to life.

'I miss them,' she said in a voice so low I had to lean forward to hear her. 'I miss my home. My family. My country. I miss my husband. I do not want to be here. Do not be . . .' (flick, flick) '. . . angry. I know this is your home. But it is not my home. I do not want this. And I know many people here also do not want us to be here. I do not want it. They do not want it. But I am here. It is possible I may never see my own home again. I am filled with . . .' (flick, flick) '. . . pain. If it was me alone . . .' she shrugged '. . . I would have stayed. I would not have come here, where I am hated and where I hate to be.'

There was a long silence.

'But it is not me alone,' she sighed.

She gazed down at the top of Yaroslav's head as he and B 'n' B launched marbles down an empty cardboard tube onto cars that shot along a track constructed from their own shoes. I think I must have been the first person for a very long time who was prepared to sit and listen to her. If nothing else, I at least provided her with an opportunity to practise her English.

There was a timid knock on the door. Nadia opened it and greeted a young, dark-haired woman, who came in, looking at me and the kids with curiosity. Nadia introduced us. The woman's name was Galina. She was from Lithuania. From a beautiful village near a lake, Nadia said. Now she lived in south London two doors up the hall from Nadia. She gave me a shy smile and sat down on the other chair while Nadia made more tea.

Galina watched the children playing on the floor with a wistful air, while I looked at Nadia's photos and wondered what it would be like to have your whole world ripped out from under your feet. Nadia placed the tea on the table and perched on the edge of one of the beds. She spoke in a gentle voice to the other woman. Galina lowered her head, her dark curtains of hair not quite hiding the tears rolling down her cheeks.

'Her mother ill,' Nadia explained to me. 'She want go home to see her. But she . . .' (flick, flick) '. . . scare no . . .' (grunt of frustration and further flicking) '. . . can return in England again.'

She laid a comforting hand on Galina's arm and asked her something. Galina nodded and sniffed. Nadia passed her a tissue and she blew her nose and began speaking.

I couldn't understand a word, of course. Which gave me a tiny insight into what it must be like for them all the rest of the time. I focused on the children as a convenient distraction. I saw Galina pull a passport from her bag and show it to Nadia. Nadia looked at it carefully, turning the pages and gazing at the photo, before handing it back with what sounded like encouraging words. I could see, even from the corner of my eye, that it wasn't a Ukrainian passport. Nadia had shown me hers with the Home Office documents and this was a different colour. I didn't know what colour Lithuanian ones were, but this one was the same colour as my British passport. I guessed Galina had found a way to travel home and then be able to re-enter Britain.

What must it feel like? A sick mother; a return to a home that could no longer be 'home'; the terror of not knowing if the passport would hold up under scrutiny . . . I wished her luck with all my heart.

We left after an hour or so. It was Friday and I would be working the market over the weekend. I invited Nadia and Yaroslav to tea the following Monday.

The weekend went well, my jewellery selling enough to raise my spirits a little. I bought some food from the deli stall that I thought might be not too unfamiliar to Ukrainian palates, and then splashed out on a toy boat made out of tin for Yaroslav. It ran on steam created by lighting a wick running into a knob of candle wax – cheap to run, small enough to pack and hardy enough to last whatever upheaval its owner might have to endure.

I was awoken in the early hours of Sunday morning by a scratching at my front door followed by pounding and slurred curses. I stumbled from my bed, pulled on a T-shirt and peered through the spy hole. I opened my door and Wee Jock fell into my flat. Jock was a Glaswegian alcoholic who lived two floors down. You would be forgiven for assuming his name was a reference to the fact that he was small and Scottish, both of which were true. In reality, the moniker had been given to him by the local kids as a result of his tendency to wander round in all weathers wearing nothing but a pair of piss-stained jockey shorts.

I hauled him up from the floor, automatically holding my breath.

'You've got the wrong floor, Jock,' I grunted through gritted teeth.

I steered him over to the lift and stabbed the button. The doors opened to reveal a fresh turd in one corner. Jock squinted at it as he lurched against me. He nodded and mumbled with pride, as though assuming I would be equally impressed by this faecal achievement. I heaved him into the lift, leaned him against the wall and pushed the button for the eighteenth floor before staggering back to bed, after a prolonged Lady Macbeth handwashing routine in the bathroom.

On the Monday morning I went to pick up B 'n' B after my gardening job. Nadia wasn't among those waiting outside. The teacher told me Yaroslav hadn't been in, but they hadn't been informed why.

Concerned, I headed straight for the church with B 'n' B in tow. The same flash cars were parked outside and the same tired woman was behind the desk. She was on the phone again.

'Yes. No problem. I'll send the transport over to get them now.' She looked up. 'Can I help you?' she inquired. 'The Nobotkins? Oh, they've been relocated.' She turned to her computer screen and pressed a few buttons. 'They're in Glasgow,' she confirmed. 'They were moved on Saturday.'

'Glasgow?' I gasped, my mind lurching back to my recent encounter with Wee Jock, though the rational part of my brain knew not all Glaswegians were Rab C. Nesbitt.

'But she never said . . . We'd arranged to see each other . . .'

'She wouldn't have known until a few hours before,' she said. 'That's normal policy.'

'But the boy was at school here. He had friends . . .'

She gave me a sympathetic smile.

'I'm sorry,' she said. 'We don't make the rules. But Glasgow's nice . . .' she finished brightly.

I imagined Nadia and Yaroslav starting again from the beginning. Struggling with a whole new area, a new set of strangers and what would seem like a whole new language. I didn't think they would consider it 'nice'.

Even though the remote chance that I could have helped the Nobotkins had faded still further, I couldn't bear to let go. A couple of days later I phoned the New Dawn Project again. Mags was with a client, but the woman who answered the phone took my number and said she'd get her to call back.

An hour later the phone rang. Mags sounded tired, her voice several notches down on her usual volume. I told her I'd heard she had been on compassionate leave and said I hoped she was OK.

'Yeah,' she sighed. 'It's been – hard.' There was a pause while I wondered if I should probe. 'Anyway . . .' There was an audible pulling-herself-together in the word. 'How are you, honey?'

I told her about Nadia and Yaroslav. I said I knew this wasn't her field, that no doubt she was snowed under with work after her absence and that I had no right to be asking anyway. She waved away my objections and said she'd get together some names and addresses of organisations and also print some stuff off the internet for me.

'Um, there's another angle I'm sort of interested in,' I said. 'Prostitution rackets, the international sex trade, corrupt lawyers . . . that sort of stuff.' There was a long whistle down the phone.

'Jo, honey. What are you getting yourself into?'

I told her I wasn't actually getting 'into' anything, just that I had met someone who had made me curious. Mags sounded unconvinced, or at least cautious.

'Listen, m'dear. This is murky stuff . . .' She hesitated, before coming to a decision. 'OK. I'll get some stuff together and send it. But before you go rushing in, you better make sure you have the resources to cope. You understand what I'm saying? Sleazy does it, girl. Sleazy does it. And you phone me again if you need to, y'hear?'

I rang off, feeling bolstered by having someone like Mags on my side. Even if I was none too sure what side that was. I paid no attention to her warnings. I was hardly in any danger. Doing a bit of research couldn't do any harm.

Mags's package arrived two days later. Fast. But not as fast as Tatiana.

10

MY MOTHER, DES, believed in the power of the subconscious. She reckoned that just by focusing your spiritual energies, you could create a sort of metaphysical climate that could result in real things happening in the physical world. It explained, she told me, why life was full of bits of general weirdness that were too synchronous, too extreme, too – well, just too damn *weird* to be down to random coincidence.

The logical conclusion of this, of course, is that you can make things happen just by wishing hard. Visualise the dream long and hard enough and it will come true. This is patently not the case, as Des's own life could testify.

Even so, her theory came back to me with force as the lift doors opened in the early hours of Friday night, Saturday morning.

I'd been round at Smokey Pete's. I'd delivered his shopping during the afternoon and had stayed for a meal. I didn't generally like eating there. The food always tasted like perfume. The essential oils and incense he used to scent the candles seeped into everything and overpowered the other embattled senses.

But Pete seemed to want the company and I always enjoyed his, so I stayed. I got a real buzz on the occasions I spent several hours at a stretch with him. As though my horizons were being stretched in unaccustomed directions. There was something about the perspective he had of the world that was unique and almost pure. It was a strange kind of innocence I suppose, unsullied as he was by the world outside his walls and its evil influence. He had no TV and didn't read the papers. Occasionally he would catch the news on the radio, but not by design or intent.

He liked to hear about it, though. He would sit and listen to me spout on about wars, famine, corruption and injustice in my block, the city, country or world, before delivering his own slant, tipping the way I had been seeing it off its axis. He had a technique that made the global personal. And made the personal universal.

His method was to take on the persona of one individual involved. 'OK,' he would start. 'Imagine you are . . .' Sometimes a victim, sometimes a perpetrator. Sometimes a key player and sometimes an uninvolved observer. He'd invent their background, analyse their thought processes, their reactions. Bring them to life. Make them real. You ended up feeling that, but for a trick of fate or an accident of birth, this could have been *you*. So that even if the people he described were sadistic thugs, they were still sadistic *human* thugs. Not demons, just real people with their own baggage and agenda.

That night, I'd told him about Tatiana and Nadia. I'd sipped my can of patchouli-flavoured lager and listened as he created for me the psyche of a man who would control women by fear, ensure their dependence and exploit their bodies. His image was of a man who was ruthless, cold and ambitious. A man of no scruples who would stop at nothing to achieve his own ends.

I remembered the brothers on Brighton pier and shivered.

Pete paid for a minicab when I left after midnight with a battered suitcase full of new candles nestling in beds of scrunched-up tissue paper.

The lift shuddered open on the top floor. She was sitting outside my door, her knees drawn up, her arms clasped round them. She looked almost too young to be out at that time of night. Not that I'd have been tucked up in bed with a mug of cocoa and a good book when I'd been her age. She was wearing a short black skirt with a halter-neck top and strappy sandals.

And she had a black eye.

'Tatiana,' I said. 'Come on in.'

She was walking strangely. She hobbled into my front room and sank onto the settee. She slipped a finger behind the ankle straps and eased her bare feet out of the sandals. I watched horrified as, released from their bonds, they swelled before my eyes. The places where the straps had been were rubbed raw where blisters had burst revealing weeping flesh which the re-morseless leather had continued to torture.

At least I knew how she had got here. She'd walked. All the way from the Ukraine judging by the state of her feet.

I bustled about, filling a bowl with warm water and putting it on the floor in front of her. Fetching a towel from the bathroom, I placed it next to the bowl.

Tatiana lowered her feet into the water, keeping her eyes down. She had barely looked at me.

'Are you hungry?' I asked.

She gave a tiny shrug. I made her a mug of hot chocolate, thinking the milk might serve as a compromise between food and drink. She took it from me and wrapped her hands round the mug. I sat opposite her, but now that my ministrations were complete, I wasn't sure what to do next.

She looked beyond exhausted. Her skin was paper pale, the dark smudge under her undamaged eye almost rivalling the bruising around the other. She was stick thin and sat with her shoulders hunched and head down. The posture of a woman at least half a century older.

I couldn't bear to question her. Part of me felt relieved – proud almost – that she had turned to me. At the same time, I suspected that her choices would not have been much greater than those of my goldfish swimming round their bowl.

I got up and fetched her a blanket and a pillow and set them down on the settee.

'Is there anything else you need?' I asked. Again, that minute shrug was the only response. I supposed it had been an un-answerable question and I felt stupid for having asked it. 'Will you still be here in the morning?'

At last she looked up at me, a pink flush staining her cheeks.

'I am sorry about your phone and the money,' she breathed. 'Both are gone . . .'

'Don't worry about that,' I reassured. 'It's not important.'

She gave me a quizzical look, before lowering her head again. I went into my own room and made a valiant but unsuccessful attempt at a night's sleep.

The next morning I eased open my bedroom door and tiptoed into the shadows of the front room. I half expected her to be gone, but she was curled up under the blanket on the settee, breathing evenly.

The post had arrived. I picked the letters up from the mat and went into the kitchen. I binned the junk mail and carried the large brown envelope over to the tiny table. I forced myself to make tea and toast and sit down before I would allow myself to open it.

Mags was a star of the first order. The envelope was full. My confidence in her resources hadn't been misplaced. I pulled out a sheaf of papers and began my new role as researcher into the global sex trade. Painfully aware of the unexpected proximity of one of its victims.

Mags had scrawled a note on a compliments slip, saying she hoped the information would be useful and repeating her injunction to take care. She also included a mobile number, where she said she could be contacted 'in emergencies'.

That really surprised me. She had never given me the number when she'd been my support worker and I would never have expected her to. It's the kind of job where you have to be careful not to get too involved. I could imagine the stress and frustration of working in a place like a drugs project. With people like me. Or at least like I used to be. I guessed you'd have to be strictly boundaried if you didn't fancy becoming a client yourself. Maybe she reasoned that our contact was no longer within the scope of the project. Or maybe it was an indication of the extent of her concern at what I was getting into. Either way, I was surprised. And flattered.

She'd sent lists of refugee organisations, their contact details and brief descriptions of the work they did as well as several pages printed off websites. I put the lists aside in a separate pile to send to Nadia. The rest of the envelope's contents were in response to my request for information that might relate to Tatiana's situation.

Facts were delivered with no dramatic embellishment. They needed none in order to invoke horror and disgust. Statistics leaped from the paper and bludgeoned me with the stark reality of human misery they represented.

- *Fifty two billion dollars* – the annual value of the global prostitution industry.
- *Five hundred thousand* – the number of women smuggled into Western Europe by the sex trade.
- *Ten thousand* – police estimate of the number of illegal immigrants working as prostitutes in Britain.
- *Seventy* – the number of walk-up flats in Soho worked by prostitutes of whom *ninety per cent* are from Eastern Europe.

- *Twenty-four hours* – the time within which women picked up by Immigration are flown home, having been seen as illegal immigrants rather than victims who could potentially give evidence against the criminal networks that brought them here in the first place. The traffickers often meet the women at the airport and bring them straight back to Britain.
- *Two years* – the Court of Appeal's recommended sentence for pimping.

My tea grew cold and my toast lay uneaten as I read through case studies of girls – teenagers most of them, but some as young as ten – tortured and exploited, isolated and terrified. Like the sixteen-year-old whose pimp had taken out her front teeth, so she could give better oral sex. I learned about 'seasoning' – a pimping term for raping and beating a girl until all resistance has been knocked out of her.

I was beginning to understand Mags's concern. The men controlling this human trade were not part of an organised mafia. They were more dangerous than that. They operated in small groups held together by blood or tribe. Their own backgrounds were often ones of abject poverty. They had little to lose and untold riches to gain. All of which meant they were utterly ruthless. I crept to the front room door. Tatiana was still asleep. As I turned back into the kitchen, I glanced at the clock on the wall.

Shit! I was late! Half an hour late. And that was if I left right now. I couldn't just walk out on Tatiana for the whole day without explanation. And I had no idea if her English skills were up to reading a note. Even if I could think of what to say . . . I pushed the papers back into the envelope and shoved it in a drawer. Then I grabbed Pete's case with its new stock of candles, my own holdall packed with jewellery and slung some essential items into a rucksack. No time to make a sandwich. I shoved everything by the front door and went back over to Tatiana.

I crouched by her side and murmured her name. To my mounting despair, she didn't respond.

'Tatiana,' I said, with greater urgency, shaking her shoulder.

She muttered something unintelligible, turned her head and opened bleary eyes to look at me. As she focused, her eyes sprang wide and she sat up with a jerk.

'It's OK,' I soothed. 'Nothing's happened. It's just that I have to go out. I have to work. I'll be out for the whole day. You can stay here. Eat or drink anything you find. Watch TV. Take a bath. Anything. I'm sorry, but I have to go.' She nodded at me, with no expression on her sleep-puffy face. 'Do you understand? Is it OK? Then, when she still didn't respond, 'Will you stay?'

She met my eyes for an instant before closing hers again and curling up under the blanket. I only just caught her whispered response.

'I will stay.'

I was on tenterhooks all day. I'd arrived late and Mick, who ran the market, had given my usual pitch to a casual, leaving me with an unfamiliar spot and a double guilty conscience to deal with. I felt bad for Pete, knowing sales would be affected. And I felt awful for abandoning Tatiana. The hours crawled past. The faster I willed them, the slower they went. It was a grey, drizzle-filled day that deterred all but the most determined punters. I phoned Nadia's mobile. Communicating by phone was even harder than face to face. She told me they had a flat of their own but it was in a 'very bad place'.

'We very unhappy here,' she told me. 'Yaroslav cry at night. He sick. I also.'

She gave me the address and I told her I would send her the list of contacts I'd got from Mags. She clutched at the thin straw with desperate hopelessness.

'They will help?' she asked.

'I don't know,' I replied with a heavy heart. 'I hope so, Nadia. I hope so.' I couldn't think of anything else to say that might make her feel better and hung up feeling worse than before.

I closed the stall down early, having clocked up less than half the previous week's takings. The only upside being that I wouldn't have to spend so much time replacing the jewellery during the week.

There were two ambulances, a paramedic's car and a cop car in the courtyard when I got home. My stomach lurched as though I had known further dramas were inevitable. The doors of the ambulances were closed. A skinny guy I recognised as a regular visitor to the dealer who lived on Mo and Claudette's floor was sitting in the back of the cop car, looking sick and miserable. Not that I'd ever seen him look any other way. A couple of kids on bikes were hanging round the ambulances, standing up on the pedals to try to peer in through the blacked-out windows. A knot of adults and toddlers stood by the entrance to the block.

I spotted Claudette among them and went over.

'What's going on?' I asked.

'Him there.' She indicated the cop car with a nod. 'He cut up Mikey real bad. One big slash down here.' She drew a line down her left cheek with a fingernail painted with a palm tree silhouette over a Caribbean sunset. 'An' more too. Only there's so much blood, you can't see where it's come from.'

'Just Mikey was hurt?'

'Seems so. Though there's nuff blood on my landing and all about to fill six Mikeys. He ran into the lift and collapsed inside the door there.'

'Huh,' I grunted, relieved that I didn't have to be directly involved in this particular drama, 'Two ambulances *and* a paramedic? How many pieces did he cut him into?'

Claudette and some of the other women barked with laughter, easing the tension.

'Gotta go, Claudette. See you later,' I called, pushing my way through the doors and into the block, skirting the blood lake on the floor.

One of the two lifts had the lights-out, no-one's-home look I know so well. When you live on the twentieth floor, you get a sixth sense about out-of-order lifts. The doors of the other were wedged open with an empty bucket, though there was no sign of anyone who might fill and use it. The lift itself looked like an abattoir. Blood was sprayed over the walls and was running down in rivulets to join the expanding sea on the floor.

My heart sank.

One day, I thought, I must time how long it takes me to climb twenty flights of stairs. By the time I reached the top, my legs were jelly, my breathing ragged and my heart pounding. I held on to the door frame and closed my eyes for a moment to compose myself before opening the door.

The TV was on. Some mindless Saturday-night gameshow. I gagged with relief. Having spent the whole day focusing on Tatiana, it would have been devastating if she'd disappeared again. I didn't stop to examine why I felt so strongly about her. It was as though I was scared to discover that my need for her was greater than hers for me. I couldn't have explained the connection, but I was becoming convinced she and I were destined to have a major impact on each other's lives.

She wasn't in the front room. But now I had my breath back, I noticed something. A smell. I've heard it said that of all the senses, smell is the most powerful, and this one evoked a reaction in me so strong that my eyes clouded with tears. It had been a very long time since I'd had an experience like that. Back before Des had checked out permanently. And then not on a regular basis.

It was the experience of coming home, breathing in and knowing someone had cooked a meal for you. Someone had cared enough to do that. For you.

I walked into the kitchen. Tatiana was putting the finishing touches to a salad, sprinkling sunflower seeds over the top. She turned and gave me a shy smile, before reaching into the oven, her tiny hands awkward and incongruous in giant oven mitts.

She pulled out a dish of pasta bubbling with tomatoes and cheese.

I felt my eyes welling up again and covered it with gabble.

'Oh, wow. That looks fantastic. I recognise all the ingredients but I could never have come up with something like that. Tatiana – you're wonderful.' She blushed and ducked her head as she ladled food onto plates.

'Phew. What a day I've had. I work in a market, you know. On a stall? Do you know what that is? I sell candles. And jewellery. I make it myself. Not the candles. Pete makes them. He's a friend. But the jewellery. I make that. I've only just started. It's not that good or anything, but people seem to like it. I'll have to show you. After we've eaten. Wow. This looks so good. I didn't eat lunch, you know.'

I couldn't stop myself babbling. She didn't say a word. Not that I gave her the opportunity. We walked into the front room and sat down next to each other facing the TV. Finally, I shut up and stared at the vacuous grins on the contestants' faces for a few moments.

'Tatiana?' I said softly. She raised her head to one side to indicate she was listening. 'Thank you,' I whispered.

She shrugged.

'It is only food,' she said. 'Your food. I find in cupboards . . .'

'No. I mean thank you for staying.'

She looked puzzled.

'But it is I who should thank . . .'

'I don't know,' I replied. 'I can't explain it. I just have this feeling that . . . that somehow you will be as important to me one day as I am to you right now . . .'

She shifted in her seat, looking a little uncomfortable. I was scared I might frighten her by my intensity. I've been told before I can come on a bit too heavy some times.

'I'm sorry,' I said. 'I'm just tired. Take no notice. Half the time I don't know what I'm on about myself.'

She didn't volunteer any information about what had hap-

pened to her since the last time we had met. And once again I
didn't probe. By the time I went to bed, I realised she'd probably
only said about a dozen words since I'd first encountered her
outside my door the previous night.

But she was still there.

11

THE FOLLOWING DAY was a bit like an action replay. Only without the last-minute panic and the evening bloodbath. I'd asked Tatiana the evening before if she'd like to come with me to the market. But she'd turned down the chance to get up early and spend the day perched on a stool getting stiff. Can't think why.

I'd also offered to go down to Mo's to collect my spare keys so she could go out if she wanted. She seemed jittery at the thought.

Some people who spend time in blocks like Boddington Heights become virtual prisoners in their homes. They're OK when they're inside. And they're OK(ish) when they're outside. But it's the getting from one to the other and back again that presents the problem. Negotiating the landing, the lifts, the entrance hall and the car park. The noise and the debris and the ever present undercurrent of barely suppressed violence.

I didn't know if Tatiana was suffering from that particular fear or if she felt some other, greater evil was lurking outside waiting for her. Either way, she turned down the offer of the keys and I didn't push it.

Coming home, I had the luxury of the lift. Unlike the previous evening. But I still hesitated before putting my key in the lock.

When you have very little, you at least have one thing that is vital for your survival. The fact that you have very little to lose. Of all people, it was Modani from the floaty silky stall who forced me to look at what was going on in the background to my helping Tatiana.

'Strikes me, sweetie, you're a bundle of emotional needs of your own,' she said in her debutante drawl.

'You can dress it up however you like and talk about how some cosmic connection or some such thing is drawing you into her life so you can "be there" for her . . .' Her voice had a nasty sarcastic twang as she drew inverted commas round the last words. '. . . But the truth is it's you who really needs her, so you can fill the emotional void in your life.'

She uttered that final bit as though stating the boringly obvious and then turned to serve a customer, leaving me floundering with my jaw hanging open. Once I got over the urge to strangle her with one of her silk scarves, I thought about what she'd said. And had to admit that, even with the nastiness extracted, there might still be a grain of truth in it.

So when I hesitated before opening my door that evening, I had a bit of a handle on what I was feeling (fear that Tatiana might not be there) and why (fear of losing her).

She was. And I hadn't. And the lentil stew was delicious.

She didn't want to go to the supermarket with me. And she didn't want to go for a walk in the park. She refused a trip out for coffee or to come along to my gardening job. I told her I'd buy her some clothes in a charity shop. She asked me to choose them for her. She didn't want to go down to Mo's. And she didn't, she definitely didn't, want to talk. Any time I asked her about what had happened after she'd disappeared the last time, or anything else remotely personal, she withdrew into herself. She'd duck her head and hug her arms round her chest. The stubborn set to her lips sending a clear message to back off.

She had my flat sparkling on a par with Mo's. And she cooked like a culinary angel. The rest of the time, as far as I could tell, she sat and watched TV or stood at the window gazing over the city. She communicated occasional small-talk froth, but nothing more, and she never asked me anything about my own past. It wasn't just because of the language barrier. I felt like so many men must feel when they have a woman at home tending to their needs whether they speak to each other or not. She was making the rules, but I went along with them. I colluded. It was power, but not of a sort I have ever wanted. It was an odd feeling. Discomforting in spite of the luxury of the unfamiliar attention. I suppose that's why I felt unable to force her to speak to me if she didn't want to.

She was the stillest person I'd ever met. Me, I'm always on the move. If I'm not pacing, smoking or munching, I fidget – either biting my nails, twiddling my hair or picking at bits of myself. Especially when I'm watching TV. But Tatiana would sit with her legs tucked under her, utterly immobile, as though she had retreated to some deep place within herself. We'd both be staring in the direction of the screen, but I could never be sure if she was taking anything in. If I made any comments on a programme, she would respond with a polite half-smile, but rarely with words.

The only time I would see her animated was when she was watching athletics. She would sit forward on the edge of the settee, urging the competitors on. I'm not into it myself, but I would pretend to share her enthusiasm. Once I asked her if she had ever played any sport herself.

'It is a dream,' she replied, and then, tantalisingly, refused to expand.

If I'd been caged and unable to go out, I'd have been climbing the walls. Yet I never saw her agitated inside the flat. On the two occasions I'd seen her outside, she'd been jumpy as a flea. Maybe, like Smokey Pete, she felt safe inside and was able to access some inner space. I had seen two sides of her. But I sensed there was more. Much more. In spite of living together in such close proximity, I was no closer to discovering the real Tatiana.

Only one strange thing happened that made me wonder if TV and window gazing were all she got up to when I was out. The Miserable Gits accosted me in the entrance hall one morning and complained about the bumping on their ceiling during the day. I had no idea what they were talking about. Tatiana was feather light on her feet. I often jumped to find her at my shoulder when I hadn't heard her approach. Maybe she was practising for her dream career as an athlete by tumbling off my settee or swinging from the light bulb . . . Anyway, I wasn't about to argue the toss with the Gits, so I mumbled my usual apologies and never bothered to mention it to Tatiana.

She gave no indication that she might not be prepared to accept this state of affairs for ever. But I wasn't. I wouldn't have dreamed of pushing her into making a more permanent move. But it was summer. The sunshine had finally kicked in and even the Old Kent Road viewed through the grimy windows looked almost fit for human habitation.

'C'mon,' I said one Thursday afternoon about two weeks after she'd arrived. 'You can't just stay cooped up in here. It's un-healthy. It's a beautiful sunny day. And we – you and I – are going to go out and enjoy it.' She did the stubborn head ducking routine, but this time I wasn't having it. 'We'll get the bus to Greenwich and go to the park. I've just made us sandwiches. We'll have a picnic and you'll get to stretch your limbs and feel the sun on your face.'

From her expression, you'd have thought I was suggesting a day trip to a morgue. She tried to protest, but I wasn't taking no for an answer. She asked if she could borrow a hat and some shades, as her skin reacted badly to sunlight. She stuffed her hair into a baseball cap, pulling the brim low over her eyes. Wearing the shades, second-hand baggy jeans and a T-shirt, she looked nothing like the girl I had first met.

She was sulky and bad-tempered all the way there. Or so it seemed to me at the time. In retrospect I can see she was probably shit scared. I've often wondered since if she hated me on that day. Was I just another person she'd been forced into dependence on who threw their weight around and made her do things she didn't want to? At the time, I treated her like a recalcitrant child. So did that make me any better than those who treated her as a woman, but one who was simply a commodity?

Most of the other people in the park were tourists, clustered round the observatory at the top of the hill. A chilly wind had sprung up. It suddenly seemed Tatiana wasn't the only person who thought sitting on a rug eating a picnic was not a good thing to be doing at that point. She was twitchy and nervous, nibbling at a sandwich I forced on her.

Ominous clouds had started an inexorable march across the sky, obliterating the sun. As though the weather was in league with Tatiana to prove what a bad idea this had been. I was determined not to write the day off. I had a feeling that if I admitted defeat, I might never prise her out of the flat again.

'C'mon,' I said, packing up the remains of the picnic. 'We'll go to the Maritime Museum.'

Tatiana pulled off the redundant shades with a sigh of exasperation. She slouched over to a bin to throw away the rubbish, while I folded the rug. I looked up as she walked back towards me. A sudden gust of wind blew off her baseball cap and she caught it in mid air and jammed it back on her head. Black clouds were rolling in from the direction of the river. People were moving through the park with a sense of urgency. A man stood on the path behind her. I noticed him because he was the only person standing still, his eyes drilling into Tatiana's back. As I watched, he pulled out a mobile phone and spoke into it.

It was only much later that I recalled this detail. At the time, my focus was entirely on providing distraction and preventing the day from being an unmitigated disaster. We hurried through the park, negotiated the crowded pavements and made our way to the museum just as the rain started to fall in big heavy drops.

Once inside, Tatiana was sucked in, as I'd hoped she would be. I didn't know anyone who hadn't been to the Maritime Museum who didn't assume it would be stuffy and boring. And I didn't know anyone who *had* been who didn't rave about its imaginative scope and sheer creative energy. We wandered through mock ice caves recreating doomed Arctic expeditions, shuddered at reconstructions of the *Titanic* and marvelled at the combination of lights, mirrors and sound used to illustrate the arcane mysteries of early navigation.

On the next floor up, we went into a giant dome filled with rows of screens chronicling the wonder of the seas and the damage wrought by pollution and stupidity. I felt tears pricking my eyes as we were told that the water on earth was endlessly recycled and was all we would ever have. That the rivers we see today carry the same water bathed in by dinosaurs. And that the damage being done, even in the time we stood there, would be irreversible.

I glanced at Tatiana to see if this affected her in the same way as it did me. I gazed at her profile as she stood transfixed, staring at the screens. Her lips were slightly parted and she held both hands clasped to her chest. She looked very young and vulnerable and I felt a surge of affection for her.

It looked like I might be vindicated after all. She was finally beginning to relax. I glowed with satisfaction. She even agreed to sit in the café for coffee, gazing about her with fascination.

'I have never been to a museum before,' she breathed in a voice filled with wonder.

Up until that day, I had always seen her as a young woman. Now I saw that she was little more than a child, but she had experienced few of the things most people associate with childhood. I started making mental plans for trips to the Science and Natural History Museums.

I'd saved my favourite part of this particular place for last. The interactive gallery on the next floor up. We went up in the glass capsule lift, just for the experience, looking down on a lighthouse planted dozens of feet beneath us on the ground floor next to a vast wave machine. Everything seemed to be on a massive scale, right up to the glass-panelled roof.

We walked along an open balcony overlooking the first floor, which was itself narrower than the ground floor below it. At the end of the balcony, there was a dizzying fifty-foot drop beyond the waist-high wall, passing the edge of the first level all the way down to the ground floor.

We passed through the double doors into the interactive area at the end, where Tatiana and I finally had FUN. We sent semaphore and morse code signals to each other from opposite ends of the room. We sat on a miniature crane and loaded cargo onto a boat. And Tatiana crawled into a low dark hold and launched missiles at enemy boats. With unerring accuracy. Every time she scored a direct hit, she threw her head back and laughed. She played like the child she had never been allowed to be, but without the need to appear cool exhibited by most English girls her age. It was shocking to realise I'd never heard her laugh before. The familiar sullen reticence was gone, replaced by flushed cheeks and sparkling eyes.

We came back through the double doors onto the balcony, giggling like the friends I so wanted us to be. I'd walked on a couple of paces before I realised she was no longer next to me. I turned back. She was standing, rooted to the spot. Her hands were over her mouth, as though she was stifling a scream, her face a mask of horror.

I wheeled round as I followed the line of her vision. At the other end of the balcony, the glass lift doors were opening, the occupants stepping out. Two men I had never seen before began walking towards us. They both wore leather jackets. One of them also wore gloves, which he adjusted as they approached. They walked as though they were in no hurry, but it was clear they weren't there to marvel at maritime adventures.

I looked back at the interactive gallery. I was sure there was no other exit. Tatiana must have thought the same. She shouted something in Ukrainian. One of the men responded in a low voice that sounded as though he meant to be reassuring but succeeded only in sounding sinister.

I couldn't believe this was happening. What were they going to do? Abduct her in broad daylight? There were cameras, security guards . . . yet Tatiana looked almost demented with terror. Surely they wouldn't . . . They *couldn't* . . .

I didn't have time to think. I reacted from gut instinct. It was Brighton pier all over again. I yelled and ran towards the men, knocking them off balance. I knew it had to be futile. The chances of her getting past them and escaping were wafer thin. But if I could just distract them long enough – and attract attention *to* them at the same time – she just might stand a chance. Because one look into the eyes of these men told me there would be none if they got their hands on her.

In the next instant, while we were still grappling, the men and I found we had something in common after all – none of us could believe what we were seeing. In one agile movement, Tatiana kicked off her shoes and leaped onto the low wall overlooking the floors below. She stood poised, just for a second, before launching herself into space. I remember being amazed at the sheer beauty of her flight. Her arms outstretched in front of her, her back arched, her toes pointed, she looked like an Olympic diver. Her baseball cap fell off, her hair streaming behind her.

The men and I shot to the edge of the wall together, momentarily united in our need to see the results of that awesome launch. I was terrified at what I would see, assuming the worst. To this day, I've never been able to work out how she did it. I suppose it's all in the timing . . .

An enormous golden propeller was slowly rotating beyond the wall. The top of its broad blades reached to a point about ten feet below us before turning to a spot about fifteen feet above ground level, where it was rooted on a metal pillar. Tatiana's launch brought her down onto one of the blades near the top of its circuit. She landed cat-like, on all fours. As the blade turned past the highest point, she shifted position. I couldn't see how she could stop herself slipping as the cycle continued. She was now standing on the blade on which she had landed, reaching to the next one above her. As the rotation dropped below horizontal, she took her weight on her arms, resting them on the flat of the upper blade. At the last possible moment, she dropped to the floor, landing in a perfect somersault, before springing to her feet and making for the nearby exit.

For the few seconds this spectacular performance had taken, there had been silence. As though the breath had been collectively sucked into several dozen pairs of lungs and held there. As soon as she landed, all hell broke loose. One of the men snarled something at me, but the other pulled him away. They ran back along the balcony and hared down the stairs. Crowds gathered, pointing in amazement, newcomers asking for an account from witnesses who were still unable to believe the evidence of their own eyes. A couple of security guards ran to the bottom of the pillar, shouting into walkie-talkies and looking up at the propeller in disbelief. I pulled back out of sight. I didn't want to be connected to what had happened and have to answer any awkward questions. To which I realised I probably wouldn't know the answers anyway.

I picked up her discarded shoes and pushed them into my rucksack. Then I went back through the double doors into the interactive gallery. At the far end I found a door I hadn't seen before. So there had been another exit after all. I made my way down the stairs and walked round the ground floor on the opposite side to the propeller. People were still running over to where the crowd were gathered, breathlessly discussing the spectacle in several different languages. No one challenged me as I made my way out through the front doors.

The rain was falling in sheets outside. There was no sign of Tatiana or her two pursuers among the scurrying figures huddled under hoods and umbrellas. I headed for home. Only because I had no idea where else to go.

I was writhing with guilt. She had been desperate not to go out. Not to expose herself. Why hadn't I been more sensitive? I never tried to bully Smokey Pete into hitting the streets. I'd never questioned or challenged the complex fears that made up his agoraphobia. Yet I had stomped roughshod over Tatiana's fears. I had no way of knowing what those men would have done if they'd got hold of her. What I did know was that Tatiana was in no doubt. No one would have taken such extreme measures if they hadn't been terrified for their life.

And, come to that, I still couldn't get to grips with the actual mechanics of how she had achieved her spectacular escape. I still can't. I've stood on that balcony many times since and stared down at the propeller trying to work out how she could have done it without being killed or at least severely injured. And the sheer *style* of her flight . . . the actual *aesthetics* . . .

The next question clamouring for attention was: where is she now? She had no money on her and was lightly clothed and barefoot. I got home, stripped off my sodden clothes and lay in the bath, trying to calm my racing heart and brain and think constructively. But the only thing in my consciousness was: what have I done? What have I done?

12

I SPENT THE evening wrestling with my guilt. I couldn't eat, I couldn't watch TV (except for the news, which didn't mention anything I might want to know about at that point) or listen to music. I didn't dare pop down to Mo's in case Tatiana came back. I wouldn't have been able to talk about my stupidity out loud anyway. I didn't want to use the phone in case Tatiana was trying to get through. Assuming she knew the number. And could find a phone that didn't require a coin.

It was gone midnight when the buzzer sounded. I was staring out of the windows, still frantic. I hadn't gone to bed, refusing to allow myself the luxury while Tatiana was still out there. Cold, wet, frightened. Or worse . . .

At first I didn't recognise the sound. I knew it wasn't the phone. And I didn't have an alarm clock. There was no TV or radio on. And I didn't have a bell on my front door. The buzz sounded again and this time I traced it to the redundant entry phone in the hall. It was linked to the entrance to the block downstairs, but I'd never heard it before. I'd always assumed it didn't work.

Either way, it was a bit pointless, since the doors never locked anyway.

I picked it up, frowning.

'Hello?'

'Uh – Peck-ham Poh-leese,' came a voice in an accent so strong it sounded as though the speaker had just stepped off a plane from Kingston. Peckham Police? I don't think so . . . 'Can you let I in please?' the voice continued.

'Who are you looking for?'

Silence. Then, 'A fren' send me.'

'So you're not the police, then?'

I don't know why I was attempting to engage him in any kind of dialogue. I assumed he'd come to see one of the numerous dealers in the block. But I suppose I welcomed the small distraction.

'Look. You is Jo Cooper?'

I sucked in my breath. He was looking for me after all. But who was he?

'Not to the cops I'm not,' I replied automatically.

'OK, So I is not the poh-leese. You know she?'

'Maybe.'

'Cos I have an important message for she.'

'Who's it from?'

'Me cyan say.'

'So what is it?'

'You is she?'

'Who are you?'

This was getting us nowhere. But my paranoia levels were heightened after what had happened earlier. I was determined to be more careful from now on.

'I is a fren' of a fren'. But me cyan talk here, y'know? If you is she, you should let I in, sistah.'

'I can't let you in,' I replied, still playing for time. 'The buzzer doesn't work.' I heard muttered cursing down the phone. I had the feeling he might give up and walk away. And that I might end up kicking myself later.

'Oh, just push the bloody door,' I told him.

'What floor you on?'

'Top. And I can't guarantee the lift will be working . . .' I added with grim satisfaction.

I was waiting behind the closed door, my eye glued to the spy hole. I heard the chugging of the lift motor and the grinding of gears over the assorted bumps and screams coming from the S&M couple's flat opposite. The lift opened and a tall skinny Rasta stepped out. He stopped and stared at the door to his right where the noise was coming from. I watched him walk up to it and stand listening. A voice from the flat moaned loud enough for us both to hear.

'Oh, that is s-o-o gooood,' followed by a swishing noise and a scream.

The Rasta grinned and turned away shaking his head, his waist-length locks writhing in accompaniment. He looked round the landing before heading to my door. I waited for him to knock, but instead he leaned forward and pressed his own eye to the spy hole.

I gave an involuntary jump back before realising the distortion from his side would prevent him seeing anything. I crept forward again. Even allowing for the fisheye view, his eye was remarkable. I'd never seen whites so bloodshot. Red is another word for high among black ganja smokers. And you could see why. I had no idea who this guy was or what he wanted with me, but I felt instinctively that I had no reason to be afraid. Being that high and simultaneously aggressive is an unlikely combination in my experience. I drew a deep breath and pulled the door open.

He almost fell into the flat, but straightened in time, grabbing the door frame to steady himself.

'Greetings, sistah,' he purred, a beatific smile on his face. 'Greetings from the Mos' High, Selassie-I, conquering lion of the tribe of Judah, king of kings, lord of lords.'

In spite of myself I warmed to him. I've always envied people who have unquestioning faith. But I wasn't about to invite him in.

'So what's this message?' I asked.

I had hoped he was bringing news of Tatiana. Now I wondered if he was a Rasta version of a Jehovah's Witness who had somehow got hold of my name. He peered over my shoulder.

'You is alone?'

The screams from the flat opposite crescendoed to a climax and a heavy silence descended. I suddenly felt vulnerable.

'Look,' I said. 'I don't know you. I don't know how you know my name or why you're here. Tell me why I should trust you.'

He grinned at me, his hooded eyes twinkling in their blood-red sea.

'You don't have to. But your fren' – she trust me. An' I man no use she. Cos I man nah use, abuse or refuse. I is strickly spiritual. I is workin' for Jah an' in this time I is doin' Jah works. An' Jah works in mysterious ways, sistah. KnowhatImean? An Jah – he sen' me to help this woman cos she oppress' by Babylon an' I man is a warrior in Jah army an' Babylon is the system I an' I mus' fight. An' he sen' her all the way from the east an' he sen' me all the way from Africa via the Caribbean so we can meet an' I can be in the right place when she need Jah help.'

I stared at him goggle eyed.

'So where is she?'

He gave me his sleepy smile again.

'She in my van roun' the corner. Jah tell I not to park in the car park. An' she tell I the same thing. These people too wicked and nasty. Them have her full up o' fear. I man give she healing herb an' it work it magic 'pon she. An' I come up ahead to meet with you, sistah, an' check out the scene. KnowhatImean?'

Oh yes. Oh yes, oh yes, oh yes. I knew what he meant. She was safe. I gasped with relief as tears filled my eyes.

'She's OK?'

'Yeah, sistah.' He reached out a hand and rested it lightly on my arm. 'I an' I go fetch she for you. You take it easy, sistah, y'hear? You two women is wrestling with the devil, f'true. Jah will guide an' provide you with the strength you need in the struggle.'

And then he was gone. Back into the lift, with that broad smile and a clenched fist. He never even told me his name.

Tatiana had liberally partaken of the healing herb all right. Her eyes were heavy-lidded and bloodshot, though nowhere near the intensity of her new friend. She wore a black sweatshirt emblazoned with a golden lion carrying a red, gold and green banner in its mouth. Her feet swam in giant flip-flops. She also seemed to have taken on some of his verbosity, and for once was prepared to recount her experience.

After her dramatic exit from the Maritime Museum she had run down, past the *Cutty Sark*, on to the embankment. She soon realised this was not a good move. The paved path runs alongside the Thames going east, with no obvious exit points. As far as she could tell, she wasn't being followed. But she didn't want to risk doubling back in case she ran into her pursuers. There was no one else around in the heavy rain, so she kept moving in the direction she had committed herself to.

I shuddered to think of her. Drenched, barefoot and terrified. Running, not *to* anywhere. Just away.

A pub loomed up in front of her. But it offered no hope of comfort. What could she say to get help that wouldn't involve her in awkward questions? She carried on past the building, into a car park, where she sat on a low wall, trying to gather her thoughts.

She looked up to see a battered van parked nearby. Focusing on it, she realised with horror that it was filled with smoke. And someone was in the front seat.

'I jump up,' she said, leaping to her feet to illustrate. 'My heart is . . .' She punched her thin chest to indicate the pounding sensation. 'I start to run . . .' Tatiana acted out the scene for me, using drama to compensate for the limitations of her vocabulary. I remembered the way she had taken the parts of herself and

Georgi the time I met her on the train from Brighton. That time she had been desperate and panic stricken. This time, it was more like a performance and I was sucked in. But then she *was* very stoned . . .

Thinking of the attention the fire would bring, she started to run away. Then stopped. She knew she couldn't leave the person inside to burn. Against all her instincts, she forced herself over to the van and yanked the door open.

And that was how she met her saviour, sitting peacefully gazing out at the river through a dense fog of ganja smoke.

13

WE SLIPPED BACK into the old routine. Except I didn't attempt to coax her out of the flat any more. That much I had learned. In spite of her enthusiastic, stoned rendition of her Rescue by Rasta, she still refused to talk about what or who she was running from. Not just Georgi and Viktor, that was clear. For her to know she risked being identified wherever she went, the net must have been cast very wide indeed. I couldn't believe they would go to such lengths just to trace a runaway prostitute. What could she have done to piss them off to that extent? I was still so consumed by guilt at having exposed her to danger, I didn't have the heart to insist on answers.

The arrangements still made me feel uncomfortable. I knew we couldn't carry on like this for ever. While one part of me dreaded the thought of losing her, another part chafed at the lack of communication and the way she held so much of herself back.

I popped down to Mo's the following day. Kirsty and Delilah were at school. I wanted someone else to know what had happened. Just in case. Just in case of what, I wasn't sure.

I wanted Mo to be as amazed as I had been at Tatiana's spectacular escape. I probably also wanted her to tell me it hadn't been my fault. In the event, I got neither wish. She was freaked out and angry with me. Not for endangering Tatiana, but for taking her back in after she'd performed her rob-and-run routine a couple of weeks earlier. For getting involved. She told me it was time to demand some answers about what exactly it was I *had* got involved in.

'It's the least she can do, Jo. If you know what it is, you can decide if you want to be mixed up in it or not. Cos from the sound of it, this lot ain't pissing about. This is serious heavy stuff. If she don't tell you nothing, it's not surprising you fuck up and get things wrong.'

I had to work hard to dissuade her from marching upstairs on the spot to interrogate Tatiana. I launched into a recitation of the visit from the Rasta to distract her. It worked.

'Here,' she said, with obvious relish. Mo loved nothing better than being able to top a story of mine. 'Talking of knocking on doors spouting on about religion, y'know Gill downstairs?'

Yes. I knew Gill. She was a vast, slovenly woman who lived on the fourteenth floor. I could never work out how many children she had. There seemed to be numberless hordes of them, aged from nought to seventeen. My heart always sank if I came into the block at the same time as her. I'd rather walk up twenty flights of stairs than share a lift with Gill. I couldn't handle the way she shrieked and cussed the children. I never heard her address any of them with what could pass for the mildest affection.

'Yeah. What about her?' I asked.

'She's been reborn,' Mo said with an expectant smirk.

'You what?'

'Reborn. You know. She's found Jesus.'

'You're having me on.'

'Oh no, I'm not. She's joined some group calling themselves the Church of Christ the Obese.' My jaw dropped. 'I kid you not.

Apparently, they reckon Jesus was really overweight and that was part of the reason he was persecuted. They say the best way to worship him is to copy his example and pile on the pounds.' I shook my head in disbelief. 'It's true! They're having a mass baptism next weekend down at Margate. That should make a few waves. Hope they've warned local shipping.'

'Mo,' I said. 'You're terrible! It's comments like that that lead people like her to look for desperate solutions.'

'Oh, stop being so bloody politically correct,' Mo complained. 'This lot are totally off the wall. Don't go analysing it and coming up with excuses. Do you know what she's up to? She's been knocking on doors trying to convert people and offering them doughnuts.'

'Blimey,' I murmured. 'That takes guts.'

Mo laughed so much, she nearly wet herself. But at least it took her mind off of running upstairs to give Tatiana the third degree.

Another week dragged by. Tatiana continued to cook and clean. I continued to earn and consume. Delilah became a regular visitor. Tatiana was more animated when they were together. It didn't matter to Dee if Tatiana shared no details of her personal life. She wasn't interested in other people. She just enjoyed the company and the novelty of having an exotic foreigner as a friend.

Dee played her the latest hits, introducing the likes of Will Young and Gareth Gates into my home, and together they pored over teen gossip magazines. It irritated the hell out of me, though I would have bitten through my own leg rather than admit it. Together, the pair of them closed me out as effectively as Tatiana did on her own. And I didn't like it. Was I jealous? Probably. And I didn't like that either.

I came home late from the market one day to find the two of them sitting next to each other on the settee looking through my old photo album. A saccharin Not Quite Girls Not Yet Women girl band chirruped at me from my stereo. I looked down and saw the page was open in a familiar place. Des stared up at them from the black and white print, her hair blowing in the wind, holding a baby me up to the camera. It was my most treasured photo. Des had a quizzical half smile and was staring straight into the lens. It was an image I had almost consumed over the years, staring into the eyes of a mother whose world had not yet come crashing down. Eyes still full of unfulfilled dreams and hopes for the future.

Seeing the two of them sitting there in my front room, on my settee, looking at my photo of my mother, was too much to handle.

'Dee,' I said. 'I'm cold and tired. I've had a rough day. I just want to relax. Would you mind . . . ?'

They both looked up at me, surprised at the uncharacteristic abrasive quality in my voice. Dee looked blank, not realising I was asking her to leave. Tatiana nudged her and nodded at the door.

'Oh right,' Dee grumbled, getting to her feet and retrieving her tape. 'See ya, Tatiana.'

She slouched past me with no further acknowledgement and slammed the front door behind her. Tatiana looked up at me from the settee with a curious expression on her face.

'Food is ready,' she said, closing the album and standing up. I took the album from her and hugged it to my chest.

'Forget the food, Tatiana. We need to talk.'

Something in my voice must have told her the usual non-response wasn't going to work this time. I didn't doubt she would have to think of a new tactic. But nothing prepared me for the one she came up with. She reached up a hand and stroked my hair.

'You are tired, Jo. You say this yourself. You need to relax. To feel good.' She carried on caressing my hair with a faraway look in her eyes. 'I can make you feel good, Jo,' she whispered.

Her voice was soft and purring. I stared at her. What did she mean? Seeing the confusion on my face, she made it clear just what she was offering. Her hand travelled down and she gently took the album from me and laid it on the settee. Her lips curved in a smile as she reached down and pulled her T-shirt over her head, revealing tiny breasts capped with dark nipples. She began to run her hands over her breasts, all the while staring provocatively at me.

I felt an ache of desire. I had never made love with a woman before. And it had been longer than I cared to remember since I had made love with a man. In fact, I wasn't sure if 'making love' was the correct expression at all for my previous sexual experiences.

I longed for someone to hold, someone to care, someone to care for. Her hands travelled down to the waistband of her jeans. She snapped open the button and began to pull down the zip.

That was when I looked into her eyes. They were dead.

Suddenly her movements no longer seemed sensual. They were the programmed responses of an automaton. This woman didn't desire me. Maybe she didn't even care for me. She was simply extending the terms of the service agreement.

I ran past her into my bedroom, slamming the door. Then I stood, my forehead pressed to the cold glass of the window, staring at a night-time city floating behind tears.

14

WE WERE CAREFUL not to meet each other's eyes after that. I wasn't angry with her. Just very, very sad. And I felt the burden of my own guilt intensify a thousand fold. I was sad that her experiences had taught her she could trade herself in exchange for food and shelter. And I was appalled that she had seen me as complicit to the bargain. And that – even if only for an instant – I had been tempted.

The guilt silenced me more effectively than any story she might have told me about herself. Fictional or otherwise. If keeping her secrets was so important she was prepared to give her body rather than reveal them, who was I to demand otherwise?

I tried to stay out as much as I could. I spent a lot of time with Smokey Pete. He was fascinated by Tatiana's story, drinking in every detail I could dredge up. I didn't tell him about the proposition she had made – I'm not sure why. Except that the confusion and embarrassment I felt as a result were too deeply personal to share with anyone. So in order to satisfy Pete's curiosity, I imbued her story with a drama and glamour that were far from the sordid reality.

I tried the same tactic with Mo, but with less success. Especially when she heard I'd stopped making the jewellery.

'Why? They was selling, wasn't they? You enjoyed doing it? Lots of people have said they really like my earrings . . .'

I couldn't tell her I'd stopped because I felt uncomfortable in my own home. But she was unconvinced by my claim to have lost enthusiasm. Mo was too astute to be taken in by an amateur like me.

'It's 'er, innit? Tatiana. How long's she gonna be there, Jo?'

Lying to Mo was a bit like how I imagined most people would feel if they were lying to their own mother. That they couldn't possibly get away with it. I'd never had to lie to Des. If anything, it had been the other way round. So I suspect I don't have the necessary experience to make a good job of it. I tend to take the stroppy road and resort to being defensive instead.

'My stopping the jewellery is nothing to do with Tatiana. And she'll be there as long as I choose, right?'

'Meaning I should mind me own business?' Mo asked, pausing in her industrial scouring of her already spotless cooker to drill me with twin beams from her narrowed eyes.

'Take it how you want,' I shrugged, looking away.

'Listen, Jo.' Mo turned from the cooker and stood directly in front of me, forcing me to look back at her. 'You're right – it's none of my business who you have in your flat. On the other hand, we've known each other for enough years now, and we've seen each other through enough shit that I reckon I have the right to say if I think you're doing something that could fuck you up. Right? That's all I'm saying. And if you don't like it and want to get stroppy with me, I'm sorry, but it's tough. I'm gonna say it anyway.'

It speaks volumes for Mo that she never pulled a guilt trip on me at that point by pointing out how much she'd done for me over the years. It also speaks volumes for me that I took advantage of her yet again.

'Yeah, well, it's my life,' I snapped back.

I turned to go, tearing my eyes away from the mixture of hurt and anger in her eyes.

'OK, Jo,' she called to my departing back. 'Just don't forget who your real friends are.'

I realised with a stab that her concern for me was tinged with envy at my assumed closeness with Tatiana. She'd probably heard glowing reports about her from Delilah. She'd never seen us together. So she didn't know the wariness with which we moved round each other, avoiding eye contact at all costs. I would have loved to tell Mo the truth. But I knew what she would say to me, and I didn't want to hear it.

I apologised to Mo the next day. She shrugged and said it was already forgotten. But there was a coolness between us that had never been there before. Even when I'd abused her friendship, ripped her off and been a general acute pain in the arse in years past. It seemed Tatiana's secret was not only a barrier between her and me. Like a physical force, it was also coming between me and my other friends.

One morning, about a week after Tatiana's unmentionable proposition, there was a tentative knock on the front door. Tatiana was already in the bathroom, so didn't need to employ her usual strategy of retreating there when we received un-expected visitors.

'Nadia!' I gasped, pulling open the door. 'What are you doing here?' I looked round the empty landing. 'Where's Yaroslav? Is he OK? Come on in. Come in.'

I directed her into the front room, where she sat down on the edge of the settee and assured me she was fine. She had come to London to meet her new solicitor. The appointment had been made by one of the refugee organisations whose details I had sent her. They had also paid for her fare. She told me they had given her details of other Ukrainian families living in the area. She had made a couple of friends, one of whom had agreed to collect Yaroslav from school and look after him until her return. She seemed tired, but somehow more confident than before.

'People help us now,' she explained. 'But you were the first.'

I felt a small drip of comfort. At least something I had done had turned out right. There was no sound from the bathroom, though I knew Tatiana must have been able to hear us. I thought she would have come out once she realised the visitor posed no threat.

'I have a surprise for you,' I told Nadia. 'Someone I'd like you to meet. She's from the Ukraine too.'

I knocked on the bathroom door. There was no response.

'Tatiana,' I called. 'Come on out. It's OK. It's a friend of mine.'

The door opened and Tatiana appeared, her head wrapped in a towel, looking round suspiciously. I ushered her into the front room, ignoring her obvious reluctance. Nadia frowned as she looked her younger compatriot up and down. Tatiana fidgeted under her scrutiny, unable to meet her appraising gaze.

I was confused. I thought they would have been pleased to see each other. Tatiana, at least, hadn't had the opportunity to converse in her own language for a long time.

'Tatiana – Nadia. Nadia – Tatiana,' I introduced with a smile that was dying on my lips as I spoke. Nadia said something that was obviously a question and Tatiana mumbled a response.

Maybe they were constrained by my presence.

'I'll make tea,' I offered, stepping into the kitchen.

I could hear a weighty silence, then Nadia spoke again. I could tell by the inflection in her voice that she was questioning the other woman. Tatiana didn't sound like she was giving any more away in her own language than she had in mine. Nadia's voice was clipped and cool.

When I came back into the room, bearing mugs of tea and a packet of biscuits, Tatiana was still standing in the same spot as when I had gone out, shuffling her feet and darting glances round like a cornered animal. I tried to make conversation, but neither of them was prepared to co-operate. I was annoyed with Tatiana. She had the manner of a sulky child, while Nadia appeared to be taking the role of the disciplinarian adult.

Actually, I felt irritated with both of them for creating an atmosphere that made me feel uncomfortable in my own home.

Nadia took a sip of tea, refused my offer of a biscuit and got to her feet.

'I go now,' she said, her mouth set in a prim line of disapproval. 'I have appointment.' She gave a brisk nod at Tatiana and held out her hand to me. 'Goodbye, Jo,' she said.

'I'll see you out,' I murmured, throwing a quizzical glance at Tatiana.

At the door, Nadia looked me in the eyes.

'Jo – this girl. She is friend of you?'

'Well, sort of . . . Why?' I asked, trying to interpret her expression and failing.

She hesitated a moment, glancing back towards the front room, before coming to a decision.

'I no like,' she whispered. 'I know this type of woman. She no good person, I think. She could bring you trouble. Jo, *you* are good person. You help me. So I say this to you – you must have care.'

I looked at her, struggling to understand what it was she had seen when she looked at Tatiana to bring her to this conclusion. I knew that Nadia was a respectable wife and mother. And I also knew from her reaction in the park earlier that she fiercely disapproved of prostitution. Had she been able to guess Tatiana's background from that short meeting? I was no closer to understanding when she disappeared behind the closing lift doors.

Tatiana wouldn't give me any response either. But that was less of a surprise.

I was determined to keep myself away from Tatiana's unsettling presence as much as possible, considering we were living together in the same tiny space. It never once occurred to me to solve the problem by asking her to leave. I felt confused and isolated, unable to share the dilemma with anyone. It was doing my head in. I knew it. But I couldn't see a way out.

Somewhere in that time, my birthday came and went. Pete gave me a candle in the shape of an open hand, with wicks protruding from the finger tips. Mo and the girls gave me a card and a strappy T-shirt. The card had rainbow-coloured fish dancing on their tails on the front. It was the only card I received.

During the days when I wasn't at the market or doing my gardening job, I'd go to the park. I'd sit nibbling sandwiches, watching the ducks and feeling miserable. One Monday, about a week after Nadia's visit, I saw a guy I used to know shambling past. He was off his face, oblivious to his surroundings. He didn't even register me, let alone recognise me. I stared at his haggard face and other-world eyes and was appalled to realise that I wasn't feeling the usual gratitude that I wasn't him.

For a gut-churning moment . . . I envied him.

The shock was almost physical, like being slapped. I leaped from the bench, scattering cheese sandwiches and ran round the lake and across the open park, stumbling and retching. I stopped and leaned against a tree, wheezing for breath, my heart pounding. As soon as I was able to function sufficiently, I pulled out my mobile and took the action I had been programmed to take at times like this. Mags was in a meeting. She'd call back. I sank to the ground to wait. Not daring to make a move in case it was a wrong one. In the wrong direction. Backwards.

A dog came and sniffed at me, but otherwise I attracted no attention. Just one lone woman, sitting in a park, her back against a tree. Not a volcano about to erupt. Not a bomb about to explode. Just one woman. As indistinguishable from the thousands of other lonely frightened people in this city as one blade of grass at my feet was from all the others waving in the gentle breeze.

The phone rang and I jumped.

'Hi, Jo. How you doing?' Mags's reassuring voice boomed in my ear.

Just hearing her made me feel better. More grounded. More aware of the solid earth pressing into my arse than the nebulous limitless molecules of air around my head.

'I'm – I –' I stuttered. Then, taking a deep breath, 'Mags, is there any chance I could come and see you?'

There was a minute pause. I could hear a wood pigeon cooing in the branches above me.

'Um, Jo. I have to tell you . . . I've handed in my notice here. I'm leaving at the end of next week. I'm just tying things up. I'm not seeing any clients. But you know you can always just drop in here, if you need to. Shall I tell one of the other workers you're coming . . . ?

'No. No, that's OK,' I mumbled. 'I don't want to come to the project. Don't worry. It doesn't really . . .' Doesn't really what? Doesn't really matter? Doesn't really matter that the one person I felt I could confide in without being judged had just told me she was no longer available?

'What's this about, Jo?' Mags interrupted. 'Is this project business? Or is it to do with that research stuff I sent you?'

'Er, nothing. I mean, neither. Well, both maybe,' I rambled. I could hear my own voice as if I was a mildly interested bystander and knew I was losing the plot. All my energy had to be devoted to retaining my grip. There was obviously not enough left over for coherent speech.

'Jo,' Mags said in her no-nonsense, pulling-it-all-together voice. 'If you're struggling, you really should come in. Even if I can't see you myself, you know there'll always be people here to help . . .'

'I know,' I mumbled. 'I do know that . . . It's not really . . . I just thought . . . It's sort of personal . . . Don't worry. Honestly. I – I'm sorry to lay this on you . . .'

I can't remember her response. Something positive and

reassuring, no doubt. I think – I hope – I wished her luck for the future before hanging up. I leaned back against the tree and stared up at the sky through a blur of tears, trying to deep breathe away the panic.

Almost anyone else in Mags's position would have given my details to a colleague and thought no more about it. I'd always known Mags was different. She was about to demonstrate just how much.

My phone rang and I answered it automatically.

'Jo,' Mags's voice penetrated the fog. 'I've been thinking.' I heard her draw a deep breath. 'Look. This isn't normal practice. I'm sticking my neck out here. But I'm almost out of the system now . . .' I held my breath, wondering what she was building up to. It sounded as though she was persuading herself of something, but I was too hyped up to try to guess what it might be. '. . . Jo, would you like to meet up? Outside the project, I mean . . . At my place . . .'

I was stunned.

'Oh Mags,' I gasped. 'That would be amazing . . . But . . . surely it's not allowed . . .'

I knew that limiting personal involvement with clients was an absolute rule, but now she was leaving . . . I didn't take too much persuasion, I'm afraid. We made an arrangement for Wednesday and I memorised the address in Peckham she gave me. I decided I would phone the day before and give her the opportunity to back down. I was convinced she'd start regretting her offer the moment she put the phone down.

On the other hand, I started counting the hours until Wednesday evening.

There was a third hand too. The one that noted the danger of depending on someone else to make everything all right. When if there was one thing Mags had tried to drum into me, it was the knowledge that only I could do that for myself. But if she trusted me enough to invite me into her own home, I was determined not to let her down. You could analyse that by saying I was being strong for her, not for myself, but the end result would be the same. I would hang on in there. I would come through this.

And, anyway, Mags also used to say that though it was essential to do it for yourself, that didn't mean you had to do it alone. Before hanging up, she made me promise to drop into the project if I needed to before Wednesday. I assured her I would be OK. And, amazingly, I thought I probably would be now.

I managed to carry on. If not forwards, at least not backwards. There had to be an end somewhere, I told myself. Even if it wasn't currently in sight. Tatiana couldn't spend the rest of her life holed up in my flat. Was she waiting for something? I had no way to tell. Maybe she just needed enough time to pass for . . . for . . . something to happen. Or maybe nothing to happen. Maybe that was the point.

I was doing my best to relax in front of the TV the following evening when there was a loud rapping on the front door. Tatiana jumped up and ran into the bathroom. I opened the door to Claudette. She didn't come in, saying she'd left B 'n' B downstairs in bed.

'I've got a big favour to ask. I've promised to take the kids to the circus on Peckham Rye on Thursday, but I just had a call. Someone's gone sick and I've been offered a gig . . . I won't be able . . .'

'I'll do it,' I interrupted. Claudette is a talented backing singer, with the kind of deep, rich voice that resonates in your guts. She's also a single parent who needs all the work she can get. I calculated a three-pronged benefit from my offer: a) supporting Claudette; b) an evening out of the flat; c) a trip to the circus! Yeah!

'Thank you, darlin'. You really helpin' me out, y'know.'

'Believe me, Claudette,' I said with utter conviction, 'the pleasure is all mine!'

I popped back down with Claudette to Mo's to see if Kirsty

and Delilah fancied coming too. Like I needed to ask. I didn't bother inviting Tatiana.

I phoned Mags later. She said she hoped I was still coming over the next day. So I had two consecutive evenings' entertainment lined up. Pretty good going for someone who a couple of days previously couldn't see beyond the next five minutes.

15

I WALKED THROUGH the back streets of Peckham to the address Mags had given me. It was a pleasant enough road, running from a low-rise estate at one end down to Nunhead Green at the other. The terraced houses were innocuous and bland. I hadn't imagined Mags living somewhere so – well, unremarkable, really.

The road was bisected by a railway bridge, next to a plot of wasteland. The house numbers seemed to change once I'd walked under the bridge. There were some missing, and my luck being what it is, Mags's was in the missing chunk.

The first building after the bridge appeared to be a shop. I say 'appeared' because it was by no means certain. There was no sign or adverts. No posters on the shuttered windows or any other obvious indication that it might sell anything. But it didn't look like a house either. I decided to chance it and pushed the door open.

The first thing that hit me was the smell. I can honestly say, with my hand on my heart, I would never be tempted to buy anything from a shop that smelled that bad. Though that might have been just as well, as I couldn't actually see much that might be on sale. The stench was a combination of nicotine and piss – both familiar to me from my own stairwell. But they were overlaid with a hideous musty smell of stale food and fabrics with a definite layer of Big Dog.

On my right was a rail of mouldy-looking old clothes and a crate half filled with bottles of milk. I hadn't seen milk in anything other than a carton for years. The place felt like it existed on the other side of a time warp.

A high wooden counter ran the width of the shop. A few bars of chocolate in faded wrappers sat in a shoebox on its filthy, pockmarked surface. On the wall behind it was a cigarette machine.

Two figures leaned on the counter, both watching me intently. One was about fifty, his chin covered in stubble, greasy, lank hair framing a cadaverous face with dull eyes. As I walked in, he grabbed the fag from his mouth and stubbed it out violently on the counter, laying his hand over it as though to hide the evidence. Unfortunately, he didn't seem to have done a very good job of extinguishing it. His eyes widened in shock and pain as he snatched his hand away, balled it into a fist and pummelled the butt several times before laying his palm back over it. All the time, he never looked away from me.

The figure beside him was a huge Rottweiler, the size of a grizzly bear, its massive forepaws resting on the counter. It also watched me as I stood there, dazed. Drool fell in a constant stream from the sides of its slack mouth and pooled between its paws.

I took a deep breath and instantly regretted it. Swallowing hard, I said. 'Um – excuse me. I'm looking for number 293a?' I paused, but neither of them seemed to realise I had asked a question. 'Could you tell me where I could find it? Number 293a?'

There was almost complete silence in the shop. I couldn't even hear breathing, but I was making every effort to keep mine shallow. The only sound was the muted trickle of the dog's dribble splashing onto the counter.

A sudden roar filled the room and the milk bottles jangled in their crate. I gasped and almost screamed before I realised it was just a passing train on the bridge outside. The human of the two figures shook his head at me. I couldn't interpret the expression on his face. It looked like disgust. But it could have been suspicion or even horror. I had no idea what I could be giving out that could justify such a response.

'Oooh, no,' he croaked. 'Oooh, no. I couldn't do that. Oooh, no.'

I turned and fled from the shop. I'd contacted Mags because I was teetering on the brink. A surreal and nightmarish experience like that might be all it took to have me hurtling into the abyss.

I stood on the pavement outside, trying to deep breathe away the panic.

'You OK?' a voice called.

I looked over. A young woman with spiky dark hair was putting a bag of rubbish in a wheely bin outside a house three doors away. She didn't look nightmarish. She looked friendly. Familiar almost.

'I – I'm looking for number 293a . . .' I stammered.

'Oh, you must be Jo. C'mon in,' she said, disappearing back into the house, leaving me no option but to follow her.

She trotted up a flight of uncarpeted stairs, calling over her shoulder to me.

'Mags just phoned. She's been delayed. She'll be about half an hour. In the meantime, you get me, I'm afraid . . .' She stopped in the hall at the top of the stairs. 'I'm Jen.' She grinned at me. 'Welcome to Nirvana.'

I was so busy staring at my surroundings, I didn't immediately take in what she had said.

'Do you like it?' she asked, looking round.

'It' was the interior decor of her hallway, the walls of which were thickly spattered from floor to ceiling with vivid drools of bright red and yellow gloss paint. Jen led me into her front room, explaining how her 'art installation' had been the result of a paint fight she'd had with Mags when they'd been decorating years earlier.

Her front room was more within the range of my experience. Apart from one rickety armchair, the seating was huge floor cushions, arranged opposite big sash windows that overlooked the railway embankment. As I sank onto the cushions, a train thundered past, the windows shaking in their frames.

Jen laughed at the shocked expression on my face.

'You get used to it after a while. And it's better than traffic or planes. I like it. It makes me feel connected . . . Coffee?' she offered. 'Herb tea? I don't have ordinary tea, I'm afraid.' She stopped, struck by a sudden thought. 'Or milk. I could pop out and get some . . .'

I thought about the dusty bottles I'd seen sitting in their crate in the shop next door.

'Black coffee would be fine, thanks,' I said in a rush.

I felt slightly intimidated by this sparky woman. She was smaller than me, but I felt somehow engulfed by her personality and confidence. I also felt a strange little nag of recognition that suggested we had met before. But I couldn't for the life of me remember where. I was grateful for the space afforded by her departure to the kitchen. That was when I remembered what she'd said in the hall.

She came back in, sat down next to me and handed me a mug filled with something that looked as though it had been scraped off a beach following an oil tanker disaster. I took a sip and almost choked.

Jen looked up, concerned.

'Is it too strong? I forget not everyone believes coffee isn't coffee unless you can slice it with a knife and fork.'

'Blimey,' I gasped. 'Now I can see where you get your energy from.'

Jen threw her head back and laughed. Laughter is a great way of bringing people together. I felt myself beginning to relax a little.

'Did I hear you say "Welcome to Nirvana"?' I asked.

'Sure. You know about Nirvana, I presume.'

'Er, yeah,' I frowned. 'It's like enlightenment, isn't it? Sort of paradise. Unless you mean Kurt Cobain's band . . .'

Another laugh. I was warming to her now.

'True on both counts. But it's also – and more importantly – the name of the co-op.'

'Co-op?' Now I was really confused.

'Didn't Mags tell you? This is a housing co-op. I live up here and Mags is downstairs. Well, not right now, of course, or you'd be down there too and we wouldn't be having this conversation. Then there's Robin and Frank next door and Ali and Gaia in the house after that.'

'What about that weird shop place?'

'Oh, that's Mrs V's. Not part of the co-op. Did you go in?'

'Yeah. I couldn't work out the house numbers . . .'

Jen grimaced.

'We do that deliberately. We've had some trouble here recently. It was a futile attempt to keep away the journos and gawpers.' She laughed again, but this time the sound had a hard bitter edge to it. I remembered that Mags had been on compassionate leave the first time I'd phoned and was tempted to ask questions. But her comment about gawpers prevented me. 'Did you meet Derek in the shop?' I nodded. 'Bet you got precious little from him, then.'

I was relieved to hear his reaction had been predictable and was therefore not personal, as my paranoia had claimed.

'About as much as I got from that monstrous dog he's got.'

'Hey,' she said with mock severity. 'Don't knock that dog. Tyson has saved my life twice before – literally. I'll tell you about it some time.'

I liked the way she assumed there would be other occasions we would meet. I was also even more intrigued now. Though she spoke lightly, there was something dark behind her eyes that hinted at some deep horror. I didn't for a moment disbelieve her or assume she was exaggerating.

'So where do you live, then?' she asked, changing the subject.

'Boddington Heights. It's . . .'

I got no further.

'Fuck me! You live at the Bod? Shit, that's weird.'

As she spoke, I suddenly realised why she'd seemed familiar. My mind lurched back to the night I'd discovered Bare Botty Man dangling outside my window. It wasn't even that long ago, but so much had happened since, it felt like several lifetimes. Like a rewind of a video sequence, I remembered peering through the spy hole at the two people getting into the lift. The woman had had a bruised face and was wearing a leather jacket and mini skirt. She had dark spiky hair.

And I was sitting in her front room chewing her coffee.

She looked no less shaken than I imagine I did. Although she couldn't have known I'd seen her that night. Before either of us could think how to react, we heard the front door slam and a familiar voice boomed out unfamiliar words.

'Coo-ee, honey. I'm home.'

'We're up here,' Jen bellowed back, recovering her composure. 'Jo and I are bonding.'

'Glad to hear it. Up in a mo.'

I heard a door downstairs crash open, followed by heavy bumps and thumps of drawers and cupboards being slammed. Then footsteps clattered up the stairs and the doorway was suddenly filled edge to edge and bottom to almost top with my former drugs counsellor.

She fell into the ancient armchair, which gave a despairing sag under the onslaught.

'Christ! I'm knackered,' she groaned. She looked over at me. 'Welcome to Nirvana, Jo. You find it all right?'

'She found Derek and Tyson first,' Jen butted in.

Mags gave the great belly laugh that I remembered so well.

'Well, if you survived that, honey, plus half an hour of verbal assault and battery by our Jen here, you can handle just about anything.'

'Thanks a lot,' Jen protested. 'If you'd given the poor woman proper directions, she wouldn't have had to endure at least half of that terrible ordeal.'

It was clear the two of them had a closeness and intimacy that could only have come through shared history. Yet I didn't feel uncomfortable or closed out. It was strange, but I felt more at ease there than I ever did in my own home. Even before Tatiana was in it.

Mags produced a carved box and pulled out a packet of Rizlas, a cigarette and a bag of ganja you could smell from the other side of the room and proceeded to roll a massive spliff.

'Do you skin up at work in front of your clients?' Jen inquired.

'Oh, very amusing,' Mags drawled, holding a lighter out at arm's length and introducing the flame to the end of the spliff.

'It's not a problem,' I rushed to say, thinking Jen was being critical of Mags for smoking in front of me. 'I smoke myself. And, anyway, I can't imagine anyone being able to do that job without something to get them through . . .'

'Yeah, well I won't be doing it much longer, m'dear. Want to hear something weird? I'd decided to take some time off before going for another job. But then I saw an ad for a worker in a refugee project. I'd been checking out the issues when you called that first time.' She took an enormous drag on the spliff, the end burning with the intensity of a flame thrower. 'Coincidence, huh?' she said through a dense cloud of smoke.

Then she and Jen both chorused together, 'Gaia says there's no such thing as co-incidence.' They both grinned at what was obviously a familiar joke.

'My mum used to say the same thing,' I mused.

Mags passed the spliff to Jen. By the time it got to me, it was still several times larger than your average joint and I was already high on breathing in what the two of them had breathed out.

'Listen, m'dears. I've got the makings for a barbie downstairs. Jen, why don't you check if any of the others want to join us? Jo and me can pop down to my place and make a start on the salad. Give us half an hour or so.'

Jen agreed with obvious enthusiasm. Mags thundered down the stairs with me at her heels. By that time I was so hooked on their easy familiarity they could have roasted me on the barbecue and eaten me if it meant I could be part of their scene.

Mags's kitchen was a bit on the dilapidated side. There was a large damp patch on one wall and the cupboards looked hand-made – but not by a carpenter. But it was clean enough to pass a scrutiny by Mo. We chopped vegetables into a bath-sized bowl and she asked some general stuff about how I'd been.

'It's OK, Mags,' I told her. 'I'm not about to rush out and fill my veins to overflowing with smack. I – I am having a bit of a crisis, but it's not a drugs-related one.'

Mags drew the information from me. I started with Nadia and Yaroslav. Mags sucked her teeth in anger when I told her about their relocation.

'But in a way it's sort of worked in her favour,' I told her. 'Thanks to the list of contacts you sent, she seems to be getting a bit of support at last. And if this new solicitor works out . . . Anyway, that hostel place was awful . . .'

I described the scene at the church. When I mentioned the beer-gutted guys hanging round outside with their flash cars, she erupted in anger.

'Parasites,' she spat. 'The kind of filth who feed on misery. It's a whole industry, Jo. There's always going to be people who see the misery of others as a unique and lucrative business opportunity. On the one hand you've got the government flinging money round to show they take the problem seriously – though of course they never fling it at the people who really need it. So you've got dodgy hostel owners and landlords cashing in on the bonanza. Not all of them are on the take, of course, but plenty are. Then you've got the contractors. They deal in all kinds of shit – all of it exploitative and most of it dangerous. They're looking to pick up cheap labour to work on building sites with zero health and safety. The government turns a blind eye to them, needless to say. Then there's people traffickers, prostitution racketeers . . .'

The knife I'd been using to slice cucumber slipped as she spoke.

'Shit!' Mags yelped. 'Shove it under the tap. Here.'

She held my finger and we both watched the trickle of blood spread and dilute into the flow of water. She grabbed a wad of tissue and I pressed it on the cut as she ran for a plaster. She stuck it on for me and then looked up into my face. Tears were flowing down my cheeks. We both knew they weren't caused by a cut finger.

'Jo, honey. What is it? C'mon, baby. What's going on?'

She guided me to a table set immediately under the damp patch. We sat on wicker chairs. And I told her all about Tatiana.

Mags let me speak without interrupting. When I'd finished, she sighed.

'Shit, Jo. That's a hell of a lot to be dealing with. For you *and* for her. I don't know if you're aware of this, but if Tatiana has family back in the Ukraine, she's going to be seriously worried for them. And with justification.'

'How do you mean?' I asked, even though I wasn't sure I wanted to hear the answer.

'OK.' Mags propped her elbows on the table, the better to use the expansive hand gestures I remembered so well from the times I had seen her at the project.

'The way these gangs operate is by fear and control. If they don't get Tatiana back, they'll take it out on her family back in the Ukraine. Vandalism, violence even murder – trafficking the remaining sisters . . . they'll stop at nothing. It's not just a question of money. It's power too. Everything depends on them maintaining their reputation. They can't allow anyone to be seen to get the better of them.'

She popped a cherry tomato into her mouth and chewed thoughtfully.

'So – they can't just let Tatiana get away.'

She offered me a tomato, but I shook my head. I was riveted by her words. They lent a context and background to some of the stuff that must have been churning round Tatiana's mind behind the blank and sullen façade.

'And from what you've said,' Mags continued, 'it sounds possible she may have done something else to provoke them apart from running away. Not that she needed to . . . But there feels to me like there's missing chunks in her story . . . I'm sorry, Jo.' Mags shook her head and reached a hand out to mine. 'I don't really know what to say. I understand you feel you can't just chuck her out. On the other hand, you've got yourself mixed up in some seriously dangerous stuff. I don't mean to freak you out, but these people are utterly ruthless. I've heard that the backgrounds a lot of these guys come from are so impoverished that they literally have nothing to lose. Chuck them in prison over here and it's still an improvement in living standard from what they'd have back home. And anyway, if you checked out the stuff I sent you off the Web, you'll know the authorities here aren't interested in tracking them down. If they were, they'd treat the girls as victims and give them protection – try to get them to give evidence instead of chucking them out as illegal immigrants.'

Mags gave a deep sigh and stared up at the damp patch on the wall above us.

'I'm worried about Tatiana and we have to work out how best to help her.' She paused and added almost to herself, 'But I'm worried about you too . . .' She hauled herself up from the table and began pouring dressing over the salad. 'I'm going to think about this. I want to talk to the others too – if you don't mind, that is. We've found before we can get whole new perspectives on stuff when we focus together. But not tonight. I don't want you to have to deal with this in isolation. And you don't have to. But tonight – tonight, honey, I just want you to chill. Relax and enjoy yourself, that's the most important thing you need to do right now.'

She picked up the bowl and handed it to me and pulled a pile of plates from a cupboard.

'C'mon. Let's go outside and I'll introduce you to the others.'

The garden was huge, stretching the width of all three houses. Jen was tending a home-made barbecue constructed of piled-up bricks with an oven rack on top. Two guys were setting up a wallpaper pasting table on a paved area. Mags and I put down the salad and plates on the table and she introduced me.

Frank was an edgy-looking guy with a soft Irish accent. He shook my hand with a shy smile. He exuded a sort of battered vulnerability that I recognised. I had no doubt that here was a man with the same kind of drugs-related experiences as I had.

The other guy was Ali, a serious-looking Asian with a tattoo of an Anarchist symbol on his forehead. He was familiar too. But for a different reason. I had seen him before. Not just his type, but the real him. Standing next to Jen in the lift on the night they'd dangled a bare-arsed man outside my window. I wondered if Jen had told him where I lived. I shuffled in discomfort as he appraised me with solemn, dark eyes.

I was grateful for the arrival of another co-op member. A heavy woman dressed in layers of multicoloured fabric and lots of tinkly jewellery appeared to float out of the third house.

'This is Gaia,' Mags announced. 'Be careful. She's just started a course in leech healing and she's looking for victims. Ooops,' she mocked with heavy sarcasm, 'I mean *patients*. Don't let her see any running sores you might have . . .'

Everyone laughed, including Gaia. It was clear they all knew each other so well, none of them would be offended by the banter with which they communicated. They related to one another like a quirky family, but without the hideous complications families so often have. There was only one co-op member missing, apparently. A guy called Robin, who they told me was in Italy for an anti-globalisation protest.

I couldn't remember when I had last enjoyed myself so much. We sat on blankets on what they called the lawn – even though it was actually a bare patch of earth filling the centre of the garden. We ate, drank, smoked and talked. I didn't do much of the talking, but I wallowed in the atmosphere of warmth and easy companionship.

The conversation was mostly about politics. I'd always been too tied down in my own piece of the world to pay much attention to the rest of it. I knew instinctively what I felt was right and wrong. Multi-culturalism was right, racism was wrong. Equal opportunities was right, the gap between rich and poor was wrong. Giving people the means to run their own lives was right, giving them war, Coca-Cola and McDonald's was wrong. And so on. But in general, all this was 'out there', remote and unchangeable. It was what it was. And that was beyond the power of people like us to change. Or so I had always thought. Until I came to Nirvana. Mags and her friends made politics seem immediate and personal. Sexy almost. I drank it in.

I learned a lot that evening about the way the world worked and the impact individuals could make on it when they acted together. I also learned that in the co-op Mags was known as Maggot. I've no idea why. It would be hard to imagine anyone less like the human equivalent of a small white worm.

The only person I was a bit unsure of was Ali, who spoke even less than I did. His main form of communication seemed to consist of minute gestures which the others responded to as if he'd delivered a learned treatise. I had no way of knowing if he was mistrustful of me or if he was always this quiet. Frank seemed to get teased a bit more than the others, but in a very gentle, affectionate way. Gaia reminded me slightly of a younger version of Des, but one who had found a place for herself and a way of living in this world. And Mags and Jen . . . well as far as I was concerned, they were the living embodiment of Cool.

The time ran so fast it was with bone-breaking reluctance that

I announced I had to get home. A silent message flashed between Jen and Ali.

'We'll give you a lift,' Jen told me as they got to their feet.

'Do you mind if I don't come, honey?' Mags asked, yawning and stretching. 'Gotta get up tomorrow . . .'

Gaia kissed me on both cheeks and mumbled something over my head that sounded like a blessing. Frank gave me an awkward embrace and then busied himself putting out the fire.

Mags walked me to the door, saying she'd ring in the next day or so once she'd had an opportunity to talk to the others. By a lucky chance, the hug she gave me failed to dislocate my shoulders.

We climbed into a battered old Transit van. Ali drove and Jen sat next to him on the passenger seat. I sat in the back, listening to Jen rant about politics. Racism, globalisation, homophobia, capitalism – you name it. All I know is, if she was on a particular side, that was the side I wanted to be on too.

The Transit lurched down the Old Kent Road and turned into the Boddington car park. I felt a great cloud of desolation descend on me as I peered through the dirty window up at the top of the block to where my flat – and Tatiana – were waiting. The contrast to where I'd just come from couldn't have been greater.

I tried not to give in to the depression. I would take the kids to the circus tomorrow. I would carry on, one day at a time, knowing that with Mags and her fellow Nirvanans on the case, at least I was no longer alone. I had to believe there would be some kind of resolution. To the immediate problem of Tatiana, if not to the emptiness in my life she had filled.

Jen twisted round in her seat.

'Here you go, then. Um – we won't see you in, if you don't mind.'

I looked her straight in the eyes and came to a decision.

'I saw you that night, y'know.'

'What night?' She frowned. 'What do you mean?'

I told them about seeing them both getting into the lift and my rescue of Mr Dangly Stripe Bum. Jen gave a bark of mirthless laughter.

'So that's how he got down then,' she said to Ali's impassive profile. 'I always wondered.'

Ali raised an eyebrow and shrugged.

'Yeah,' Jen went on, her jaw set, her voice controlled. 'I'd half hoped he was still up there. We'll tell you about it some time, Jo. Not tonight though . . .' Her voice tailed off.

'Hey,' she said, her voice resuming its former high energy and humour. 'You realise what this means, don't you? You're one of us now.' She put on a theatrical tone I recognised as an impersonation of Gaia. 'The lines of energy, karma and synchronicity have linked us inextricably. The threads that have woven us together in the rich tapestry of life cannot and will not be broken.'

She laughed and even Ali turned the corners of his mouth into a genuine smile.

Her words and the sound of her laughter stayed with me as I walked across the gravel of the car park and into the block.

16

'ME! ME! ME! I wanna be her right-hand man!'

Blythe clung to my hand with the grip of a Black and Decker Workmate, while shoving a Nike-clad shoulder into Bliss's chest.

'That's not fair!' Bliss wailed. 'Jo, why can't *I* be your right-hand man?'

'You be my left-hand woman, honey,' I soothed.

Fat chance. The two of them tugged at me, pulled at each other and tripped all three of us up until I resorted to the assertive adult routine.

'Right. Stop right here, both of you. *All* of you.'

I pulled up so abruptly Kirsty and Delilah cannoned into us from behind.

'OK. We're going out to have *fun*. Understand? F-U-N fun. And *this* – this is not fun. If you two don't get your act together and stop fighting, we're going to turn straight round and go back home again. You hear? And, Delilah, if you don't stop giving me dirty looks – or at least explain *why* you're looking at me like I'm Cruella De Vil – you can go home too. Now, what's the verdict? In five minutes' time we can either be going into that big top over there, or we can be catching the bus back home again. Your choice.'

There was much growling, muttering and shuffling of feet, which I took as grudging acquiescence.

'OK. Let's go, then.'

We set off over the open expanse of Peckham Rye towards the circle of trucks, caravans and motor homes ringing the huge, striped marquee. We bought the cheapest tickets, which still amounted to a large chunk of my weekly income. I was glad Mo and Claudette had insisted on contributing their money, if not their presence.

There are regular circuses on the Rye. Usually, they're fairly upmarket. No doubt hoping to attract the Dulwich denizens who could afford the entrance fee, full-colour brochure, assorted merchandise and snacks and a photo of their children in the ring with a Shetland pony.

This one was different. The tent was tatty, the seating seedy and the whole place smelled musty. We ran a gauntlet of performers doubling as souvenir sellers. Up close, you could see the boredom and fatigue etched on their faces beneath the pancake make-up. Wearing stockings and a sequin-covered costume to sell candy floss doesn't make the drudgery any more glamorous.

Not that the kids noticed any of this, of course. At least they weren't squabbling any more. Now all my energies had to go into refusing requests for battery-operated light sabres and furry antennae. We took our seats, the lights dimmed, the drums rolled and the squirming finally ceased, to be replaced by wide-eyed breathless expectation.

My thoughts turned to Tatiana, sitting alone in my flat. Even though I knew she wouldn't have come if I'd invited her – and even though getting away from her discomforting presence was a relief – I couldn't help remembering her childlike joy at the Maritime Museum. She would have loved this. I gave myself a mental shake and settled back to watch the show.

A short, grizzled man, wearing a faded red coat several sizes too big, a scuffed top hat and an irritated expression, ran into the ring like a cut-price Father Christmas. I was surprised to find myself feeling cheated. I thought ring masters, like Santas, were supposed to be big and jolly.

'La-dies and gen-tle-men. Welcome to Cosmo's Cir-cus.'

Even with the mike, his voice sounded reedy. He introduced the acts, feigning annoyance (without too much effort, I thought) at the antics of a couple of clowns who looked like rejects from a Ronald McDonald audition. The first performer was an African fire breather – cue lots of leopardskin and jungle drums – and the second was a pair of juggling twins.

Blythe elbowed me in the ribs.

'Me an' Bliss could do that,' he whispered, awestruck, as the performers chucked vicious-looking swords and flaming brands to each other. Having seen B 'n' B throwing things *at* each other numerous times, but never *to* each other, I reckoned they'd have a lot of work to do to brush up their technique, but smiled encouragement.

The next act was a family of Russian acrobats, three men and two women called the Flying Poliakovs. At least, they were introduced as a family, but none of them bore the slightest resemblance to each other. The two women, one dark and statuesque and the other thin and mousy, pirouetted from ropes, which they scaled with a lot less effort than most people use to climb stairs. While they hung upside down, twisted and spun, the men performed hand stands and tumbles on the mat. For the finale, they all climbed to two facing trapezes and proceeded to chuck each other about as though unaware of the twenty-foot drop to the floor, and undeterred by details such as the absence of a safety net.

I looked at the children's profiles. Their eyes were wide with wonder, their mouths hanging open. Even Kirsty's, and she doesn't usually allow that to happen.

Next up was a display of knife throwing and whip cracking by the ring master and two young women. He'd swapped his red coat for a black silk shirt. The women's costumes were skintight black leather, seamed tights and stilettos. They did lots of feline crawling round on the floor while the ring master cracked his whip over them. Then the women stood and one of them spread-eagled her partner against a backboard and secured her wrists and ankles. She returned to the ring master and presented him with a tray of gleaming knives. The bound woman stood impassive as the knives swished through the air and thudded into the backboard behind her. The fetishist overtones seemed inappropriate in this setting, but the children were oblivious to such concerns. Delilah shrieked a couple of times. B 'n' B were utterly silent. Kirsty grinned at me. Everyone happy.

Next, a diminutive Chinese girl climbed on a plinth carried on to the stage by the fire breather and one of the clowns. She wore a plain blue backless leotard. Her hair was cropped so close you could see her skull shining in the spotlight. The juggling twins brought a table laden with long white candles in small holders and placed it next to the plinth, where the Chinese girl sat cross-legged, her eyes closed as if in deep meditation. The twins lit the candles.

'La-dies and gen-tle-men,' wheezed the ring master. 'Exclusively to Cosmo's Circus . . . it's my honour and privilege to present for your entertainment this evening . . . from the mysterious Orient . . .'

As he spoke, the girl moved onto her front and lay prone with her hands outstretched over her head, the palms flat on the plinth. The twins placed a lighted candle on the back of each of her hands. '. . . *superb agility . . . mesmerising grace . . .*' She bent her legs at the knees and raised her feet so they were parallel with the plinth. Two more lighted candles were placed on the soles of her feet, a third on the small of her back. '. . . *the suppleness of a cat combined with the strength of a tiger . . .*' She raised her head, her spine bending backwards against its natural curve. '. . . *unbelievable feats of contortion . . .*' Her head and shoulders continued to rise until her head was pushed back so far her face pointed to the ceiling, her toes almost touching the top of her skull. '. . . *courage . . . strength . . .*' The candle on the small of her back wobbled and fell, spilling melted wax from the bowl. One of the twins leaped forward and replaced it carefully. Only then did I notice the Chinese girl's skin was mottled with red sores. '. . . *bravery in the face of pain . . .*'

I'd seen enough.

'I'm going to the loo,' I told Kirsty. 'Watch the kids.'

I didn't need the toilet. I ran out, stooping low to avoid blocking the view of the audience, who were glued to the performance with a kind of appalled compulsion, like voyeurs at a crash site. Outside the marquee, I took a few gulps of fresh air. I pulled out a cigarette and looked round at the circle of battered vehicles that housed the circus equipment – both human and otherwise.

The hoped-for escapist element of the evening's entertainment had drained away with the wax from that fallen candle. I would find no release here from my current obsession with vulnerable women far from home.

I stared at a poster advertising the circus. The shrivelled ring master stood in the centre, arms outstretched to encompass a montage of the acts. The Chinese girl stood in crucifixion pose in the top corner with a row of candles on each extended arm and an elaborate blazing candelabra balanced on top of her head. The red sores had been airbrushed out.

The Russian family were directly below her, the three men forming the base of a human pyramid. Two of the women stood on their shoulders. A third woman stood on the top to complete the structure. I peered closer. Only two of the women had performed that night. I recognised them as the two in the middle. The third woman – the one on the top – was much younger. I drew my breath in sharply as I realised I recognised her too. That incredible feat I'd witnessed at the Maritime Museum flooded into my mind. And made sense at last. Because the third woman, the woman standing triumphant and smiling a plastic smile on the top of that human pyramid, was Tatiana.

I gawped in disbelief, my mind churning to take in this new and unexpected piece of information. I ground my cigarette butt under my heel and strode back into the big top.

There was a short corridor before the main arena, marked out by a strip of muddy carpet. On one side was a stand selling snacks. I bought two huge tubs of popcorn and four cardboard cartons of Coke from the middle-aged woman with blood-red lips behind the counter.

'Brilliant show,' I gushed, handing over what seemed like an extortionate sum.

'Glad you're enjoying it, love,' she smiled.

'Those Russian acrobats are amazing . . .'

'The Poliakovs? Oh, yes. They're a real class act.'

I took my time pocketing the change.

'I couldn't help noticing there were six of them on the poster outside . . .'

Did her eyes flicker in suspicion? Or did I imagine it?

'That'll be Irina,' she replied, after a short hesitation. She leaned towards me. 'She's up the duff,' she said, in a conspiratorial whisper, as though it had been a bit of a scandal.

'Oh, right. Well, I suppose it's not the sort of job you can do if you're pregnant . . .'

'Mmm.' She nodded in agreement.

'Reckon she'll be back?'

It was a question too far. The woman shrugged and turned away to fiddle with the popcorn machine. I could see I would get no further information from her. I struggled back to the kids with my arms full of potential tooth decay. They were roaring with laughter as two short, fat men on unicycles weaved round the ring. They accepted the popcorn and drinks without a sideways glance. I doubted if they'd even noticed I'd been gone. Let alone have any awareness of the inner turmoil churning up my guts. After the drought of detail of the past few weeks, this sudden new and unexpected insight into my house guest's background had knocked me sideways.

I have no recollection of the rest of the show. All I could think about was the significance of what I had learned. And what I should do with it.

The circus finished and the lights went up, revealing the full extent of the seediness of the surroundings. The big top was faded and patched. Empty cartons and containers littered the ground under the scuffed seats. The boundary of the arena was formed by a ring of coffin-shaped boxes coated in flaking red paint.

The performers had reformed their gauntlet along the corridor to the open air. From artiste to tat seller in one fluid movement. One of the Russians was standing at the end of the row. Like the others, he looked glassy-eyed and exhausted. I stopped to buy a brochure from him.

'What happened to Irina?' I blurted.

I didn't actually plan to say it, the words just tumbled out.

His head jerked back as he focused on me.

'How you know Irina?' he muttered in a low tone.

'She – she's on the poster.'

His eyes narrowed in suspicion. We both knew her name wasn't on the poster.

'She return to Russia,' he said with an air of finality.

'C'mon, Jo.' Bliss tugged at my sleeve. 'Can I be your right hand man on the way home?'

Poliakov, or whatever his name was, held my gaze for another long moment. His eyes were the palest blue I had ever seen. With reluctance, I allowed the children to pull me away.

I could feel the intensity of his stare boring through my spine as we walked out into the open air.

The Coke had shot through the children's digestive systems and slammed into their bladders. I paced up and down outside the prefab toilets trying to work out who was lying. By the time we had all assembled again, I'd decided probably everyone was.

If I was distracted on the way home, the kids were too hyped up to notice. I was planning how to confront Tatiana with my new knowledge. To my utter frustration, by the time I'd dropped the children off and arrived home, she was fast asleep, stretched out on the settee. I considered waking her up but decided against it. Instead, I stood and stared at her.

I had been avoiding her for so long, it had been some time since I'd really looked at her. And it also felt as though each time I *had* looked at her, I had never really *seen* her. Who was this woman? She looked so young and peaceful lying on her back, one slender arm thrown over her head, her lips slightly parted. I had lived in the closest contact with her for weeks, yet I didn't even know her name. More to the point, I hadn't even realised I didn't know it. Was she Tatiana? Irina? Maybe something else altogether . . . Was she an acrobat? A prostitute? Or was her story even more complex?

Whatever the truth, it was clear things were more complicated than I had realised.

I pulled out the brochure I had bought. It was cheaply printed on flimsy paper. Only half a dozen pages including the covers. I turned to a fuzzy photo of the Flying Poliakovs. It was the same one as I had seen on the poster. They were wearing white satin costumes studded with rhinestones.

I looked from the Irina in the photo to the Tatiana on my settee and back again. Any residual doubts I might have harboured that they were the same person vanished. But I would have to wait until the morning before letting her know I had discovered at least a part of her secret.

I spent a long time staring out of my bedroom window. Twenty floors below me, I watched a fight between rival gangs unfold on the Old Kent Road. With ant-like industry, they set about inflicting maximum damage on each other. It looked like a choreographed ritual from this distance and perspective. As though the participants were not fully human. Screams, yells and the unmistakable sound of a gunshot over the wail of approaching sirens floated up through the night air and filled me with a heavy sense of dread.

I walked away and lay down on my bed. I had no desire to

watch the cops trying to establish control and bring order out of the savage chaos. I had enough on my hands trying to do the same in my own life.

I lay awake for hours. When I eventually fell asleep, I had strange silent dreams of faceless women bursting into flames. They seemed to be participating in some sort of grisly mock ballet. Each would take turns to whirl and spin, sending flames and sparks spiralling through the air, before passing the fire to the next performer and then dissolving in a heap of smoking ash.

I woke late with the taste of cinders on my tongue. I could hear Tatiana in the kitchen, but couldn't face her yet. I padded through to the bathroom and soaked off the night sweat in a bath.

When I emerged, Tatiana was scrubbing the kitchen sink. She didn't turn as I entered the room. I stood for a moment, staring at her back.

'Good morning, Irina,' I said in an unnaturally loud voice.

I watched her shoulders stiffen, the hand scouring the stainless steel pausing for the time it took my heart to beat three times. The room was so silent I could hear us both breathing. Then she continued the interrupted scouring motion as if nothing had happened.

I went and stood next to her, watching her impassive profile.

'I said good morning,' I repeated.

She ducked her head without looking up.

'You want tea?' she murmured. 'I make.'

She turned away from me to grab a towel and started to rub her hands dry. I walked round her, manoeuvring in the tiny space so I could see her face again.

'You don't have to do that,' I said. 'I can do it myself.'

I allowed a long pause before adding 'Irina'.

She turned away from me again, back to the sink, but again I moved so that I was next to her, crowding her, staring at the side of her face. She stepped sideways and tried to duck past me and out of the kitchen, but I grabbed her arm. She gave a little gasp and tried to swivel her head so I couldn't see her expression.

'Irina!' I shouted, as though the name was an accusation. 'Irina Poliakov!'

She shook her head. I moved round yet again to see her face. Tears coursed down her cheeks. I calculated I had managed a full five minutes of assertiveness before the inevitable return of the familiar guilt.

I released her arm.

'It's OK, you know? You can tell me. Whatever it is . . . I won't judge you. You don't have to lie to me . . . I went to the circus yesterday. I saw your picture . . .'

She gave a little moan and covered her face with her hands. Her shoulders trembled with the effort of holding in the pent-up emotion.

'Look,' I said, coming to a decision. 'We don't have to talk now if you don't want to. I'm going gardening, then I'll get some shopping in. We can talk later. But we do have to talk, OK? I'm sorry I bullied you . . . As far as I'm concerned, it doesn't matter who you are or what you've done. But I have to know. Do you understand?'

She nodded her head, though I could still see the tears trickling through her fingers.

I knew I was taking a risk by going out. There was always the possibility she would be gone by the time I returned. It depended on whether her need to keep her secrets was greater than her fear of what might be waiting for her on the streets.

But I couldn't see how else to play it. And if she disappeared and I never saw her again, then so be it.

But I had a feeling my part in this woman's story was far from over. And on that point I was right, at least.

Sergei Poliakov stared at the woman with the long red hair standing in front of him.

'What happened to Irina?' she had said.

He reeled in shock as he gawped at this stranger with her retinue of children, one white, one mixed race and two black.

'How you know Irina?' he asked.

'She — she's on the poster,' she replied.

But Irina's name was not on the poster.

'She return to Russia,' he lied automatically.

It was clear she was not satisfied with the answer, but she allowed the children to drag her away. He watched as they walked out of the big top towards the toilets. He seized the opportunity. Nikolai was standing opposite him, having heard nothing of the previous conversation. Sergei handed him his remaining brochures with a muttered excuse and ran towards his trailer.

Feverishly, he ripped off his costume and changed into jeans and a sweatshirt, all the while peering through the filthy window towards the prefabs housing the toilets. She was still there. With a wad of tissues and lotion, he scoured the pancake make-up from his face. He crammed a baseball hat onto his head, the peak low over his eyes, and jumped from the trailer just as the children emerged and the group began to move off.

Following them was easy. The children were excited and happy, behaving like children do all over the world when they've just seen a circus. Even one as impoverished as Cosmo's. The woman seemed distant and distracted as she herded them onto a bus.

They got off on a main road in what looked like a poor area of the city. He followed them past some shuttered shops and down a side street into a car park. Above them, a massive tower block loomed up into the night sky.

The woman pushed open the door to the block. Sergei was relieved to see she hadn't used a key. He flattened himself against a wall and peeped inside. They were standing waiting for a lift. As he watched, the lift doors shuddered open and they disappeared inside.

Sergei sprang through the entrance. To his right, double doors with a cobweb of smashed glass led to a concrete staircase. He bounded up the steps, pausing on each floor to check if the lift had stopped. The stairs and landings were littered with empty bottles, cans and used syringes. Every so often, he jumped over a pool of piss. In spite of his fatigue, he was fit and strong. By the time he saw the group pile out on the fifteenth floor, he was barely out of breath.

He stopped on the landing, flattening himself against the wall again. The woman knocked on two doors. They opened and two of the children ran through each, still chattering excitedly. The woman exchanged a few words with the people behind the doors and then stepped back into the lift.

So she didn't live there. But was the lift going to go down again, or rise up higher? He took a risk, on the grounds that if he got it wrong, he could run down faster than up. He continued his climb upwards.

Five more flights. Right at the top. The lift doors opened again and the woman reappeared. This time, she used a key to open a door opposite the lift and went inside.

Now he just had to wait. And he was prepared to do so for as long as it took. He had to be disciplined. The stakes were too high to let this unexpected opportunity slip away.

17

I'D WALKED ALL the way to the bus stop before I realised I couldn't carry on. And the reason was practical, not emotional. Caroline Harrington, whose Dulwich garden was the weekly subject of my tender ministrations, wasn't going to be there today. She'd told me last week when she'd given me her spare keys. The keys that were still hanging on the hook in my kitchen.

I slapped my forehead in exasperation and retraced my steps. I hoped Tatiana wouldn't think I'd changed my mind about giving her some space and had come back to bully her. I needn't have worried. Some other bully had got in first.

When I got out of the lift on the top floor, I barely registered the raised voices. Without even thinking about it, I assumed they were coming either from the lads' flat or the S&M couple. It wasn't until my key was in the lock that I realised they were coming from my own flat. And they weren't English.

I didn't hesitate. I threw open the door and ran inside. Tatiana and the guy from the circus – the one I had questioned at the end – were facing each other in my front room. They were so busy screaming at each other, they didn't notice me at first. Then Tatiana spotted me, but barely paused in her torrent of abuse. The words may have been incomprehensible, but uncontrollable rage is pretty much the same in any language. The man still hadn't seen me. The two of them stood so close to each other, their noses were almost touching. Spit sprayed in a verbal battle so fierce and intense it was clear nothing else existed for either of them.

I was superfluous. Closed out of this deeply personal confrontation on every level – language, history, understanding, culture . . . But it was happening in my front room, so I couldn't just pick up the keys and leave.

Just as I was wondering how to go about establishing my claim on the territory, Tatiana upped the stakes. She leaped at the man, fingers extended, claws out ready to rake his face. He grabbed her wrists and they grappled together, lurching round the floor. I launched myself forwards, yelling at them both to stop. They still didn't respond to me, blinkered as they were by their private drama. Adding a third person and a second language into the scrum made little impact.

I don't know how it would have ended if it hadn't been for the unexpected interruption of Jamie, one of the lads from the flat next door. When I'd run in, I'd left the front door open. I don't know how long he'd been standing there trying to get our attention. Once I'd sprung into action to try to pull Tatiana and the man apart, I'd been sucked into their circle of oblivion.

Jamie let out a bellow, so loud, so long and so penetrating, it shocked the three of us into reacting. For an instant we froze. Then, as if out of respect for the sheer volume of sound he had produced, we all dropped our arms simultaneously. Tatiana took a step back from the man, but the two of them still didn't take their eyes off each other. They stood, breathing heavily through flared nostrils, their expressions filled with hate and passion.

I looked at Jamie. He ran a hand through his tousled hair.

'You OK, Jo?' he grinned.

He looked casual, as if he'd just popped in to borrow a cup of sugar.

'Um . . . I'm not sure,' I replied. 'I think this guy's just leaving.'

The Russian acrobat turned and looked at me for the first time. I stifled an involuntary shudder at the venomous hatred that streamed from those impossibly blue eyes.

'You heard the lady. C'mon, mate,' Jamie said in an affable let's-go-down-the-pub tone.

The man swivelled his gaze to Jamie. His eyes brushed over him as though assessing the threat he represented and rejecting it as negligible. He turned back to Tatiana, who still hadn't taken her eyes off him. Her face was twisted in fury, her fists balled at her sides.

'Go away, little boy,' the man sneered, his lip curling in scorn.

To my utter despair, Jamie shrugged and walked back out the front door. It took an instant for Tatiana and the stranger to pick up where they'd left off. In that same instant, my despair ricocheted back again to dizzy relief as Jamie reappeared in the doorway. The hall behind him was filled with a milling posse of hard-faced, gum-chewing, gimlet-eyed youths.

I should have known. I had no idea what went on in the lads' flat and I'd never tried to find out. They were always unfailingly pleasant and polite to me. Whatever scams they might have been pulling were their business. All I do know is they always moved round in packs. There were half a dozen regulars, including Jamie, and at any time there seemed to be at least another half a dozen either hanging round or passing through.

It didn't take too much effort for the Russian to realise he had fewer choices than a battery chicken. He muttered something to Tatiana. In response, she drew her head back and spat full in his face. I could feel the waves of energy set off by his effort to control himself. He swivelled, strode past me and pushed his way through the crowd in my hall. We heard the double doors to the landing slam and his feet thunder down the stairs.

'Anything else you need, Jo?' Jamie asked in a cheery voice.

'Er – no thanks, Jay. I'm cool.' I turned to his mates. 'Thanks, guys.'

'No problem.'

'That's OK.'

'Any time,' they chorused. And let themselves out, closing the door carefully behind them.

I turned to Tatiana. She was still standing on the same spot, trembling, her arms wrapped round her body.

'Who is that man, Tatiana?' I breathed.

It was warm in the room, but her teeth were chattering. I put my arm round her shoulders and guided her to the settee, where we sank down next to each other.

'You didn't seem scared of him,' I mused, as much to myself as her. 'Not like the men on the pier at Brighton, or at the museum.'

Tatiana's eyes blazed.

'Why should I fear him?' she replied through clenched teeth. 'He is my brother.'

18

VERSION TWO OF Tatiana's story differed in many ways from the previous version, though you could say the essence was the same. Sergei and his sister were brought up in grinding poverty. He was the eldest, she the fourth of eight children. Both longed to escape. And both had always been agile and fearless. When the circus came to their village, their parents were only too happy for them to join. They were unlikely to earn enough to send money home to help support the family, but at least there would be two fewer mouths to feed.

They travelled through Eastern and Central Europe. It must have been a strange and lonely life for a girl in her mid-teens. On the way, performers would leave the circus and others would join, the acts remaining fluid. Sergei and his sister were joined by two married couples, one from Hungary, the other Romanian, and together they formed the Flying Poliakovs.

I was right in thinking that life in the circus held no glamour. Two shows a day for five days, then one day spent dismantling the marquee and equipment, before moving on to a new site in a new town or a new country. No breaks. No holidays. The time spent not performing, spent in breaking down, setting up again, practising routines, cleaning, maintaining equipment, flyposting, publicity . . . In return, they received little more than basic food and somewhere to sleep. The ring master ran the whole show behind the scenes as well as in front. He was wily and cunning, finding ways through the system so they could perform in Western Europe, where he promised the rewards would be greater. It made little difference to the performers. If any rewards were forthcoming, they didn't come in their direction.

Sergei had two ways of relieving the tedium and exhaustion in their bleak lives. And both cost money. Cocaine and gambling. He amassed debts that he couldn't hope to pay off in a lifetime. Yet if he didn't, it seemed that lifetime would soon be brutally foreshortened. Tatiana told me the men he owed the money to were operatives for a gang notorious for its ruthless approach to debt collection. He had only one thing he could trade in order to pay off his debts and keep his throat intact.

I gawped at her in disbelief.

'He *sold* you?' I gasped. 'Your own brother *sold* you to pay off his debts?'

She shrugged.

'It was my life or his,' she replied in a wooden voice. 'He chose his. If I was in his position, I would have done the same. But I am not in his position. I am in mine. And so I hate him.'

'But . . .' I floundered as I tried to reconcile this new information with Tatiana's earlier versions of her past '. . . but that's what you told me Georgi did . . .'

'It's true,' she replied. 'Georgi did this too. He did not use me to pay off his own debts, but he still exchange me for money. He is a man. This is how men see women. This is true everywhere, I think.'

I baulked at such bitter cynicism coming from someone who under different circumstances might still be wearing a school uniform.

'So, the story about your parents dying and Georgi rescuing you – that was all lies?'

She stood up from the settee, disappeared into the kitchen and emerged holding an empty carrier bag. She began picking up the meagre bits and pieces she'd accumulated from my forays into junk shops on her behalf and pushed them into the bag.

'I cannot stay here now. I cannot trust Sergei.'

'Where will you go?' I asked in a hollow voice. I'd just realised that I must be directly responsible for this new development. The only way he could have tracked her down was by following me from the circus. If I hadn't given in to the impulse to confront him . . .

Tatiana shrugged.

'I don't know. I will keep moving. But I must leave here.' She paused, as though struck by a sudden thought. 'You also, Jo. There is danger for you here now.'

I stared at her, struggling to take in the full impact of her words.

'But – but, this is my home . . .' I stuttered, stating the obvious.

She responded by stating the obvious back at me.

'If they come to look for me and find you, they will think you know where I am . . .' She spread her arms. It was an impotent gesture. But not as impotent as I felt. 'I'm sorry, Jo,' she murmured.

I fought to get a grip on my churning thoughts. Mags had warned me. So had Mo. I shouldn't have been so shocked. I should have been better prepared. Or just prepared full stop.

'How – how long will I have to stay away?'

She looked down, unable to meet the intensity of my gaze.

'They will never stop looking for me,' she whispered, so low I could tell myself I hadn't heard right.

She disappeared into the bathroom and came back clutching a toothbrush. She wrapped it in a strip of cling film and dropped it into the carrier bag.

'Wait! Wait!' I said. 'Let me think . . .'

Where could I go? No, where could *we* go? Because I knew without a doubt now that our paths were inextricably linked. I remembered what Jen had said the other night about the threads of the tapestry of life weaving us all together. She'd been joking, but there was nothing funny about the undeniable connection I now had with Tatiana.

I knew Mo would take me in without question. But she'd never allow Tatiana through the door. And anyway, staying in the block was too close. I wasn't prepared to expose Mo and the girls to any potential danger.

We had to go somewhere out of the immediate area. Somewhere with no kids or anyone else too vulnerable. We needed help from people who were resourceful and tough.

I grabbed my mobile from the top of the fridge, called up the entry for the number Mags had given me for emergencies, and pressed call.

I held my breath. Signals bounced off satellite dishes and aerials and connected. The phone was answered on the third ring, but the voice wasn't Mags's.

'This is Jo. Who's that?' I fought unsuccessfully to keep the tremor from my voice.

'Hi, Jo. It's Jen. How you doing?'

I gagged with relief at the solid sound of her voice.

'Jen – I – did Mags tell you about – about Tatiana?'

'Yeah. Look, Jo. Are you OK? You sound freaked.'

'Um. No, not really. It's a bit long to explain. But we're not safe here. We've got to get out . . .' I tailed off. I'd only met the woman once. Unless you count the time she was in the lift with my front door between us. And here I was, laying my mega-crisis on her and expecting her to come up with instant solutions.

The amazing thing was, she did. She didn't even hesitate.

'We'd better come and get you. What number is your flat?' I gave her the number, giddy with relief. 'I'll see who else is around and we'll be there in half an hour. Hold tight, Jo.'

I hung up. I couldn't believe she'd come to the rescue without asking a single question. But then there were a lot of things I was having trouble believing. I also couldn't believe I would have to leave my home for the foreseeable future. Or that I'd brought this whole hideous situation about by my own stupidity.

'It's sorted, Tatiana. I've found somewhere for us to go. They're going to come and pick us up.'

I'm not sure what reaction I'd expected. Gratitude? Relief? I got neither.

'OK,' she shrugged, and sat down on the settee as if she was waiting for a minicab.

I bit back an angry response. Apart from that brief apology, she had shown no sign of remorse. Or any indication that she had taken on the implications of the effect she was having on my life.

I looked at her, perched on the edge of my settee, still clutching her carrier bag. Her face was pinched and pale, her shoulders rigid with tension. Her expression was blank, but her eyes, staring unfocused into the middle distance, told the story of what was going on behind the façade. They weren't frightened. They weren't angry. They were just somehow lifeless. As though she accepted the inevitability of her situation. As though she'd known it would only be a matter of time before her secrets caught up with her. She would come with me to the next haven. For a while. And then she'd move on again. Always moving on. Never relaxing. Never knowing the luxury of feeling safe. Until, eventually, the day would come when she didn't move fast enough.

It wasn't her fault I had been caught up in the situation with her. I had got involved of my own free will. I'd known early on what the result could be, even if I'd chosen to ignore it. What had I expected? That I could just waltz into her life and provide the magic remedy to make everything come out right?

I shook myself. I would need to get some things of my own together. I walked into the bedroom and pulled the suitcase off the top of my wardrobe in a shower of dust. I threw in clothes picked at random and some toiletries. I folded the fluffy white bathrobe on top. As I snapped the locks shut, my mind drifted back to the circumstances in which I'd got the bathrobe from Bare-Botty Man. If it wasn't for him, I'd never have seen Jen and Ali through the spy hole. I'd never have got the five hundred quid and I wouldn't have taken Kirsty and Delilah to Brighton. And Tatiana would have been helped by someone else in that toilet on the pier. Or not.

I pulled myself together with an effort and went into the kitchen. I packed the contents of my fridge into a carrier bag. My mind was racing. I would have to tell Mo. But should I tell her where I was going? And why? Might it be better if she didn't know? I shuddered. I was in uncharted territory and had no means of navigating my way through it.

Would I still be able to work for Smokey Pete? He couldn't cope without help. What about my gardening job? I slapped my head in exasperation. I'd been on my way there before this had all happened. I'd have to phone and apologise for not turning up. I pulled my mobile from my rucksack where I'd put it with a couple of books and some other odds and ends. Personal effects, I think they call them. I was already seeing myself as a victim. I called Caroline Harrington's number and was waiting for her answer machine to kick in when there was a knock at the door.

'It's OK,' I called to Tatiana, who was disappearing into the bathroom. 'It'll be my friends.'

I embarked on a grovelling apology to Caroline's machine as I walked up the hall. I pulled the door open just as I hung up.

How stupid can you get? I had never opened the door without checking first through the spy hole. The only time I didn't check was the only time I should have done. I could try to justify the lapse by saying I was expecting Jen . . . I was reeling from shock . . . I was distracted by leaving the message. It was less than an hour since Sergei had left. Surely it would take longer than that for him to alert the men hunting for Tatiana.

Like I say, how stupid can you get? If all I had to do to get someone over was pick up the phone, why should I have expected it to be harder for Sergei?

The door was flung open with a force that threw me back down the hall. A dark-haired man, big and heavy in a black leather jacket, stepped into my flat, slamming the front door behind him. I turned to run, but before I'd gone a whole pace, he grabbed me from behind. One arm wrapped around my throat, choking me. Something cold and hard dug into my right temple. From the corner of my eye I could see what it was, and my blood turned to ice. I didn't even think of trying to fight back. What chance did I have? Would a kick in the shin or a squeezed bollock make him drop the gun? Would it stop him killing me?

My fingers clawed at the leather of his sleeve. I could feel my windpipe constricting and bright sparks of exploding light pierced my vision. The rushing noise in my ears failed to drown out his heavy guttural voice. I didn't need to understand the words to recognise their murderous intent.

He dragged me backwards through the front room. My body was limp, my feet scurrying to keep up so as not to increase the pressure on my throat. He paused to look in the empty kitchen before moving to the closed door of my bedroom.

He kicked the door open. At the same moment, I felt the gun leave my head as he pointed it into the room. He must have expected Tatiana to fight back. Either that or he knew threatening to kill me would not be sufficient incentive for her to surrender without a struggle. He dragged me into the bedroom, the gun pressing into the side of my head again. He yanked open the wardrobe door, repeating the routine with the gun.

Frustrated, he pulled me back into the front room. Only one room left now. The bathroom door opened into the hallway. Through the swirling fog, I had time to wonder if she'd managed to slip out the front door while he'd been checking the bedroom. I don't know if I hoped she had, to be honest. I also don't know what would have happened to me if she wasn't there. Though I've got a pretty good idea.

He kicked the bathroom door. It didn't budge. Satisfied he'd found what he was looking for, he upped the volume of his discourse. I felt nothing but despair. The total absence of hope. This was the end.

He kicked the door again. And again. If I'd lived anywhere else, I might have expected a reaction from the neighbours. A call to the cops even. But not in Boddington Heights. He'd taken the gun from my head, and although the force of his efforts had me shaken like a rag doll, the grip round my throat had eased slightly.

With a splintering crash, the door caved inwards. I don't know what instinct caused me to take my hands from his sleeve and put them over my face. Probably I just didn't want to see what he was going to do to Tatiana. Through the gap in my fingers, I saw her standing against the back wall. She held my tooth mug in her hand, filled with a clear liquid. In the split second it took to register this, I remember the sense of disbelief I felt, thinking she was going to chuck a glass of water over him. I ducked my head and squeezed my eyes shut.

The sound of the gunshot reverberated round the enclosed space, the echo bouncing off the tiled walls. At the exact same time, the man roared and released his grip on my neck. I fell forward onto my hands and knees, gagging, convinced that Tatiana had been shot.

I felt a tugging at my shoulder. I looked up. My attacker was holding his hands over his eyes, still roaring and bouncing off the walls of my hall. I realised with a combination of relief and horror what the tooth mug had contained. Peroxide. Tatiana used it to bleach her hair.

She was pulling at my arm now, careful to keep out of reach of the man. I lurched to my feet, sick and dizzy. It was *her* turn to drag me now. But this time to the front door. She bent and picked up my mobile, which was still lying on the floor where I had dropped it. She slammed the door shut behind us and I had my one lucid moment. As she stabbed the lift button, I double locked the door with the key that was still mercifully in my pocket.

We fell into the lift and leaned against the walls, breathing heavily. Neither of us spoke, until Tatiana said in a leaden voice, 'He will not have been alone.'

My heart, which had begun to slow down to a rhythm that was almost bearable, started to pound again with the force of a pneumatic drill. Once again it was Tatiana who kept her cool and displayed the presence of mind I totally lacked.

'Your friends . . .'

Yes. Of course. My friends. I have friends. She handed me the mobile and I called the Nirvana number for the second time that day.

'Jen!' I gasped. 'They're here.'

'Shit! Where are you now?'

'In the lift.'

'OK. We're just coming into the car park. We'll come right to the door. Be ready.'

Tatiana and I stumbled from the lift. As we reached the front doors, the white Transit screeched up. The back doors were flung open and we jumped in, pulled by several hands. I lay on the floor, next to Tatiana. I think I might have been whimpering. Someone slammed the doors shut. I looked up to see Frank gazing down at us with concern.

'Get us the fuck out of here, Ali,' Jen shouted, banging on the back of the driver's seat with a large baseball bat.

A tall, skinny guy with long hair in a plait squatted by the back doors. He peered through the grimy windows as the Transit sped out of the car park.

Georgi's mobile chirruped an electronic version of 'Kalinka'. The illuminated screen told him the caller was Mikhail.

'Good,' he thought. 'He must have the little slut by now.'

He leered in anticipation as he pressed the answer button and put the phone to his ear. Instantly, his hand shot away, as a combination of screeching, cursing and howling burst at him from the earpiece.

'Mikhail, Mikhail!' he shouted. 'What is it? What's happened?'

With an audible effort, Mikhail spluttered the bad news. The peroxide was still burning his eyes. He'd splashed copious amounts of water into them, but his vision was blurred and the pain was excruciating. And, on top of that, the English bitch had locked him in and that bastard Sacha, who was waiting for him in the car park, had his fucking mobile turned off.

And Tatiana? She was gone, of course.

Georgi swallowed his rage with an effort that shaved ten years off his life. While Viktor went to rescue Mikhail and take him to Casualty, Georgi paced the floor plotting his next move.

It wasn't so hard. Obvious really. All was not lost. It only took one call. Trash the English bitch's flat. Show her the consequences of meddling in their affairs. Then wait. Sooner or later, she would return. Be patient. Be alert. You can't miss her. She has long red hair. Take shifts. But never let up. Not for an instant. When she turns up, don't let her see you. Follow her. Stick with her. Don't let her out of your sight. I know these bleeding-heart liberals. She won't be able to let Tatiana go. She will continue to interfere. It may take days. It may even take weeks. But eventually she will lead us to Tatiana.

And keep your fucking mobile on.

19

WE WERE ALL in Jen's front room. I'd phoned Mo earlier. I told her I'd gone to stay with friends and would be in touch again soon. She was suspicious, of course, but in the spirit of the new coolness that had developed between us, didn't press me for details.

I also called Smokey Pete and gave him a fuller version on the grounds that the knowledge wouldn't compromise or endanger him in the way it might Mo. And that he wouldn't be tempted to have an I-told-you-so go at me. Though to presume Mo would was selling her short and was more to do with my own guilt than her inclinations. Pete was horrified and took a lot of persuading that Tatiana and I were both OK. He spoke about Tatiana with an almost protective air, as though they were close friends. It would be easy to forget they had never met. I told him I might have problems getting to the market the next day. He assured me his cash flow could survive the slump and that he had enough food to last several days, so not to worry about his shopping. He also made me promise to call him if we needed any help he might be able to give.

Mags arrived home from work and we lolled on Jen's cushions, smoking and drinking herb tea. I discovered an unexpected taste for camomile tea sweetened with honey. Every so often I'd find myself starting to relax in the congenial atmosphere. Then I'd look up and see Tatiana looking tense and uncomfortable, sitting cross-legged on the floor. Reality would kick in with a savage force and set my mind spinning with the implications of leaving my home. My gut hurt from retching each time I remembered the details of the attack – the pressure of the leather-clad arm on my throat and the sensation of utter hopelessness and despair I'd experienced.

'I thought I was going to die,' I kept saying over and over, shaking my head in disbelief.

Tatiana sat silent and remote, seemingly calm, responding politely to direct inquiries but, true to form, offering no detail. She spoke in monosyllables that had little to do with her limited English and everything to do with the characteristic reticence that the new developments had done nothing to dent. When it became clear I would have to tell her story if she wouldn't, she sat listening with head bowed as I recounted the events that had taken place since I'd last been in Nirvana. She didn't comment or react when I told the others about my trip to the circus and my discovery of her other life as Irina Poliakov. The one she hadn't told me about. The Nirvanans allowed me to speak without interruption. They seemed silenced by her presence. It was hard discussing her secrets in front of her, as though she had no voice of her own. But they had to know what they were letting them-selves in for. And Tatiana seemed to accept the exposure as the price she had to pay for refuge.

I would have preferred her to tell her own story. I got the feeling the others would have felt more comfortable with that too. By refusing to speak, she was conferring yet another power on me that I'd never desired. But before the familiar guilt trip set in, I decided that losing my home meant I'd paid my dues. Even though I was responsible for inadvertently leading Sergei to her, as I narrated her story, it was clear even to me that eventual exposure had been inevitable.

There was a long silence when I finished speaking, broken only by the occasional roar of a passing train. Robin, the guy with the plait, gave a long whistle. Frank looked miserable. Mags looked angry. Ali – like Tatiana – looked blank. And Jen – to tell the truth – she looked wired, excited almost.

'Peroxide? Good thinking, Tatiana!' she blurted, with obvious admiration. Tatiana looked surprised to be addressed directly.

'You know what I thought?' Jen went on, in the same enthusiastic tone. 'I thought – bathrooms, aerosols, candles maybe – I thought you'd go for the old aerosol blowtorch bit. You know, you shoot out a spray of deodorant or whatever and ignite the burst. Gotta watch out for the blow-back though, or the whole can explodes in your hand.'

I wasn't sure how much of this Tatiana had understood. The Nirvanans responded by grinning and shaking their heads. Frank giggled.

'That's our Jen,' Mags said, with obvious affection.

Their response amazed me. For an instant I struggled with the feeling that they were making light of the horror I'd just been through. But I soon realised their practical support and lack of judgement was more important than their verbal response.

'There is a problem about being here though, Tatiana,' Mags went on.

The others straightened and all assumed serious expressions. It was obvious that whatever Mags was about to say had already been discussed among themselves.

Mags drew a deep breath.

'We had some trouble here at the co-op recently. The details are not important right now, but it meant we got a lot of unwanted exposure in the media. We still get the occasional journalist snooping round, asking questions and trying to sniff out scandal. You need to be somewhere inconspicuous, and I don't think this is it. You're very welcome to stay tonight, of course.

And Jo, you can stay as long as you like, but we feel we need to find somewhere else for you, Tatiana. Do you understand?'

Mags stopped to gauge Tatiana's reaction. I could have told her there wouldn't be one. Tatiana nodded and shrugged. I don't know if she believed Mags's story or if she thought it was an excuse to get rid of her. Maybe in the end it didn't matter to her either way. She couldn't afford the luxury of analysing people's words and actions because she was too busy surviving. As for me, until that point, I hadn't realised it *was* a luxury.

'Right,' said Mags, once she'd realised she wasn't going to get any further reaction from Tatiana. 'Ideas, people.'

There was some mumbling and shuffling. A few suggestions that were soon rejected as unsuitable, including one from Frank that Tatiana go to stay with some tree-dwelling eco-warrior friends of his. I felt panic gnawing at my innards again. Then an idea struck.

'Pete,' I said.

I explained Smokey Pete's circumstances to the others. He was the least conspicuous person imaginable. And if Tatiana stayed there, I would still see her regularly. On the other hand, Pete was so reclusive, I wasn't sure he'd be able to handle the disruption and intrusion. It was time to test how seriously he had meant his earlier offer of help.

I called him on my mobile. To my relief, I'd never heard him so excited and enthusiastic about anything that wasn't made of wax. I told him I would deliver his house guest the following day.

I spent the night downstairs on Mags's settee, while Tatiana slept on Jen's cushions. To be accurate, I don't know if she slept. Against all the odds, I did.

20

ALI PARKED THE van outside Pete's flat. We'd agreed he'd drop us off and I would find my own way back so Pete wouldn't feel too overwhelmed by the sudden influx of visitors.

Tatiana was enchanted by the waving, waxen stalactites of candles hanging from Pete's ceiling. She wove her way around them, touching them reverently with the tips of her fingers, looking for all the world like an erotic elf in an inverted forest of wax.

Pete, it was clear, was enchanted by Tatiana.

They were awkward and shy with each other, but her obvious fascination with his candle creations soon broke the ice. For a horrible, cynical moment I wondered if she had instinctively known this would be her best tactic for endearing herself to him. Pete had no experience that I knew of that might help him deal with someone like Tatiana. He'd been agoraphobic since his late teens and if he'd had any sexual relationships, he'd never told me about them. I felt fiercely protective of him and wondered if this had been such a good idea after all.

I told myself I was just being jumpy. Why shouldn't she admire his candles? They were exquisite, weren't they? I picked up Pete's shopping list and left them to bond over the vats of molten wax.

By the time I got back, she had deposited her carrier bag of possessions in the box room he had cleared for her. As I put toilet paper in the bathroom, I noticed her toothbrush nestling next to Pete's as if they were an old established couple. They barely noticed me as they stood shoulder to shoulder at his desk, poring over sketches of new designs.

'They are so beautiful,' I heard her breathe. 'You think if this part is a little more big and perhaps colour red would be good?'

Pete cocked his head to one side and followed her pointing finger.

'You're right,' he beamed. 'That would really work. You have an instinctive eye for colour and form.'

He turned and smiled at her and I saw her blush. He flicked over a page.

'What do you think of this? I wondered if it was a bit too heavy at the base . . .'

I carried the rest of the shopping into the kitchen. I didn't want to hang around too long. Their burgeoning intimacy already had me feeling a bit like a third leg. I recognised a pang of envy. Not that I've ever fancied Pete. I love him to bits and I know it's mutual. But I'd never experienced the crackle of electricity that he and Tatiana seemed to be giving out. Not with Pete or with anyone else for that matter. And that I suppose was the heart of the problem.

I arrived back in the boring Peckham street that I now knew housed several far-from-boring people and was faced by an unexpected dilemma. Which of the three doors should I knock on? The first house, the one next to the shop, was where Gaia and Ali lived. Gaia I knew less well than the others, as she'd been out the day before when I'd arrived with Tatiana. Ali I knew less well, because – well, because he was Ali. And the more time I spent with him, the more I realised his silence wasn't an indication of his mistrust of me, but was just his way. Nevertheless, the yawning gaps in conversation still left me feeling uncomfortable in his company.

Robin and Frank lived in the middle house. Robin seemed fine, even if he did have the poshest voice I've heard outside Modani's aristo set. Frank, however, was shy and awkward round me. And there was something else about Frank too. There was no doubt in my mind that Frank had an intimate relationship with drugs. Maybe not right now, but certainly in the not-too-distant past. Although on one level that meant we had something in common, I knew that getting too close to someone who had first-hand experience of that sweet smack-rush hurtling through their veins would always be dangerous. How long before we would start reminiscing? How long before hard-won distance turned to nostalgia and nostalgia turned to need, shared memories effacing the bad times and leaving only the irresistible urge to go there one more time? These would not be healthy memories to share. Yet inevitably, if we spent too much time alone together we'd end up exploring the common ground. I knew heroin too well to deny its seductive nature. Frank was no doubt a lovely guy. But I needed to be careful around him.

The last house was Mags and Jen's. Mags would still be at work. Jen no longer intimidated me, though I was still a bit in awe of her. Even so, I reckoned she was the safest bet, so I walked up her path and gave a timid rap on her letter box. No response. I knocked harder. Just as I was beginning to wonder which of the other houses would be my second choice, the door opened.

Jen was dressed in cut-off jeans and a white T-shirt with 'Eat the Rich' emblazoned on the front in dripping red letters.

'Excellent timing,' she grinned. 'C'mon through.' I followed her inside, expecting to climb the stairs to her flat. But instead she pushed open Mags's door and walked through her kitchen and towards the back door.

'Tatiana settle in OK?' she called over her shoulder.

'Better than OK,' I replied. And then I heard myself say, 'I think Pete's fallen in love with her.' I don't remember deciding to say that, but the words tumbled out all the same.

Jen stopped in the doorway and peered over her shoulder at me.

'You OK with that?' she inquired.

So she wasn't just tough and funny. She was astute too.

'I suppose so,' I shrugged. 'It's not like I fancy him myself or anything.'

'Hmmm,' Jen replied, as though she was unconvinced. Or at least suspected there was more to tell. But she didn't press me and I was duly grateful.

We walked out into the back garden.

'I need some help with the Lawn,' she said, indicating the vast expanse of bare earth between the vegetable and herb borders.

'Why *do* you guys call it the Lawn?' I asked, only too happy to change the subject.

Jen gave a snort of laughter.

'Cos it used to be covered in grass.'

'So what happened?'

Jen stared at me, as though challenging me to tell her she was weird. As if I'd dare . . .

'I lost it one day and dug it up to work off an excess of energy. We've been wondering what to do with it ever since. Anyway, we've come up with an idea we all like and you've arrived just in time to help me put it into action.'

She led me round the side of the house, where dozens of bulging bin bags were piled up against the wall.

'In a few hours' time, the Lawn will be transformed into the Beach. And you and I, my new friend, will be completely and utterly knackered.'

I goggled at the sacks.

'You mean . . .'

'Yep,' Jen nodded. 'Sand. Real beach sand. Not that earwax-coloured stuff you get down the builders' merchants. The best the Kent coast can provide. The only problem will be if it's contaminated by radiation from Dungeness. But we won't think about that now. C'mon.'

She hefted the nearest sack onto her shoulder, carried it to the far end of the earth patch and ripped it open, spilling the contents onto the ground.

I picked up a sack and staggered under the weight. Man, she was strong. Smaller than me, but her wiry frame must have consisted of muscle groups mine didn't know existed. After another two trips of mine, coinciding with four of hers, the pile of sacks didn't appear to have diminished. Whereas the spilled sand covered the equivalent of a very small stamp on a very large letter.

'Is no one else around to help?' I asked.

The pile of sacks intimidated me more than Jen did, enabling me to assert myself when normally I wouldn't have dared.

'Huh,' she grunted. 'The others are a bunch of lazy gits when it comes to the garden. You couldn't hold them back when I suggested driving down at night and nicking the stuff. We had to draw up a rota. Took a whole week of nocturnal raids to shift this lot. But some kind of collective paralysis comes over them when it comes to the unromantic hard slog.' She gave a disapproving sniff. 'Oooh, look.' She bent and picked up something from the sand at her feet. 'There's a crab in this one. Oh, shit.' She frowned in disappointment. 'It's a dead crab. I'd better bung it back in the sack. If Gaia sees it, she'll demand we perform some kind of ceremony to mark the rites of passage for its life force or something.'

We worked in silence for a while. I was beginning to see the attraction of this. The sun was shining and there was a gentle breeze. The smell of the sea was tumbling from the bags with the fine sand, crushed shells and strips of sea weed. The beach had come to Peckham and I was part of its journey. The effect was as far from the garden where I worked in Dulwich as the sea was from the city. I'd never done anything like this before, though the element of working together to bring a fantasy to life was reminiscent of the intermittent good times I'd shared with Des.

If Des had been part of a community like this, maybe it would have given her a space in which she could have retained her sense of self. Although I think of her every day, I had never before found myself anywhere I could imagine her thriving and happy. With a sharp stab of pain, I wished with all my being that she could see me now.

Jen must have picked up on my mood. She dropped the sack she'd just lifted and stretched.

'Spliff break, I reckon,' she said. 'I'll get the makings.'

She returned a few minutes later with a tray laden with a jug of orange juice, two ice-filled glasses and a small tin. We lay on the warm sand, which now covered a quarter of the earth. Jen rolled a spliff and flopped back onto her beach, squinting up at the blue sky.

I lifted a handful of sand and let the fine grains trickle through my fingers.

'Jen,' I said. 'About that time I saw you at Boddington Heights . . .'

'I wondered when you'd get round to that,' she murmured.

'I presume it's connected to the trouble you had here that Mags mentioned,' I went on. 'But if you'd rather I didn't ask . . .' Then, when she still didn't respond, 'I mean, it's none of my business . . .'

'No. It's OK,' Jen drawled, executing a perfect smoke ring and watching it dissipate like a tiny lazy cloud. 'We – I – no, we . . . Oh shit, get on with it . . .' She shifted and pulled herself up onto one elbow, facing me. 'The guy you rescued from your roof – it's complicated, but he was indirectly involved with this bunch of fascists who wanted to take over the world and decided to start with Bermondsey.'

'What?' I gasped.

'Hmm. Well, it's a long story.'

The way she said it made it obvious she didn't want to go into too much detail. On the other hand, she couldn't just drop something like that into the conversation and expect me to react as if she'd told me about a shopping trip.

I remembered the news broadcast I'd seen weeks before and grasped at the connection.

'I saw a big demo in Bermondsey on the news . . . Mags was there,' I said.

'Yeah. That was us. So we exposed the bad guys, but along the way two really good mates of mine wound up dead.'

Jen's brow darkened, her jaw working as she ground her teeth. She passed me the spliff and threw herself back onto the sand, one arm flung over her eyes.

'I'm sorry,' I murmured. 'I didn't know . . .'

'How could you?' came her muffled reply.

'I knew Mags had been on compassionate leave . . .'

'Yeah, well, it was a really shit time. Still is, I suppose. It's not that long ago. You probably heard about it. It was in all the papers and stuff . . .'

There was a silence broken only by the sound of a passing train and Tyson, next door's Rottweiler, headbutting the fence. Something clicked in the memory section of my brain.

'You mean . . . you don't mean . . . the business with the train, the dog and . . . and . . . *the head* . . .' I tailed off, appalled.

'Yeah. That was us,' Jen responded with a bark of laughter that was totally devoid of humour. 'The train was the Eurostar, the dog was Tyson there. And the head . . . the head was Nick's.'

The words were intended to shock, but her voice sounded brittle. She gave a convulsive shudder.

'Nick lived there.' She jerked a thumb in the direction of Robin's flat. 'Does it bother you?' she asked, raising herself on one elbow again and challenging me with a direct stare.

I responded with a sideways move Des would have described as pure Cancerian.

'I – I don't know how you deal with it,' I said. 'If it was me, I'd be in bits.'

Jen didn't say anything. She stared at me for a moment longer. I felt horribly aware of the inadequacy of my response. But what would have been a more appropriate reaction? She flung herself back on the sand, one arm over her eyes again. She could have been shielding them from the sun. Or she could have been hiding something else.

I racked my brain, trying to remember the details of that grisly murder a while back. I could recall something about a body on a railway line and a severed head bouncing down an embankment into the jaws of a playful Rottweiler. When I'd read about it, I'd had the same horrified reaction any other reader would have had. I had no way of knowing that it was about to touch me personally. One thing I knew now for sure: Nirvana might be amazing. But it sure as hell wasn't paradise.

I had lots of questions I wanted to ask, but was too intimidated by the sheer scope of the horror Jen and the others must have gone through to think how to phrase them. On the other hand, I couldn't resist the urge to fill the silence, if only to show that I was still there.

'Shit,' I said. 'If I was you, I reckon I'd bawl so much I'd probably need to be hospitalised for dehydration,' I blathered, conscious of how lame I sounded.

Jen leapt to her feet. She pulled up the end of her T-shirt and wiped the sweat from her face.

'Yeah, well I don't do tears,' she grunted.

She strode to the sand sacks and in a burst of energy that made me feel like I was watching a speeded-up film, shifted half a dozen in quick succession before I'd finished the spliff.

My head was whirling with a combination of having to take in this new horror plus the ganja and the sunshine. I struggled to my feet, my muscles complaining. The rest had done them no good at all, allowing them the opportunity to seize up, whereas Jen was now toiling like a demonic worker ant on amphetamines. She sussed that we were in different leagues and we shifted tasks, me ripping the bags and spreading the sand, while she did the heavy lifting.

Even when there was no more earth visible, she kept going, piling the sand deeper and deeper.

'Well, we've got to put it somewhere,' she muttered. 'And I'm fucked if I'm taking it back to Kent.'

With exquisite timing, Mags appeared at the back door, just as I emptied the last sack and Jen had begun collecting the discarded bin bags.

'Looks cool. Knew it would,' Mags grinned.

Jen squinted at her through narrowed eyes.

'I swear you've been lurking in there waiting for us to finish,' she accused.

'As if . . .' Mags protested. 'Come on. I'll reward you both with rice and peas. Fancy grating coconut?' she asked in an innocent voice.

'Don't you dare,' Jen warned. Then, noticing the puzzled expression on my face, she asked, 'You ever hand-grated coconut? It makes the work you've just done look like taking a piss in terms of effort required.' She turned back to Mags. 'You use coconut cream or I swear we'll bury you up to your neck in sand. Head first.'

The thought of Jen tipping Mags's mighty frame on end and burying it had me giggling. I stopped abruptly at her next words.

'You cook. We bath. Then we all decide what we're going to do about Tatiana.'

We sat at Mags's battle-worn kitchen table. The food had been cooked and eaten and the plates washed. We'd run out of diversions. My eyes focused on the damp patch on the wall, while my mind searched out strategies to prevent it focusing on the problem at hand. Luckily for Tatiana, Mags and Jen were more disciplined.

Mags opened a notepad.

'OK,' she said, picking up a pen with a mini troll stuck on the end. 'Brainstorm. Just ideas. Words even. No matter how unlikely, we'll jot them down and then look at each one in detail.'

'This,' Jen explained in mock solemn tones, 'is the way of Nirvana. You with us, Jo?'

I dragged my wayward attention from the troll's head. Its long silky hair had been plaited in an elaborate cane row. I had been wondering if Mags had bought it like that or if she'd created the effect herself.

'Sorry,' I mumbled. 'I'm not feeling very constructive. Erm . . . could we get her a change of identity maybe? Though I can't see how that would work . . .' I fizzled out, dismissing the suggestion even as I made it.

Mags jotted down *change ID* in the notebook.

'Like I say,' she encouraged, 'we shouldn't discount anything at this point. Let's just list the ideas as they come, so we can see clearly what our choices are.' I thought the very concept of choice was alien in this situation, but I didn't say so.

'How about her applying for asylum?' Jen offered.

Mags nodded and wrote *asylum* under the previous entry. After reading the stuff Mags had sent and hearing about Nadia's experiences, I knew that wouldn't work. Tatiana would stand more chance of being admitted to an asylum. I allowed my attention to drift back to the damp patch.

'Cops,' Mags muttered, adding it to the list.

'Yuk,' Jen grimaced.

I was with her on that one.

'Media exposure.'

This was from Jen. There was a heavy silence. I glanced round and noticed they were both staring at the damp patch too now.

Mags sighed and put the pen down.

'This is not good,' she said. 'Just about all of these except Jo's suggestion are non starters – and for pretty much the same reason in each case. They all entail Tatiana coming forward and making herself visible – and therefore more vulnerable – without offering her any guarantee of protection. Maybe we need to come at this from another angle.'

She put the pen down and started to build one of her mega spliffs. Jen and I watched the craftswoman at work.

'O-K,' Mags said, drawing out the syllables as she exhaled two mighty lungfuls of smoke. 'Howzabout direct contact with the bad guys?'

I shivered. I'd encountered these guys. Direct contact didn't sound like a good option to me.

'It goes without saying,' Mags continued, 'we don't have a hope in hell of actually stopping their operation. So the way I see it, the only thing left is to come up with something they want enough that they'd agree to let Tatiana go in exchange.'

'Sounds good,' Jen asserted. 'So what do we have that a vicious gang of Russian mafiosi would want? Access to enormous sums of money, vast quantities of drugs and an endless supply of vulnerable women not being part of our resources?'

Mags ignored the sarcasm.

'What about passports?' I offered. 'I read somewhere there's this really big trade in stolen identities . . .'

'Uh-uh.' Jen shook her head. 'Even if we were able to set that up, it would mean we were facilitating their traffic in people. If we're going to persuade them to exchange Tatiana's life for anything, it can't be at the expense of other women's lives.'

There was another long silence. This wasn't exactly heartening. It couldn't be said that we were coming up with any concrete plan that was either possible, practical or had any remote chance of success. Let alone all three. The only upside was that at least I wasn't looking into this empty ideas barrel on my own.

Jen picked up the pen and stared into the troll's grotesque grinning face, as though willing it to supply the answer. I said nothing but I reckoned she had a better chance with the troll than with me. I was seriously overdrawn at the proactive ideas bank.

'There's something missing from Tatiana's story,' she murmured. She turned to me. I preferred it when she'd appeared to be addressing the troll. 'You say she was scared to go out. Where did you say the house they kept her in was?'

'Whitechapel.' I was OK on the factual stuff.

'And you live in the Old Kent Road. And the guy who spotted her was in Greenwich. There must be people looking for her all over London. And she must know that . . .'

I tried to look as if I knew what she was getting at. If I did, it was an Oscar-winning performance, because in reality I had no idea. But Mags had.

'You reckon it's over the top if all she did was run away?' she nodded. I was with them now.

'I thought that too,' I said eagerly. 'But when Mags said that stuff about these people maintaining their reputation, I assumed that explained it.'

'You were right in the first place,' Mags said. 'Never allow anything I might come out with to get in the way of your instincts.' She yawned and stretched. 'It's true. If we're to have any chance of success on any level, Tatiana has to tell us everything. We can't risk blundering in half cut when we don't even know what we're dealing with. You let her off the hook, Jo. I can see why – respect for her privacy and so on. But it's gone beyond that now. If she wants our help, that's going to have to change.'

21

SMOKEY PETE OPENED the door of his flat. His hair was wet and his face pink, fresh from the shower.

'I'm sorry, Pete,' I blurted as I walked through his door and weaved my way through the hanging candles. 'I couldn't face working on the stall today. I've missed the whole weekend. I've never let you down before . . . I'll definitely go next week.'

Pete assured me it wasn't a problem. I looked round the room. There was no sign of Tatiana.

'She's sleeping,' Pete said in hushed tones. As though the fact was a source of fascination and wonder and he expected me to feel the same amazement that Tatiana could perform such a prosaic function.

I didn't. I was too hyped up. I'd done a great deal of work to psych myself up to confront her. I couldn't handle the possibility of any further delay.

'Sorry, Pete.' I seemed to be doing a lot of apologising. 'I need to talk to her. I'm going to wake her up.'

I started towards the box room door.

'She's not in there,' he interjected.

I turned to face him.

'She's in my room,' he whispered with a shy smile. I stopped and stared at him. Blimey, that was quick. 'It's not what you think,' he blurted. 'She . . . He wriggled in discomfort. 'She came into my room and – and – offered herself to me.'

My heart sank. Pete sounded so quaint and old-fashioned. He would be so easy to manipulate. He saw the look on my face and tripped over himself to explain.

'You have to realise, Jo,' he said, his eyes pleading for understanding, 'it's all she knows. She's been forced to see herself as a commodity. And – she's so beautiful. It would have been so easy to say yes.' He took a deep breath. 'But I couldn't. Not like that, anyway. It would have been taking advantage. So – we just lay together. We spent the whole night talking. She said she'd never had any experience like that. But then – neither have I . . .'

OK. So I could imagine Tatiana being captivated by this gentle, sensitive man who was my friend. But I still needed to speak to her. I moved towards the bedroom door, but Pete grabbed my arm.

'Please don't wake her up,' he begged. 'I – I can tell you what you need to know.'

I gazed at him, puzzled. It was too much to take in. He seemed to be suggesting that, in a matter of twenty-four hours, Tatiana had already confided in him all the details it had taken me weeks not to get. I felt a stab of irritation.

'When you first told me about her, you made her life seem like an adventure,' he said, in an accusatory tone. 'But it's been full of horror. Tatiana's damaged, Jo. Seriously damaged. But she's still filled with beauty and light.'

He broke off with a smile. 'I've never felt like this before,' Pete went on after a moment. 'I – I'm so *happy*. I never knew it was possible . . . I never thought . . .'

He tailed off, the strength of his emotions too great to be put into words. I melted. For one glorious moment, my heart soared with happiness for him. Everyone should have the chance to feel like Pete did at that point, at least once in their lives. Not that I ever had. But the possibility that I might one day was one of the things that kept me going. What were the odds against Pete having that opportunity?

But the leap of joy only lasted an instant. In the ensuing painful clarity, I realised that for Pete that deluded instant had stretched to encompass his entire present and any vision he might have of the future. The details didn't have to be clear. The chances of a fairy-tale ending couldn't stand too much scrutiny. The moment was all.

I was filled with a great rush of fear for him. How could this possibly end well? Tatiana had convinced Pete, but I couldn't be sure of what she felt for him or if his obvious love for her was reciprocated.

The agoraphobic candle maker and the runaway Ukrainian prostitute . . .

What possible future could they have together?

Oh, Pete.

He saw the look of concern on my face and rushed in to head off any potential objections.

'I know. I know. It's not going to be easy. Don't think I haven't thought about that. We've talked about it. No one knows she's here. There's no way to trace her . . .'

'Pete,' I stumbled. 'You must see . . . She can't . . .'

'Please, Jo,' Pete begged. 'Please don't . . .'

What could I say? Nothing he would want to hear. And would my saying the unhearable change anything? I could see no moral or practical justification for forcing him to confront the im-possibility of his dream. And every justification for allowing him to enjoy the sensation for as long as possible.

There was only one tiny chance. My mind lurched back to the conversation with Mags and Jen. Maybe there *was* something we could do to change things – some kind of deal. Of course, there was always the possibility that if we were successful in removing the threat to Tatiana she would leave Pete anyway. But there was that remote chance . . . And he was so clearly besotted with her that I knew he would find excuses for her if she left him. But before we even knew if there was any point trying for a deal, we had to know what it was she was hiding.

I explained the dilemma to Pete, while not questioning the assumption that, whether we were able to help or not, the two of them would still be together.

Pete told me Tatiana's story. The missing part. The part that finally exposed the truth lying hidden beneath her earlier versions.

22

'WE'RE MEETING SOME *associates in Brighton,' Georgi told Tatiana. 'We will be taking you with us. These are important men. Men to impress. So you will be a good girl. Don't show us up with any of your bad behaviour, you understand?'*

Tatiana understood only too well what the consequences of any 'bad behaviour' would be.

She had been in Brighton once before, as Irina Poliakov with Cosmo's Circus. It was by the sea. Away from the dingy flat and the smoky city. She sat in the back of the car. Georgi drove, his brother, Viktor, was in the passenger seat. Their conversation – about deals waiting to be struck and profits to be made – didn't interest her and she phased it out. Instead, she gazed out of the open window at the rolling English countryside; the swollen folds of the South Downs, the vibrant yellow of the rape fields, the gentle undulating pastures dotted with sheep.

They pulled up outside a seedy hotel in one of the back streets of Brighton and she followed the men inside. There was a smell of fried food and spilled beer. A bored-looking woman with dyed black hair and a pale, sagging complexion confirmed their booking and handed them a key with no comment and even less interest.

Their room was on the first floor, over-furnished with twin beds, a rickety sofa bed, a chest of drawers and a single wooden chair. The plastic padded seat of the chair was ripped, grey stuffing exposed like an old wound. A TV was bolted to the wall in one corner and behind a grubby concertina screen against the opposite wall was a toilet and sink. If the sofa bed was pulled open, the only way to cross the room would be to clamber over the furniture.

Tatiana walked over to the filthy sash window that overlooked the street. If you leaned out and craned your neck sideways, you could see the grey metallic sheen of the sea. The room was hot and stuffy. Georgi took off his jacket and hung it on the back of the chair before closing himself off behind the concertina screen. Tatiana could hear his zip being pulled down and the splashing as his piss hit the toilet bowl.

There was a knock at the door. Viktor opened it, just as Georgi came out from behind the screen, zipping his fly. Tatiana turned from the window and watched two burly strangers squeeze their bulky frames into the tiny space.

The men greeted each other and embraced. Georgi indicated Tatiana and the men looked her over, nodding their heads in approval.

'Why don't we discuss our business in comfort at the bar?' Georgi suggested. 'And then return here to seal the deal with a bottle of vodka and some entertainment.' He leered, licking his fleshy lips. The men agreed, one of them rubbing his crutch in anticipation, and they filed out of the room.

'You stay here and don't cause any trouble,' Georgi warned as he closed the door behind them. Tatiana heard the key turn in the lock.

She turned back to the window. She put her hands on the sill and leaned out as far as she dared. There was the sea, slate grey and featureless apart from the tiny white dots of sails. The air smelled sharp and salty. Gulls wheeled overhead, screeching their raucous cries. She looked down. A marmalade cat ran under Georgi's car, which was parked at the kerb outside. The men hadn't come out of the hotel, so they must be sitting in the bar downstairs. She had seen it as they came in, to the left of the entrance, directly below their room.

A Union Jack fluttered in the stiff breeze from a flagpole protruding from the wall a couple of feet below their window. Tatiana looked at the flagpole. She twisted her neck to look at the horizon, where the grey sea met the blue sky. She turned and looked back into the dismal room, then back out of the window. She looked down and imagined Georgi, Viktor and the two strangers sitting in the bar below her, negotiating deals that would transform human misery into hard cash. She thought of the four of them returning to the room, drunk with vodka, lust and power. Down below on the street under the window, wrought-iron railings with spiked points bordered a flight of concrete steps leading to the basement. Tatiana looked at the flagpole again, calculating distance, velocity and drop.

She jerked her head back inside the room and sat down heavily on the side of the bed, her heart pounding. What was she contemplating? She must be crazy. This life had driven her crazy. She would switch on the TV and switch off her mind. Switch off the craziness. The remote control was on the chest of drawers. As she reached for it, she noticed Georgi's jacket, hanging on the back of the chair. One side hung low with the weight of whatever was in the pocket.

Tatiana reached inside and pulled out a bulging Filofax. Georgi carried it everywhere with him. He was always making entries or consulting its well-thumbed pages. She flicked through and realised why. Names, addresses, meticulously kept accounts, lists of operations . . . Tatiana's eyes flickered over the entries as she realised its significance to Georgi. And now, potentially, to her.

She stood for a moment, motionless and barely breathing. Then she grabbed her bag, shoved the book inside and looped the strap over one shoulder and across her chest.

She pulled off her strappy sandals and shoved them into the bag as well. Then she jumped onto the bed and sprang onto the wide window sill. She crouched for an instant, gathering herself with a couple of deep breaths. There was no one in sight on the street, just the flick of the marmalade cat's tail from underneath Georgi's car. She tensed the muscles in her legs and pushed off from the sill, out and down, grabbing the flagpole with both hands. She ignored the wrench to her shoulder blades and began to swing her body. There was a ten-foot drop to the pavement below. Less to the top of the spiked railings.

She heard a grinding noise. Her body gave a sickening jolt as the pole shifted, working loose from the crumbling brickwork. She convulsed her body to increase the momentum of her swing. At the highest point of the arc, she released her hands and launched herself into space. She cleared the railings by millimetres and, twisting in the air, landed on the pavement on all fours. The cat peered out from under the car at the human with the feline grace.

At the same time, there was a shout from inside the bar. Tatiana looked up to see Georgi and Viktor on their feet, staring out of the window in disbelief. She sprang up and hared down the road towards the seafront, the bag swinging against her hip.

What had she been thinking? What was her plan? When she told the story to Pete, she said that she hadn't had one. She hadn't thought it through. No forward planning, see? She had been too scared to contemplate escape until she had found the Filofax. It seemed to her to be a sign. She had a dim, unanalysed feeling that if it was important to Georgi, it could be important to her too. Perhaps she could use it to barter with . . . Exchange it for her freedom . . .

Even as she raced along the seafront, she realised the stupidity of her action. These were men who were experts in extortion, blackmail and terror. Did she really think she could beat them at their own game? She had made them look foolish in front of people they wished to impress. They would never forgive her. And that was before they knew about the theft of their crime bible.

There was a big crowd in an open space to her right. Maybe she could lose her pursuers in the melee. She ran through, colliding with tourists and tat sellers. As she fought her way round performance artists and push-chairs, she became disorientated, dimly aware of fairground stalls, packed bodies and bare wooden boards.

She didn't know. She didn't know she had run onto a pier until it was too late. The brothers were closing in behind her. She reached the giant roller coaster at the end, behind which there was nothing but sea and sky. Georgi and Viktor had split up and were moving to cut her off. She ran

across the dodgems arena, ignoring the angry shouts, and into the ladies'
toilets.

There was a woman in the toilets. She had long red hair. There were
two children with her. The woman was kind. She helped Tatiana escape
from the pier by creating a diversion and holding up the brothers' pursuit.

Where could she go now? She couldn't stay in Brighton . . . And she
had no money . . . She followed the signs to the station. There was a train
at the platform. The sign said it was going to London. There was no one
checking tickets. She jumped on board the train and locked herself in the
toilet. She had been frightened before in her life, but never like this. Never
before had she been so totally alone. With everywhere and nowhere to
go.

The train began to move after a long wait and still she huddled in the
cubicle, terrified of being discovered. When she was, it was by the same
woman who had helped her on the pier. Her name was Jo. She said
Tatiana could stay with her, in her flat in south London.

During the restless night on Jo's settee, Tatiana at last came up with a
plan of sorts. She knew another man. His name was Nikolai. He used to
visit Georgi. He had been gentle with her, kind almost. He told Tatiana he
liked her. He said if she ever wanted to leave Georgi, he would be happy
for her to come to him. He had given her an address. It was in north
London. A place called Finsbury Park.

She would go to this Nikolai. She knew he was in a similar line of work
to Georgi, but she couldn't allow that to deter her. He had said he liked her.
And with Georgi's Filofax as a bargaining tool, she felt justified in hoping
for both welcome and protection.

Jo's mobile phone was lying on the table. Tatiana picked it up and
slipped it into her bag. She rifled through the pockets of the jacket hanging
on a hook in the hall and came up with £25. She felt guilty for deceiving
and stealing from this woman who had been so kind to her. She hoped Jo
would feel £25 and a mobile wasn't too high a price to pay for her one
chance of survival.

It wasn't easy for her, negotiating the transport and the streets. She had
never been on either of them on her own before. A kind of desperate
resourcefulness was all she had on her side. She found the address Nikolai

had given her in Finsbury Park. It was a flat on a busy street above a massage parlour. Tatiana was undeterred by the familiar aura of seedy sex.

The door was opened by a girl of about her own age, who stared at her, eyes narrowed with suspicion. Tatiana asked for Nikolai. The girl hesitated before closing the door in her face. But people with no choices cannot afford to be swept aside with such ease. Tatiana rang the bell again. When there was no response, she pressed the buzzer and kept her finger there.

She could hear footsteps thundering down the stairs. The door burst open. Tatiana was unable to prevent herself stepping back as she registered the anger on Nikolai's face. She almost sobbed with relief as his contorted features relaxed into a smile.

'Tatiana. Little bird. Have you come to be with Nikolai? Come on in.' He led her up the stairs and dismissed the other girl with a curtness that produced conflicting emotions in Tatiana. On the one hand, she could understand the look of smouldering hatred the girl shot at her. On the other hand, she experienced an unaccustomed surge of power at her sudden elevated status. The feeling was seductive and she flashed a look of triumph at the other girl's departing back.

She started to speak, but Nikolai put a finger to her lips, silencing her. He led her by the hand to the bedroom and undressed her with a tenderness she had never known before. They made love on the bed and, in spite of the stained sheets, the roar of the traffic and the dozens of men before him who had used and abused her body, he made her feel special. Afterwards, they lay next to each other while he smoked a cigarette and traced patterns on her belly with a gentle finger.

'I have a gift for you,' she said, eager to give him something in return.

They were the first words she had spoken to him. She rose and padded over to the pile of clothes on the worn carpet. She lifted the Filofax from the bag and carried it over to him in both hands, with the reverence of a supplicant making an offering.

'What is this?' he smiled, taking the book from her.

He flicked through the pages, then shot upright as he realised the significance of what he was looking at. He leaped from the bed, his eyes *wide with panic. Pacing the room, he turned the pages with mounting horror. Tatiana watched his unexpected reaction and felt her blood run cold.*

'How did you get this?' he demanded. 'No! Don't tell me.' He threw the book onto the bed, as though mere contact with it could prove lethal. 'Why did you bring me this? Are you trying to kill me? Is it a trap? Tell me!' He strode over to her and grasped her arms, shaking her. 'Did Georgi send you?'

'No!' she gasped. 'I swear. Please. Please don't hurt me . . .'

He dropped her arms and resumed his pacing, clasping tufts of his hair as though to order his churning brain.

'I'm sorry,' she whispered. 'I thought . . .'

He stopped and stared at her.

'It's OK,' he said after a while. 'But I must think. I have to think what to do . . . You have handed me a ticking bomb, little bird. I have to decide what to do with it.'

Tatiana stayed with Nikolai in the flat. He still treated her with kindness, buying her new clothes and trinkets, but as time went on, his attitude became cooler and more distant. She assumed he was busy and distracted and was grateful nevertheless.

One evening, after she had been there a couple of weeks, he came in.

'Take your things and go downstairs,' he said. 'One of the girls is sick. I need you to work.'

His voice was rough and impersonal. He didn't look at her as he spoke. She reeled in shock and horror.

'But I thought . . .' she stammered.

'You thought what?' he sneered, wheeling round to face her. 'You thought you could buy your freedom? Don't you know girls like you cannot buy anything? You can only be bought.'

She shrank at the contempt in his voice.

'You should consider yourself lucky we are not handing you over to Georgi. But he doesn't matter any more. You have started a war, Tatiana. And Georgi and his operation will be among the casualties. If you stay here, you will be under my protection. Leave, and Georgi has sworn to

hunt you down and kill you. Even as the loser in this war, his resources are still formidable.'

'No!' Tatiana screamed. 'You cannot do this! You say it is a war. But if you win this war it will be because I provided you with the weapon. I deserve better than to be made to work in your stinking brothel!'

Nikolai strode over to her, but she stood her ground. Without warning, his hand snaked out and hit her hard on the side of her face. She fell onto the bed, sobbing.

'You little slut,' he hissed. 'Did you think you would be queen in this universe? You work or you go. And it is only because I have a soft heart that I give you this choice.'

Tatiana ran from the room and hurtled down the stairs. She hit the street, gasping, her mind reeling. She could think of only one place to go. Back to Jo's – the woman who had helped her before. The woman she had robbed. She couldn't even return the mobile she had stolen from her. Nikolai had taken it, saying she had no further use for it.

Grateful for the dark, without a penny in her pockets and oblivious to the throbbing pain in her face, she began the walk from Finsbury Park to the Old Kent Road.

When Pete finished telling Tatiana's story, he sat slumped in the chair, his head down. In contrast to the joy he had radiated earlier, his body language now spoke only of utter desolation and misery. I took a deep breath and let it out slowly.

'Pete,' I said as gently as I could, 'you know what this means, don't you?' He looked up. My heart convulsed at the pain I saw reflected in his eyes. It was clear he understood only too well.

'Yes,' he whispered. 'It means there's no chance of a deal with Georgi. They'll never stop looking for her. And when they find her . . . they'll kill her.'

23

I LEFT AS soon as I could. I didn't want to see Tatiana. And there was nothing I could say to Pete that either of us would want to hear. I sat on the bus back to Peckham teetering on the brink of despair. I'd known all along that Tatiana was hiding something. Finding out what it was brought anything but satisfaction. The only glimmer of comfort was that it seemed I no longer had to deal with this alone. Maybe.

I still had no keys. While I was waiting to see if Mags or Jen were in, I examined the fear that went with knowing this wasn't my home. Sooner or later I would have to leave Nirvana and return to Boddington Heights. How long would they let me stay? So far I had slept in both Mags's and Jen's front rooms. Would I be passed round the co-op? Perhaps they'd draw up a rota . . . Do anarchists have rotas?

I was churning this over in minute detail. It was painful, but if I blocked it out, the vacuum would be filled by an even more hideous crisis. *Tatiana's* hideous crisis. It was some time before I realised no one had answered the door.

I took a pace sideways and rapped the letter box next door, still lost in my quagmire of insecurity. Frank appeared without my even noticing the door had been opened. He looked flustered, running his fingers through his tousled hair and tugging at his baggy T-shirt.

'Oh, I'm sorry,' I blustered. 'Is this a bad time? I mean, I tried next door but no one's . . . But it's OK. I could go away. I mean, I could go and come back. Later.'

I started to back away up the path.

'No!' Frank blurted. 'No, no, no, no. No. I mean, no. I mean . . .' He yanked a handful of hair in frustration, trying to get beyond the insurmountable barrier of those three words. He took a deep breath. 'I'm not going out. And I'm not busy. So . . . so . . . you . . .'

'Oh, just fucking well ask her in, for Christ's sake,' came Robin's voice, almost at my elbow.

I jumped back a good yard, banging my shoulder on the wall. Robin was in the act of climbing out of his own front-room window.

'I, however, am just on my way out,' he grinned. 'See you later, guys.'

He pulled the sash window closed behind him and set off up the road.

Frank looked at the bemused expression on my face and burst out laughing, ending in a wheeze and a cough.

'Robin often uses the window,' he explained. 'It's because he's lived in squats so long. He can't get used to having a key and going in and out the front door.'

I followed Frank up the stairs, wondering how long it would be before Mags or Jen got home and whether I'd hear them when they did. I sat down on the front-room floor and prepared to wait. I didn't want to spend too much time alone with Frank. On the other hand, it would be hard to find a man so – well, so *un-threatening*. That sounds awful, I know. About as miniscule as a compliment can get without being an insult. But I didn't mean it like that.

He went out of his way to make me feel welcome, making tea and offering me biscuits from a battered packet of custard creams. His front room was painted matt black with a tin foil ceiling, creating the sensation of being in a giant roasting tin.

I decided to tell him Tatiana's story, to prevent any awkward silences being filled with anything more personal. I could see he was struggling to follow the intricacies of the detail, but the tortured expression on his face showed he'd grasped the essentials. He was a man who recognised hopelessness when he saw it.

'Poor Tatiana,' he gasped.

'Yeah. And poor Pete too,' I muttered.

I could have added 'Poor me', but thought it would sound petulant. Anyway, I was determined to keep the focus firmly away from myself.

'I wish I could help more,' Frank murmured. 'The others would know what to do. Maybe if my brain wasn't so scrambled . . .'

He looked so dejected, I felt forced to reassure him, even though it meant moving closer to forbidden territory.

'I'm sure your brain works just fine, Frank.'

He ducked his head with a gesture of pleasure and embarrassment that made him appear very young, though we were about the same age.

'Jo, you're kind. But you're also wrong. I – I've done a lot of drugs, y'know,' he confided.

So there it was. I knew we'd get there in the end. No matter what diversions and distractions I created.

'Yeah,' I shrugged. 'I know that. So what?'

'You know?' He looked up in surprise. 'How did you know that?'

I looked at his gaunt face with its prominent cheekbones and not quite bright eyes.

'I – I can just tell,' I stammered, hoping he wouldn't be hurt by the revelation and trying at the same time to retain some vestige of control over the direction this conversation was taking us.

'Wow.' Frank looked impressed, as though I had displayed special powers of clairvoyance. 'Hang on!' He jerked his head as though a thought had hit him with physical impact. 'Mags said she knew you from the project. Do you work there too?'

I couldn't help it. I had to laugh.

'No!' I shook my head. 'Frank – I was on the other end of the needle. If you know what I mean . . .'

Shit! See? I hadn't been there half an hour and we were already embarking on a stroll down Smack Memory Lane. *Resistance is futile*, a seductive voice whispered in my ear. *No it bloody well isn't*, I replied.

Meanwhile, Frank's puzzled frown indicated that he didn't in fact know what I meant at all. He mulled my words over for a moment or two while I watched him. He had a nice face, a bit battered and lived-in, but that's OK. It was an open face. Everything was there on the surface to see. There was no cunning or artifice in Frank. But that didn't stop him being a danger to me. Or me to him.

His brow cleared as he looked me straight in the eyes.

'You don't mean . . .' He struggled with his disbelief. 'Surely . . .'

I nodded. 'This time two years ago . . .'

A big grin broke out on that nice face. As though he'd found a kindred spirit. Exactly the reaction I most feared.

'But you . . . you're so together . . .'

I laughed again. That wasn't the reaction I'd been expecting. Laughing was good. I realised how little of it I'd been doing lately.

'I don't *feel* very together, I can tell you.'

'Why not?' he urged. 'You can be whatever you want to be.'

I dunked a stale custard cream into my camomile tea.

'OK,' I countered. 'But if that's true for me, it must be true for you too . . .'

'No.' Frank shook his head, his mouth set in a stubborn line. 'You can't compare yourself to me. It's not just the gear that scrambled my brain. There was the alcohol plus every other pharmaceutical you've ever heard of . . .' He rubbed his palms over his eyes and took a deep breath. 'But what mostly done for me was the years of sleeping rough. That's what did my head in.' Frank's eyes narrowed, as he drifted off for a moment. With a visible effort, he pulled himself back into the present. 'But you're different,' he said. 'There's plenty of people who were once users and who've gone on to do stuff they couldn't have dreamed of. Look at Daniella Westbrook.'

He ended on a triumphant flourish, as though producing a trump card that proved his point beyond further argument.

Amazing! I'd been scared we'd embark on reminiscences that could end up with us feeling the urge to recreate the past in our present. Instead, here was Frank giving me a pep talk! I didn't know whether to feel relieved, flattered or irritated. I settled for deliberately obtuse.

'But I'm not a C-list celebrity and I don't want to go on reality TV shows,' I protested.

'You don't have to,' Frank replied, either not realising I was joking or refusing to see any humour in the situation. 'Like I say, you could be anything you want.'

I swallowed hard. This was turning out better than I'd feared, but it was still dangerous territory. There was a long silence.

'I'm not sure if I should be here,' I murmured. I'd assumed I'd only thought the words, but when I looked at Frank it was clear from his expression that I'd spoken aloud.

Frank goggled at me, his mouth opening and shutting as he struggled to follow this unexpected turn in the conversation. His expression and the movement of his jaw were reminiscent of something . . .

'Shit!' I leaped to my feet. 'My fish! I forgot about my fish!'

Here at last was a crisis we both could understand and deal with. A manageable crisis. Right here in the present.

'We have to go and get them,' Frank said, leaping to his own feet. 'I'll phone the other houses and see who's in. You can't go back there alone.'

'Phone?' I frowned. 'You mean next door? Why don't we just knock?'

Frank gawped at me as though I'd suggested something truly radical.

'Wow,' he breathed, as though the possibility had never occurred to him before.

24

JEN WAS THE only one home, having arrived back a few minutes earlier. Maybe she would have preferred to stay in and put her feet up. She certainly looked pale and tired. Frank told me she'd gone to visit her brother, who was hospitalised in some psychiatric unit. I had a fleeting vision of some crumbling nightmare institution. A cross between *One Flew Over the Cuckoo's Nest* and *Oliver Twist*.

Anyway, Jen reacted as though she'd like nothing better than to go on a mercy mission to Boddington Heights to save a couple of goldfish from imminent starvation. The three of us set off together. Ali had taken the van, so we went on the bus. On the way, I recounted Tatiana's story for the second time, knowing I would have to repeat it yet again for Mags and the others later. Tatiana had kept her secret so long but now it was out, it was as though it was destined to be told over and over until a solution could be found. Except I still couldn't see it. And Jen likewise failed to come up with any suggestions.

If she was shocked, she didn't show it. But maybe that just

wasn't her style. I was beginning to see she was a woman who wouldn't be easily shocked. She was astute too. Astute enough to spot that I would be torturing myself over getting Pete involved.

'Don't feel bad about Pete,' she said to me, as we stepped down from the bus and started walking along the Old Kent Road. 'From what you've said, I reckon he'll always be grateful to you for bringing Tatiana into his life. Whatever the outcome . . .' I thought she was probably right, but it didn't make me feel any better. Especially that bit about the outcome.

Maybe it was the sight of Boddington Heights looming ahead of us on our left that added to my mounting despair. Boddington Heights. My home. Not the Nirvana housing co-op, with its ready-made community.

I had Mo and the girls, of course. And Claudette and the twins. And a dozen or so other people I knew well enough to make small talk with if we landed up in the lift together. Not enough to weave together into a shelter against the isolation. To provide a network of support to offset the private dramas played out behind every door on every floor. No doubt the Nirvanans had their dramas too. But at least they weren't private. And if the door was closed, there was always the window, as Robin had demonstrated earlier . . .

We made our way round the burned-out wrecks and piles of rubbish in the car park. Someone had tried to set fire to the front door to the block. Maybe it was frustration at its lack of co-operation in producing satisfying flames that had caused the would-be arsonists to pull it from its hinges. It lay charred, splintered and rejected on the ground by the entrance. I knew how it felt.

I thought nothing could happen to make me feel worse. Until I saw who was waiting for the lift. Mr and Mrs Miserable Git were standing in the lobby, habitual sour expressions in place. Opposite them was one of the lifts, its doors open and lights off. Meaning we had three alternatives. We could walk up twenty flights of stairs. We could let them get in the lift alone and wait for them to reach the nineteenth floor and for the lift to lurch its way back down to us several lifetimes later. Or we could share the stinking, battered upright box with them, breathing the same fetid air and praying the lift didn't break down between floors.

If I was horrified at the sight of them, it seemed they were positively delighted to see me. Mr Git leaped forward, not needing the surreptitious push in the back his wife dealt him.

'You!' he snarled. 'I'm glad to see you. We're sick and tired of this. We're not prepared to put up with it any more.' He was so incensed he was spitting venom, showering me with a fine spray of saliva. His wife stood behind him, a spiteful smile of triumph twisting her thin lips. She was wearing a belted beige raincoat, in spite of the June sunshine. Maybe they carried their own personal dark cloud and chill wind around with them wherever they went. 'That racket yesterday was the final straw. We're going to report you to the Neighbourhood Office.'

'Anti-social behaviour, that's what it is,' squawked Mrs Git, nodding her head vigorously. Her helmet of hair, drilled and sprayed into savage regiments of curls, moved with her, not a hair daring to stray.

My heart sank. I didn't even point out that I hadn't been in the flat the previous day. People like the Gits don't want to be confused or defused by little things like facts. The thought of Boddington Heights being my home may have filled me with despair, but if not there, where? Frank's words about the damage inflicted by sleeping rough surged back and I fought a mounting sense of panic.

Mr Git hadn't finished with me yet, though.

'People like you make me sick,' he blustered. 'No consideration. No respect. You're filth, that's what you are. Filth!'

That was too much for Frank. He leaped forward, almost pushing me aside in order to get between us. Jen caught my arm and steadied me. She looked tense and drawn, her lips pressed together in a thin line as if to stop anything spilling out.

'Don't you speak to her like that,' Frank protested, his face an angry red. 'Who are you to . . .'

'It's OK, Frank,' I muttered, tugging at his T-shirt. It's not that I wasn't touched by his protective impulse, but I didn't have the stomach for the fight. At that moment, the lift arrived, the doors shuddering open, releasing a rush of dank air smelling of stale piss.

The Gits got in first, taking up position against the side wall. I hadn't decided if we should share the lift or not, but while I hesitated, Jen walked in. Frank and I followed and the three of us stood, backs to the opposite wall, our noses only three feet away from those of the opposition. I looked at the floor. Jen appeared fascinated by the top corner of the wall opposite and only Frank glared defiance by meeting the smouldering gazes burning from the opposite side.

We had only reached the fourth floor when Mrs Git broke the claustrophobic silence.

''Ere, I know you,' she said to Jen. 'You're Jack Stern's daughter, intch yer?' I turned to look at Jen, who acted as though no one had spoken, continuing her scrutiny of the opposite wall.

'Look, Bill.' She jabbed her husband in the ribs with a rain-coated elbow and jerked her head in Jen's direction. 'It is 'er, innit?'

'So it is,' he said. 'How is old Jack then?'

'He's dead,' Jen replied in a wooden voice, still not looking away from the wall. I stared at her. What was this all about? Her jaw was set rigid and she looked awful, like she might throw up any minute. I wasn't sure how I was supposed to be reacting in this situation. I'd never been involved in any conversation with the Gits, even indirectly, in which they hadn't been telling me what a selfish waste of space I was. They were being almost friendly, but Jen didn't seem impressed.

'Oh, shame, shame,' chorused the neighbours.

'Sorry to hear that,' Mr Git said, in the softest voice I'd ever heard him use. 'He was a good sort, old Jack. There's not enough like him these days.'

I heard Frank's sharp intake of breath and felt the waves of tension radiating from him. What was going on here?

Jen, meanwhile, had finally torn her gaze from the opposite wall and was drilling Mr Git with twin lasers emanating from her eyes. But when she spoke it was in a quiet, controlled voice.

'Not enough like him?' she said in little more than a whisper. 'What, not enough twisted, savage, vicious, abusive, perverted, sadistic, sick bullies in the world for you?'

Her soft tone belied the bitter content of the list. My head was swimming with this unexpected turn of events. It took the Gits a moment or two to gather themselves and launch their counter-attack.

'I might have known,' Mr Git muttered. 'Seeing you with *her.*' He indicated me with a snarl. 'You're all as bad as each other. Jack deserved better than you lot. Your mother always mooning round, acting like she was something special. And that psycho brother of yours . . .'

Beside me, I heard Frank groan. There was a slight thud as the back of his head hit the lift wall. There was a tiny pause during which it felt like all the air had been sucked out of the confined space, before Jen launched into the most savage, articulate invective that it has ever been my honour to hear. Her eyes flashed as she ripped into them.

'You know what?' she hissed. 'It's people like *you* – ' she stabbed a finger at them and they shrank back against the wall, '– so-called respectable, pillar-of-society, upright, good fucking citizens like *you*, who allow scum like my father to carry on abusing their wives and kids.' She was well into her stride now. It was clear nothing was going to stop the stream of abuse. Her voice rose in volume and momentum, shifting up a gear. 'Sanctimonious tight arses, who are so quick to point the finger at anyone who doesn't fit into your rigid view of how to be in this world that you're prepared to defend the most unspeakable acts of violence because the perpetrator looks like one of your own. You're so quick to criticise others. Well, let me tell *you* what those *others* think of *you* . . .'

She carried on steaming into the Gits as though she no longer had need to draw breath. She was wonderful. I could only stand and gawp in respect and awe. The torrent of articulate abuse lasted from the fifth to the nineteenth floor without a pause. She utterly demolished the Gits, their way of life and all they stood for, leaving her targets no opportunity to do more than bristle and bluster in righteous indignation. There goes my last chance of talking them into withdrawing their complaint, I thought. But at least it went with style.

The doors closed behind them on the nineteenth floor. The last vision I had of the Gits was him leading her away, supporting her as she wheezed and clutched at her chest. My sense of triumph evaporated, leaving me feeling empty and depressed. I swallowed hard, but the bad taste lingered in my mouth. Jen's diatribe wouldn't have made the Gits rethink their perceptions. Instead, it must have confirmed their worst prejudices, just as their behaviour confirmed ours. We were all trapped by our labels.

I had no doubt Jen had every reason for responding in the way she had. The Gits had obviously seen her father as an affable and pleasant neighbour with a lot to put up with. It was clear that the view from inside Jen's family's front door had been as different as it possibly could be.

I touched her arm.

'Are you OK?' I asked.

In fact, she looked much better than she had before she'd launched her attack, as though she had got something out of her system. There was colour in her cheeks and she seemed relaxed, almost dreamy. She took a deep breath.

'I used to live here,' she said in a conversational tone, as though she hadn't just verbally destroyed a pair of pensioners. 'I spent my formative years at the Bod.' She turned to Frank. 'Cheer up, Frank. Don't look so worried.'

That seemed enough to reassure Frank. I was about to ask Jen which flat she'd lived in and when as the lift juddered to a halt on the top floor and we spilled out.

There was the usual racket of whooshes and shrieks coming from the S&M couple's flat. It was amazing how much of their time seemed to be devoted to sex. Jen stood and listened with a wry smile, while Frank's eyes widened to double their usual size.

I knew there was yet another problem as soon as I put my key in the door and it swung open, revealing the smashed lock.

'Wait,' Jen breathed, a restraining hand on my shoulder.

She looked around before striding to the overflowing rubbish chute and picking up a couple of bottles, one of which she handed to Frank. I felt my stomach lurch. We crept through the door. As it turned out, the bottles weren't needed. It seemed whoever had visited my flat had done what they had to do and had left again. Probably yesterday, which would account for the Gits' complaint.

They'd trashed my home. And everything in it. I know I've gone on about hating living in Boddington Heights, but the fact remained that it was My Home. The things that were in it, were My Things – and all that I had to show for my existence on this planet.

I gasped in disbelief as I looked round. Drawers had been pulled out, their contents strewn on the floor. Furniture was slashed and smashed. Books ripped, bottles shattered, clothes shredded. A chair leg protruded from my TV screen. Tomato ketchup and brown sauce were sprayed over the walls and the floor.

And in the middle of the debris, silent and predatory, was a giant turd.

Frank and Jen put protective arms round me as I gazed at the wreckage of my life. My table had been smashed in two, the shattered goldfish bowl visible among the splintered wood. There was no sign of the fish. I wasn't about to go looking for them.

Among the shredded pages of books, I saw leaves ripped from

my photo album, the pictures torn and shredded. With a stifled sob, I crouched and rummaged through the fragments until I found what I was looking for. An old black and white photo. I picked it up, holding it in trembling hands. Des still smiled up at me, as she always had done. But the tear had wrenched the baby me from her arms. It must be here somewhere. *I* must be here somewhere. I couldn't allow myself to be severed by some vicious symbolism.

I dropped to my knees and began sifting through the debris. I found the other half of the photo, wiped the smear of ketchup on my jeans and fitted the two pieces back together.

That's when the tears came. I sat back onto my haunches, my body racked with sobs. Jen sank down next to me and held me, crooning soothing words.

'Come on,' she said after a while, her voice soft but firm. 'There's nothing here for you, Jo. Let's just go.'

She eased me back onto my feet. I looked at Frank. He was crying. He spread his arms in a gesture of helplessness and frustration. I could see he was desperately trying to think of something positive and comforting to say. What he managed was, 'Well, look at it this way. The council would probably have chucked you out anyway.'

I stared at him in disbelief. Could he not see how appalling this was? Before I knew it, I felt myself start to laugh, giggles and hiccups bubbling up from my chest.

'That's true,' I spluttered. 'Just because I've lost everything I've ever owned . . . Maybe I should look on this as really good timing. Liberating even. After all, I couldn't have stored this lot in a cardboard bash in Waterloo, could I?'

Frank grinned back a little uncertainly. He wasn't sure if the laughter meant I was OK. He was having trouble reconciling it with the bitter words I'd spoken.

Jen had no such problem.

'You're not going to be living in a cardboard bash, Jo. I promise you that,' she said, radiating reassurance. Though without giving me any reason to believe her. 'Now, unless there's anything else you want to look for and try to salvage, I reckon we should leave now.' She stood in front of me and gripped my upper arms with both hands. She made sure I had her full attention before saying, 'Say goodbye, Jo. You're moving on. I reckon you've needed to for a long time. Only now events have conspired to give you a push. So you're right about the timing being good in a way.'

I struggled to come to terms with what she had just said. I knew on one level she was probably right. The trouble was, I had no idea where I was moving on to. And that scared the shit out of me.

Jen seemed to understand that too.

'Life's like that sometimes,' she went on. 'This,' she indicated the devastation in my home, 'is Life telling you it's time for radical changes. Whether you want them or not. And whether they scare you or not. I'm not going to stand here and tell you it's going to be painless. Radical change rarely is. But one thing I do know, is that you *are* going to come through this. And one day you'll look back and understand why things had to happen this way. But right now, we need to leave. Are you ready?'

I looked at her and then at Frank and gave a silent nod. I wasn't laughing any more, but I wasn't crying either. I gave one last look round at the wreckage of my home before leading the way up the hall and out of the front door.

'I suppose this is down to Tatiana's lot . . .' Frank said as the lift creaked downwards.

'Not necessarily,' I said with a disconsolate shrug. 'After she bleached the guy and we ran out, I locked the door behind us. He would have had to bust out. The door would have been left hanging open – anyone could have got in and trashed the place.'

Jen frowned but said nothing.

We spoke little on the journey back to Nirvana, each lost in our own thoughts. Uppermost in my mind was where I was going to live once the Nirvanans got tired of me dossing in their front rooms. I fingered the two halves of the photo in my pocket and tried to make a mental list of all my possessions that I no longer possessed. It was curious, but when I thought about it, there wasn't much I would really miss. Some of the books and tapes, I suppose. Maybe the rest of my photo album, though it mostly contained school photos of me through the years, peeping out from behind curtains of hair and scowling at the camera.

It didn't amount to much for nearly thirty years on the planet. In a way, though, Jen had been right. Everything I had is everything I was, I thought. Now everything I have is everything I am. And that's just going to have to be enough. The rest is just window dressing.

There was something about the acknowledgement that did feel a bit like liberation.

25

THE EMERGENCY MEETING was held in Jen's flat. She had written out an agenda on a big sheet of paper. It sat on the floor in the middle of the room, next to the overflowing ashtray and a pile of nibbles. There were three words on it, written one under the other. Gaia, Jo and Tatiana. I wasn't sure how I felt about being an item on an agenda, but at least I wasn't alone. And if people were going to be talking about me, I'd rather be part of the discussion.

Jen had told me a bit about Gaia earlier. It appeared that for a number of years Gaia had been engaged on a kind of spiritual and cultural shopping spree. She had sampled just about every alternative on the ethnic smorgasbord, trying a little of this and a little of that, blending them together in unlikely and often contradictory combinations. Now it seemed she had at last found what she had been looking for and had become what Jen called a 'Turbo Pagan'.

Gaia held the floor. And it was clear she was going to make the most of it.

'My friends,' she said, looking round with a melodramatic air. 'Loved ones, sisters, brothers, fellow spirits, companion travellers, kindred souls, sharers of the life force . . .' Jen had told me about the no interruption rule at meetings, but I heard Mags give a derisory grunt as she lit her spliff. '. . . this is the eternal moment from which all future paths will run.' Gaia was speaking in a strange, theatrical monotone. She closed her eyes and hummed a long note (slightly off key). This didn't sound very pagan to me, but what do I know? When she opened her eyes again, she grinned round at all present and spoke in her normal robust voice.

'So that's it. I'm off then. I leave next week. I'm going to check out my parents in their croft first, then take the ferry over to the island. If all goes well, I'll stay a year. If all goes really well, I'll never come back.' Gaia frowned, as if she was still in the process of working this out. 'On the other hand,' she went on, 'if all goes mega badly I might not be back either. So my continuing absence might not be the best barometer of how I'm doing . . .'

I turned to Jen and mimed a question.

'Gaia's going on a retreat to a remote island off the coast of Scotland,' Jen explained. 'It's something she's been thinking about for a while but she's been waiting for the right moment for the spiritual and physical journey. Speaking of which, how *are* you getting there, Gaia?'

'I'm walking,' Gaia replied with a beatific smile. Frank looked shocked. The others just looked sceptical. 'Only joking,' Gaia confessed. 'Actually, Ali's agreed to drive me up.' Ali raised his eyebrows. Frank looked shocked again. 'OK, OK,' Gaia smirked. 'I'm going on the train. Or at least I am if you guys let me hang on to my last housing benefit payment.'

Nobody objected. Gaia turned down the suggestion of a farewell party. I could tell that, in spite of her flippancy, she was very emotional to be leaving. I would be too, if I was her. I couldn't imagine anywhere I'd prefer to live than in this co-op. I wondered how they dealt with filling vacant flats. I assumed they must have some kind of policy.

'Right,' said Mags. 'We ready to move on to item two on the agenda? Jo,' she said, turning to me with a beaming smile. 'Welcome to Nirvana.'

I frowned in confusion. What did she mean? It wasn't like I'd just arrived. I looked round at the others, who were all grinning encouragement at me. Even Ali.

'It's yours if you want it,' Mags said.

'I'm sorry,' I stammered. 'What – what are we talking about here?'

I *thought* I knew what she meant. But I couldn't quite believe it. I wouldn't *allow* myself to believe it. In case I'd got it wrong. The disappointment combined with the embarrassment would be too much to handle . . .

'Gaia's leaving,' Jen explained. 'And you're homeless. It's obvious, isn't it? We'd like you to join Nirvana. No pressure, of course. If you feel it's not right for you, you can just stay until you've found something else . . .'

'No!' I yelped. 'No! I want this! Oh, I can't tell you how much I want this . . .' I tailed off with a nervous laugh. I didn't want them to think I was too intense.

'It takes commitment,' Jen warned. 'If there's a problem, you don't just phone the council to sort it out. We operate totally collectively. We do our own building work, repairs and stuff. We pay a nominal rent to the trust who owns the properties and the rest covers tools and stuff, running the van, funding the parties . . .'

Jen carried on, but I have to admit I'd stopped listening. It wouldn't have made any difference if she'd said the commitment entailed daily barefoot walks over flaming coals. There was nothing I wouldn't have been prepared to do to live there. My mind was spinning like a beyblade. It was incredible to think only four days had passed since I'd first come to Nirvana. In that time, I'd been to the circus, discovered Tatiana's other identity, met her brother, been attacked in my flat, delivered Tatiana to Pete, found out her story and had my flat ransacked. I'd gone from housed to homeless to housed again, all in the space of a single day. It was too much to take in. To cap it all, Mags had handed me the spliff, which did little to order my tumbling thoughts.

Through the fog, I heard Gaia addressing me. She was saying something about the spirit of the place being compatible with my life force and the karmic synchronicity of our travelling paths.

Then she uttered the words that penetrated my stupor. They cut through the murk and plunged icicles into my heart. I might have known. I might have known there would be something. Something that would mean it couldn't happen. Amazing opportunities like this were not for the likes of me. The euphoria had been fantastic. But so very, very short-lived.

The words she said were,

'And I know the cats will love you too.'

Cats. Gaia had cats. Lots of cats. I love cats. So what would Gaia and the others make of my karma when I told them that five minutes in the company of a single cat would have me clawing off my own skin?

'I – I'm sorry,' I murmured, forcing the words over my frozen lips. 'I can't move in after all. I – I'm allergic to cats . . .'

I swallowed hard. I didn't want to embarrass them by breaking down. Holding it together at that point was one of the hardest things I'd ever had to do. And I've done some hard things in my time.

'That's not a problem,' I heard Robin say through the fog of despair. 'I'm not used to staying in one place for long anyway. I'll move to Gaia's and you can have my place . . .'

And that was all it took. Item two on the agenda sorted. Jen leaned forward and crossed through Gaia's and my name with a red pen. I was about to become a Nirvanan. If my emotions could survive the violent battering they were being subjected to . . .

I assumed item three would prove insoluble even to these resourceful and flexible people, who had assumed collective godlike status in my mind at that point. I was wrong there too. I had a lot to learn. Though to be fair, they gave the credit to me.

'So,' said Mags. 'We're left with the only possible course of action. But how do we go about it?'

I thought I'd been daydreaming again and had missed something.

'Sorry,' I grimaced. 'What course of action is this, then?'

'You should know,' Mags asserted. 'It was your idea. We have to get her a fake ID. Then she can get out of London or better still the country. Where to isn't a problem. We have contacts in Amsterdam who could look after her initially and get her somewhere to live. The problem is how. Anyone got any ideas on how to get hold of a reliable forger?'

There was much muttering and shuffling, but nothing more constructive.

'I have!' I yelled. It was like an electronic circuit being completed in my brain. 'Nadia's friend. Galina. She had a false passport, I'm sure of it . . .'

I explained what had happened that day I had visited Nadia and Yaroslav at the hostel. I could barely contain my excitement. I rang Nadia's mobile straight away. She sounded pleased to hear from me. Apparently the new solicitor was really on the ball and was optimistic that she would be given leave to stay. One of the other groups on the list I had sent her was trying to put pressure on to get Yuri released and able to join her. I told her what I needed. She hesitated, but not for long. It was clear from everything I'd seen of her that she had always taken pride in being a respectable and law-abiding citizen. Until the law in two different countries had to all intents and purposes colluded with the criminals against her. In the circles in which she now found herself, it probably wasn't so unusual to get a phone call asking for details of people who provide false passports, or any of the other paraphernalia needed to get round a rigid and unforgiving system. She asked me no questions and I volunteered no further information. She said she would have to make a couple of calls herself, but she would get back to me.

In the meantime, there was nothing to do but wait.

26

NEXT DAY, I lay on the beach in the back garden, enjoying the warm sunshine and trying to visualise myself living in Robin's flat. I didn't know if I felt more delighted about leaving Bodding-ton Heights or coming to live at Nirvana. The combination of the two had me feeling giddy with excitement. And a bit scared. I'd never had so much to lose . . .

A vision of Mo filtered into my mind. I'd have to get her over here. The girls would have a field day in this garden. Meanwhile, I realised with a guilty stab, she didn't even know what had happened. I grabbed my mobile and called her.

Mo was shocked and angry in equal measure. She hadn't been up to my flat, knowing I wasn't there, and so didn't know it had been trashed. Her immediate reaction, as I would have anticipated if I'd had my wits about me, was to blame Tatiana. Nothing I could say would persuade her that Tatiana was as much a victim of the attack as I was, if not more so.

'It's *her* life, Jo. *Her* problem,' she exploded. 'I told you not to make it yours. I warned you, didn't I? Now look what's happened . . . You've lost everything − your home, all your stuff . . . I knew she'd be trouble right from the beginning.'

I had to fight to be heard over her tirade, but eventually she calmed down long enough for me to tell her I might have lost one home, but in so doing I'd gained an alternative that was light years better.

There was a long silence.

'So you've gone then. For good. Just like that . . .'

'Mo!' I cried. 'It's not like I had any choice. Go up now and take a look at the state of the place. Even if I could handle cleaning it up, do you really think I could handle going back to live there after all this? Even if it *was* safe? And even if the Gits didn't succeed in getting me evicted? Anyway, can't you see how much better off I am here? Joining this co-op is a dream come true, Mo. It's the best thing that's ever happened to me.'

'I see,' Mo replied in a wooden voice. 'Well, thanks for letting me know . . .'

'Oh, Mo,' I pleaded. 'Please don't be like this. Can't you at least be happy for me? Of course I'm going to miss you and the girls. Desperately. But it's not like I'm going to be very far away. We'll still see each other.'

'No we won't,' Mo grumbled, giving voice to her real fears. 'Maybe at first a bit, but then you'll drift off. You know full well we're not going to fit in with your new friends . . .'

'That's not true,' I shouted, shocked. 'How can you think that of me? What are you saying? That you reckon I'd just somehow drop you after all these years? I can't believe you'd think that, Mo. Really I can't . . .'

There was another loaded silence. I heard a squeak of a cloth and knew Mo was polishing something that was probably already sparkling while we were talking.

'I don't,' she eventually replied with a sigh. 'I don't really believe that. I'm sorry, love. I suppose it's just a bit of a shock. It's all happened so fast . . . I'll really miss you, Jo, but I *am* happy for you. Heaven knows you needed something. It's a great opportunity. I reckon once you're away from Boddington Heights, you'll get a chance. This place is poisonous. It was never good for you here.'

'I wish you didn't have to be there either, Mo,' I whispered, aware of a growing ache in my chest.

'Yeah, well no one should have to live in a place like this,' Mo sighed. I heard the sound of water filling a bucket and a mop being dunked. 'But we're OK here. The girls have never known anything different. Truth is you've always needed to get out of here. Now we're going to find out just how amazing I've always known you could be, given the chance.'

'Thanks, Mo. I don't deserve you,' I croaked, swallowing the lump that had developed in my throat.

The call may have been painful, but at least it ended on a positive note. I was sure that once Mo met the others, she would realise they weren't the kind of people to judge and reject her. And I was determined not to let her down. When I hung up, my mobile gave me details of a missed call from Nadia. I phoned her back and she gave me a number to ring. She said the man was expecting my call and everything would be arranged. He would tell me what we needed to do. She must have guessed I needed the passport for Tatiana. But she'd come up with the goods even though she had disapproved of her when they had met.

I took a deep breath and called the number. A gruff voice answered. Working-class London accent. I told him I was a friend of Nadia and he explained what he needed. Physical details – height, eye colour, distinguishing marks, etc., date of birth, two passport photos. And three hundred quid in cash. He gave me a post office box number to send it all to. He didn't tell me his name or ask me mine. It was strictly business with no more information asked or given than was necessary. We could expect to receive the finished article in three weeks. It was a huge risk, of course, sending that amount of money to a nameless, faceless, addressless recipient and trusting him to come up with the goods. But it was a risk we had to take.

Three weeks. Three weeks for Tatiana to stay in Pete's flat. I didn't think that part would be a problem for either of them. The real problem I could visualise was how Pete would cope when she left. I couldn't bear to imagine that. I couldn't think that far ahead anyway. Three weeks? A lifetime. Look at how much had happened in the last week alone. I had enough to do trying to wrap my head round the present. The future would have to hang on until I got to it.

Mags was enjoying her first day of unemployment and had celebrated by sleeping in. She surfaced late morning, looking refreshed and relaxed, and settled herself next to me on the beach. Jen appeared soon after, carrying a couple of kids' buckets and spades.

'Fancy making a sand castle?' she beamed.

'Sand's too dry,' Mags objected, curling up in a lazy heap of reluctance.

'Thought of that,' Jen replied, disappearing round the side of the house and returning with a hose that she'd hooked up to Mags's bathroom tap. She soaked one corner of the sanded garden and then used the hose to fill a big tin bath. 'For the moat,' she explained. Mags and I lay back and squinted at her through the bright light. The sun sparkled through the drops of water spraying from the nozzle of the hose, creating dancing rainbows of colour. Jen turned the hose onto the borders and the air filled with the smell of damp earth and aromatic herbs.

I though I'd died and gone to heaven.

We built an amazing sand castle, the likes of which would even have impressed Des's creative sensibilities. Turrets, moats, drawbridges – this one had the lot. And no day trippers to kick it over, or tide to eat away at it, or dogs to shit on it. Strange how I felt closer to Des here. It was the only place I'd ever been where I could imagine her thriving. I popped down the road to Nunhead Green and bought some crusty bread hot from the oven and fresh salad stuff.

The three of us ate and talked. And what we mostly talked about was, of course, Tatiana.

'The fact is,' mumbled Mags through a mouthful of bread, 'getting her a false identity isn't exactly a solution. It's not going to stop them looking for her. It just means that, with luck, they won't find her. And it also doesn't do anything about the broader issues of women like her being trafficked, abused and exploited . . .'

'Yeah. Well we have to know our limitations,' Jen demurred. 'It'll be little short of a miracle if we're able to save Tatiana, let alone do anything more long term to help other women in her position. The thing that worries me,' she went on, voicing a concern I had been feeling since Mags had first mentioned it to me, 'is that getting her a new ID does nothing to protect her family back in the Ukraine from reprisals. If we fail to help Tatiana, we fail. But if we succeed, we still fail. If we're successful in keeping Tatiana out of these guys' clutches, it automatically exposes her family that much more.'

I took a handful of sand and allowed it to trickle between my fingers. The sun glinted off the shiny fragments of shell among the soft grains. Thousands of years ago, each would have been a part of a living creature. The thought made me feel very small and insignificant.

'Pete told me he'd talked about that with her,' I said, smoothing the sand flat around me with wide sweeps of my open palms. 'He says she can't allow herself to think about what might happen to her family. She said if anything happened to them, the responsibility would be her brother's, not hers. He was the one whose debts started this whole spiral in the first place.'

'She said that, did she?' Jen's expression was one of dubious respect. 'Tough little cookie, our Tatiana, isn't she?'

'She'd have to be, wouldn't she,' protested Mags. 'Just to survive this long. I bet there are plenty who don't. Women who get beaten to death or top themselves . . . We don't get to hear about them because we're supposed to think they don't count. They're women, they're prostitutes, they're foreign . . . worthless, in other words.'

I shuddered at the harsh analysis, but I'd learned enough to know this couldn't be dismissed as left-wing propaganda. For women like Tatiana, this was the reality they faced every day of their lives.

'Anyway,' Mags went on, 'which of us, in all honesty, can put their hand on their heart and swear they wouldn't do the same? If you were faced with the choice of saving your own life when it's under *immediate* threat, or protecting your family from a *potential* threat, what would you do?'

Jen appeared to contemplate the dilemma for some time. I already knew my answer. Jen's eventual response showed she'd come to the same conclusion.

'Dunno,' she replied, shaking her head.

'Precisely,' Mags retorted. 'Unless we've walked in her shoes, we can't possibly judge her. Who feels it knows it.'

We all sat and thought about that for a while. I lay back on the sand. The summer sun plus the full belly was having a soporific effect, intensified several times over by the enormous spliff Mags had produced. I was almost drifting off, when Jen's next words jerked me from my stupor.

'When are you going to go and see her?' she asked. 'She doesn't even know about this yet, does she? You shouldn't go into much detail over the phone . . .'

'Tomorrow, I suppose,' I said, my heart sinking. It felt like I was coming to the end of a holiday. Today the beach. Tomorrow back to reality. The break hadn't been long enough. They never are.

'No point dragging it out,' I sighed. 'I'll go to one of those booths with her and get some passport photos.'

There was another problem I had to talk about, uncomfortable though it was.

'Um – about the money – I've got a bit, but nowhere near three hundred quid. And Tatiana has nothing. I'm sure Pete will cough up some, but I'm not sure he could get it all together – especially since I missed last week at the market . . .'

'Don't worry about that,' Mags replied. 'Between us all, we'll get enough together.'

'There's something else,' I said, determined not to be too reassured. 'How do we go about getting her to Amsterdam? They're going to be looking for her. We already know how effective their network is from what happened that time in Greenwich.'

'We've thought about that too,' Jen said. 'Stop worrying so much, Jo. Worrying changes nothing. It doesn't stop bad things happening. It just makes you feel shit in the meantime.' I certainly didn't feel too reassured by that.

'Ali's agreed to drive her. They'll get the train through the tunnel,' Mags said, exhaling a dense cloud of smoke. 'It'll be a long journey, but we checked out how it works and she'll be able to stay in the back of the van all the way. No one need see her. We've already alerted our friends in Amsterdam. They're waiting for us to give them the go ahead when and if Tatiana agrees to what we're doing. They'll find a place for her to stay. They'll rent a flat for her in her new name and then look after her until she's settled.'

'They'd be prepared to do that?' I asked, amazed. 'Without even meeting her?'

'That's the anti-globalisation network for you,' laughed Jen. 'See? The bad guys don't have the monopoly on resources . . .'

I sat up and fidgeted with my mobile for a while. It wouldn't be easy phoning Pete to tell him we'd come up with a plan that could save Tatiana's life, but if successful would tear the two of them apart for ever. I told Jen and Mags what was on my mind, hoping they wouldn't think I was always focusing on the negative aspects.

That was when Jen made her suggestion. I was flabbergasted. It was so simple, but I had no idea if it could work.

Or if Pete would agree to it.

27.

THE FOLLOWING DAY I went to Pete's on the bus on my own, having turned down offers of company. I owed it to Pete to say what I had to without cowering behind anyone else. And I wanted him to be able to react as he needed to, without feeling constrained by the presence of strangers. My mind was in a turmoil. I couldn't begin to imagine how he would react to Jen's suggestion.

The scene in his flat was a picture of domestic harmony. I'd picked up some shopping for him on the way. Tatiana took the carrier bags from me with a shy smile and began putting the contents away in the kitchen, which I couldn't help noticing had never looked so clean and organised. Pete showed me some sketches of new designs he'd come up with. Tatiana had inspired him to take wax in new directions, he told me, flicking through the sheets of paper. The charcoal drawings looked sombre and dark to me, almost sinister in comparison to his usual life-and-light-imbued creations. I told him how wonderful they were, though I wasn't sure how well they would sell. I felt my stomach flip as I remembered the information I had come to impart could make the saleability or otherwise of Pete's candles in Greenwich Market irrelevant.

Perhaps in order to delay the inevitable life-changing decision I was about to force him to face, I told him instead about my move to Nirvana. He was delighted for me, as I'd known he would be, hugging me and asking for full details of my fellow co-op members so he could visualise them. I gave him physical descriptions and any snippets that I'd picked up about people's backgrounds and their idiosyncrasies. As I spoke, I had to keep reminding myself that these people were more than just new neighbours. And coming to Nirvana was more than just a change of address. The contrast to life at Boddington Heights couldn't have been greater. I told him about the beach in the garden, at which point he said with a grin that he knew I was going to be 'just fine there'.

I didn't mention the trashing of my flat and its contents, which had meant I had no choice but to move. Pete's candles were safely stored in the basement of a newsagent's near the market, so he didn't *need* to know. I was aware that Tatiana could hear me from the kitchen. I saw no point in frightening either of them with details of the wanton destruction of my previous home. Especially as we couldn't be certain the culprits were connected to Georgi's men anyway. I remembered the sceptical look on Jen's face when I'd suggested that to her and Frank. But the fact remained that we couldn't be sure. I could see no justification for making Pete and Tatiana more frightened than they already were. They had enough to think about. Or would have shortly.

Tatiana brought in mugs of tea, weaving her way through the hanging candles with an effortless grace, as though she'd been negotiating waxy mazes all her life. Pete's eyes followed her through the room. He smiled at her as she set the mugs down on the table and perched on the arm of his chair. He circled her waist with his arm and tore his gaze away from her for long enough to give me a look so full of childlike wonder that my heart ached for him.

I took a deep breath and told them the plan to get Tatiana a false passport and resettle her in Amsterdam. Tatiana watched me with a grave expression of concentration. Pete's eyes had become huge in his thin face. He seemed to be devouring her in an attempt to drink in as much as he could before the inevitable time when he would lose her.

When I'd finished, Tatiana turned to him and cradled his cheek in the palm of her hand. It was such a tender gesture. Her eyes expressed a devastating combination of loss and love. It was light years from the hollow façade I had seen when she'd made her proposition to me in my flat. I had known then she hadn't really been attracted to me. It had been merely expedient for her to dissemble. She had been using the only bargaining tool she believed she had. This was something different entirely. Any lingering doubts I might have been harbouring about her feelings for Pete melted away as I watched the two of them struggle with their emotions.

'You have to go,' Pete whispered to her. 'It's your only chance . . .'

She shook her head, tears shining in her eyes.

'I do not want to leave you . . .'

At other times I might have left them to it, rather than continue to intrude on their intimacy. But I still had the second half of the plan to relay. Pete was shocked rigid by the suggestion I made. He turned so pale, I thought he might be sick. His breathing quickened and beads of sweat broke out on his brow. Tatiana gave a little cry of alarm. She put her arms round him and cradled his head on her shoulder.

That's it, then, I thought to myself. If this is how he reacts to the mere suggestion, there's no way he could go through with it. I slumped in my chair. Giving him the option, only for him to be unable to handle it, suddenly seemed unnecessary and cruel. It would have been better if he'd never had the choice. I thought I'd been offering a possible solution. Instead I'd just made him feel worse.

Just as I'd arrived at that conclusion, he raised his head and pulled back from Tatiana.

'Explain to me how it would work,' he croaked through pinched lips.

'Peter . . .' gasped Tatiana, but he silenced her with a shake of his head. I took a deep breath. The way I presented this to him now was crucial. I'd rehearsed it so many times, I hoped it wouldn't come out too pat.

'Ali brings the van right to the door,' I said. 'We black out the back windows and we can even put up a screen behind the driver's seat, so you can't see through the windscreen from the back. We drive onto the Eurostar and go through the tunnel. They've checked the procedure. We park in a car park before driving on. Someone has to get out of the van to find out the times and so on. But there's no reason at all why you and Tatiana should have to get out. We hand over the passports and tickets. It's all legit – we have nothing to hide and the authorities have no reason to be suspicious, which would be the only reason they would want you to get out. Ironically, what we have going for us here is that they're not looking for people being smuggled *out* of England. You stay in the van all the way and he delivers you direct to the door of the flat in Amsterdam these people rent for you. We explain that one of the criteria when they get a place should be that there's parking space immediately outside.'

Pete was deathly pale, his skin as waxy as his candles. But he listened intently, sitting on the edge of his chair and looking from me to Tatiana and back again. Hope and despair competed with each other across her face. I could imagine what might be going through her mind. Relocation to a new city. A new country. A new chance. A chance of life. But terrifying too. How much better it would be if she wasn't alone. If this man, who so clearly adored her, was able to come too.

'I'd need drugs,' Pete whispered.

'Jen thought of that too,' I replied, keeping my voice calm and even, not daring to hope . . . 'Apparently, she's got a stash of barbiturates and valium left behind by some former house-guest . . .'

I tailed off. I didn't want to put any more pressure on him, but I could see how badly he wanted to be able to do this. I remembered what Jen had said to me in the wreckage of my old flat about Life sometimes giving you a push. I decided I should act as Life's agent and give Pete a bit of positive visualisation.

'Amsterdam's brilliant,' I said. 'It's a really alternative scene. Your candles would go down a storm there. You could get most of your stuff – apart from the furniture of course – into the van and take it with you. Jen and Mags say their friends won't just abandon you once you're there. They'll help sort things out. And once you were settled Tatiana would be able to go out. She could get the shopping and deal with the places selling your candles . . .'

Tatiana twisted on the arm of the chair to face Pete, her every fibre radiating desperate hope so intense I felt physical pain for her.

Pete was trembling and his breathing had become laboured again. He lowered his head into his hands.

'What's keeping me here?' I heard him whisper in a strangled voice. 'Nothing. Nothing but fear. Nothing but fear . . .' He looked up and locked eyes with Tatiana. 'I'll do it.'

He had to force the words out over his taut lips, but once they were said, the effect was little short of miraculous. Tatiana stared at him, her eyes wide, her balled fist over her mouth.

'I'll do it!' he repeated in a stronger voice. 'I will. I'll do it. I'm going to do it!'

Tatiana erupted with a cry of amazement and the two of them flung their arms round each other, laughing and crying. Then Pete disengaged himself from her arms and came over to me and wrapped me in a giant hug.

'How can I ever thank you, Jo?' he murmured into my hair.

'You've always been an amazing friend to me, right from when we first met. And now . . .' He looked over his shoulder at the exultant young woman standing behind him before turning back to me. 'Thank you. Thank you so much. You're the only thing I'll miss here . . .'

'Oh, I'll miss you too, Pete. So much.' I brushed a couple of tears from my cheek. 'Not least because I'll be losing my income . . .' I said with mock severity.

'Oh, Jo! I didn't think . . . How will you manage?' he gasped.

'Don't even think about that,' I admonished. 'That's the least of our worries. I've still got the gardening. Anyway, who knows, I might even keep the stall on and sell my jewellery on it.'

'That's a brilliant idea,' Pete said with a relieved smile. 'You've already got the contacts. I reckon you could do really well . . .'

I shook my head in amazement.

'Isn't it weird how we're both moving on at the same time,' I said. 'And so dramatically!'

'Yes,' he agreed. 'And for both of us, it's down to one person . . .'

We turned to Tatiana. Pete caught her hand and drew her forward.

'I want to thank you also, Jo,' she murmured in her soft voice. 'You help me when I have nothing and no one. I always remember you.'

'You won't get a chance to forget me,' I warned. 'I'll be looking forward to regular cheap holidays in Amsterdam from now on.'

Tatiana didn't laugh. Humour is always the hardest part of a culture to get to grips with. And it was clear she thought this situation was as serious as it could get. She was right of course.

Pete gave a nervous giggle, but I could see he was still filled with terror at the thought of the ordeal to come. I can't say I felt too confident about it myself. But neither of us was going to express those concerns right now.

Right now was the time to celebrate.

After cracking open some lager and sharing the spliff Mags had thoughtfully provided, the continuing constriction in my chest told me it was time to get down to the practical details. We'd examined the dream, seen where it would lead us and, against all the odds, we were all on board. But I was aware that the measures that still had to be taken could scupper the dreamboat before it was even launched.

I took another deep breath, which made my head spin in a way that was not entirely unpleasant.

'Pete . . .' My voice came out louder than I'd intended. 'You're going to need a passport too . . .'

Pete gave me a sleepy smile, his bloodshot eyes testifying to the power of Mags's supply.

'Not a problem,' he drawled. 'I've already got one.'

Tatiana and I both swung our bleary focus to him in surprise.

'When I got it, the panic attacks had just started,' Pete explained through a mouthful of chocolate brownie. 'It was another year before they kicked in so hard and frequent I had to stop going out. And that was seven years ago . . .'

My fuddled brain struggled through the mental arithmetic.

'So it's still valid!' I cried in triumph.

Pete laughed and nodded, holding his can of lager aloft in acknowledgement of my mathematical prowess. So I wasn't Carol Vorderman. But I was very stoned.

Tatiana stood up and stretched. She walked over to Pete's stereo, selected a tape and pressed play. The clear unsullied tones of Enya filled the room. Pete and I both watched her. Maybe she was aware of the attention. Maybe it brought out the performer in her and we were the audience. But when she started to move, it seemed to me she was doing it entirely for herself.

Slowly, hesitantly at first, she began to sway, her head thrown back, her eyes closed and a look on her face close to ecstasy. There's some deep essence that folk music around the world seems to have in common. Maybe that was what touched Tatiana's soul as she began to move around the room with more confidence and abandon. She swooped and twirled around the hanging candles, her movements so fluid and lithe the waxy stalactites seemed to ripple with her. As though she was the breath of wind and they were the waves.

It was breathtaking to watch. Not spectacular, like her demonstration at the Maritime Museum. But achingly beautiful. Her lack of self-consciousness made me feel I was almost intruding on her by watching.

But to look away was unthinkable.

I didn't really know Tatiana at all, I thought to myself. Everything I had seen had been the product of her experiences. The fear, the suspicion, the reticence, the manipulation – they were all reactions. They don't make up a whole person. It was clear Pete had seen far more of that whole person in a couple of days than I ever had in the time she'd stayed with me. Watching her now, I could see why he'd been captivated. He hadn't fallen in love with a romantic fantasy, as I'd first feared. He'd fallen in love with Tatiana.

The music ended and Tatiana stood in the centre of the room with a dreamy smile on her face.

'I love to dance,' she murmured. 'When I was a child I wanted to dance in the ballet. It was a big dream for me. But my mother say girls from poor families like ours do not dance in the ballet. When Sergei and I joined the circus, I had pretty costume. Like ballet dancer. Sergei, he say to me, I have big chance now. People will come to see me. They will clap and cheer. It will be like my dream.'

Her shoulders slumped. I took a swig of lager to try to wash down the lump in my throat. Then she looked up and smiled brightly at Pete. She looked very young and very beautiful.

'Now I have a new dream,' she beamed.

Pete gave a delighted laugh and ran over to hug her.

'What happens now, Jo?' he asked me, extricating himself from the clinch. 'What's the timescale?'

'Once we post off the photos and the details – and the dosh, of course – it takes about three weeks,' I replied. I turned my attention back to Tatiana.

'Speaking of which, you do realise, Tatiana, we're going to have to make a trip out for the photos . . .' I saw her stiffen, the smile fading from her face. Pete put a protective arm round her shoulders. 'I've scouted out the nearest photo booth,' I went on, determined to get the information out, no matter how hard it might be for her to take on.

I felt cruel. But someone had to be practical and hard-headed if this had any chance of working. I was also slurring a bit. The ganja gave the whole scene an unreal quality, as though we were acting. 'It's in the supermarket. We can walk there in ten minutes max.'

I picked up my rucksack and pulled out a couple of items.

'Why don't we do it now and get it over with?' I said.

Tatiana paled at the sight of the baseball hat and shades I held out. She shrank into Pete's side, trembling. They weren't the same ones she'd worn in Greenwich. But I knew what she was thinking.

'There's no reason for them to be looking for you in this area,' I said. 'It was different that day in Greenwich. We were wandering through the park, taking our time. We sat and had a picnic. Ample opportunity for someone to see you and hang round long enough to be sure it was you. This time we walk straight to the supermarket. I checked the booth was working when I did the shopping. The only time we're hanging round is when we're waiting for the photos to be churned out. And you can stay in the booth 'til they're ready. Then we walk straight back here.'

Pete looked at Tatiana as she fought with her fears. Pete, of all people, knew only too well what that felt like. She made up her mind, straightened her shoulders and turned to Pete. She gave him the briefest of kisses on the lips and said to me, 'We do it now.' Her voice was resolved, with only a hint of a tremor. Pete was the one who was sweating by proxy. I heard him give a repressed retch as Tatiana bundled her hair into the baseball cap and pulled it low over her forehead. She put on Jen's mirror shades and strode to the door, leaving me no option but to follow. I suddenly felt panicky. We weren't acting and it wasn't an adventure. I wasn't too sure I was ready myself. But Tatiana may have been over a decade younger than me, but she had far greater experience of not letting an opportunity slip away.

Pete groaned and swayed slightly. I gave him a swift hug.

'We'll be fine,' I reassured. 'We'll be back in half an hour.'

28

BEING STONED DIDN'T help in a situation where paranoia was justified. If Tatiana wanted to look like someone with something to hide, I reckoned she was doing a bloody good job of it. It's not that she was shifty, darting glances round and jumping at shadows. Quite the reverse. But it still felt to me that her body language made her conspicuous. It was a hot, sunny day and most people were ambling along with the slowed-down rhythms enjoyed by people living in warmer climates. Tatiana strode along, head down, shoulders hunched, hands in pockets. She never looked right or left as far as I could tell behind the mirror shades. She didn't need to. People instinctively moved aside for her. She radiated tension so palpable I was bouncing off the waves of it at every step.

For some people, sunshine induces a more laid-back attitude. For others, it would take more than a sunny day to sort their heads out. We arrived at the supermarket without incident. As we were making our way through the car park, an argument broke out. A man pushing a full trolley had a go at a woman who was packing her shopping into a big fuck-you people carrier.

'Excuse me,' I heard him say. 'You're parked in a disabled spot, but I don't see any orange badge . . .' The woman ignored him and carried on as though she hadn't heard him. 'It's because people like you park there out of sheer laziness that people who genuinely need to be close to the exit have to cross the whole car park,' he went on, stung by her rudeness.

'I don't see what business it is of yours,' she threw over her shoulder.

'It's my business,' he went on, keeping his voice even with obvious effort, 'because I *do* have the right to park there and can't because *you're* there.'

'Well, I don't see why you need it more than I do,' she retorted, squaring up for the fight. She slammed the car boot shut and shoved the now empty trolley aside so it blocked the car next to her, before turning to face him, her hands on her ample hips. In response, the man used his right hand to hold up his empty left sleeve. Game, set and moral match, I thought. I reckoned without the capacity some people have for utter contempt.

'So? Nothing wrong with your legs, is there?' she replied, turning her back on him in dismissal.

I hesitated. Under normal circumstances, I would have had to get involved in this one. The man shook his head in disbelief as he steered his wonky wheeler across the tarmac as best he could with one arm. Today, I could do no more than give him a sympathetic grimace. Tatiana strode ahead, seemingly oblivious to the whole episode.

We walked through the automatic doors into the cool atmosphere of the air-conditioned supermarket. I could see the booth ahead. There was no one in it. Good job I had the forethought to make sure I had the right coins. Except I hadn't, I realised with a sickening jolt. The coins were sitting in the pocket of my denim jacket. My denim jacket was sitting on the back of the chair in Pete's front room. So was my mobile and all the rest of my money. My stomach lurched. Damn that fucking spliff. Just when I most needed a clear head . . . I patted the pockets of my jeans in desperation. Relief flooded through my every fibre as my fingers curled round Pete's cash card that I used to pay for his shopping.

'We have to go back out to get money from the machine,' I muttered to Tatiana.

She gave a repressed groan and swung round and back through the doors. My hand was shaking as I fed the card into the hole in the wall. I drew out two hundred pounds, the amount Pete had said he could afford to contribute to the cost of the passport. I congratulated myself on killing two birds with one stone – compensation for having been too stoned to remember my jacket. Just as I was pocketing the money, I realised I would have to buy something to get change for the photos.

I strode straight past the booth, to Tatiana's despair. I could feel the electricity crackling from her as we queued at the kiosk to buy a packet of fags. She plucked at my sleeve and jerked her head in the direction of the booth. Two small children had climbed in. One was tugging at the curtain. It sounded as though the other was kicking the screen. My heart was pounding. I wasn't sure if Tatiana could handle any further delays. I had visions of her doing a runner and the whole fantasy edifice crumbling round our ears. As we watched, a harassed-looking woman grabbed the children and pulled them away and out of the store. I was next in the queue and could barely hide my impatience as the young assistant dawdled over to the shelves behind her to get my cigarettes. My senses were unnaturally heightened. The lights were too bright. It felt to me as though everyone was moving in slow motion, as if they were under water.

At last I had the coins. We almost ran to the booth and Tatiana flung herself inside. I fed in the money and pressed the button for her.

'Take off your hat and shades,' I hissed. 'And try not to look too tense!' Huh! Advice I should have taken myself. I hyper-hopped from foot to foot as the flash burned four times in succession. Tatiana stayed inside while I waited for the strip of photos to appear. I've never known a five minutes to drag on so long. There must be some mathematical law that governs the passage of time to explain how five minutes can last anything from five seconds to several hours, depending on how you are spending them: *x amount of stress equals y amount of time multiplied by 1,000 minus z years shaved off your life.*

At last the slimy strip appeared. I clutched it by the edges and gave the pictures a quick glance to make sure they were usable. They were, though they were not what you'd call flattering. No matter. They were for a false passport, not a modelling portfolio.

'Let's go,' I muttered to Tatiana, twitching the curtain aside.

She exploded out of the machine, the baseball hat and shades back in place, and almost ran to the exit doors.

We strode along side by side back through the dusty streets. We didn't speak. My main fear was that we looked so suspicious that we might get pulled over by a watching cop trained to pick up on the kind of body language I knew we were exhibiting. There was nothing I could do, though, to modify my own be-haviour at that point, let alone Tatiana's.

It was an eternity before we were outside Pete's flat knocking at the familiar door. He flung it open and grabbed Tatiana, who collapsed sobbing onto his shoulder. I sank onto a chair and sat, my head between my knees, and tried to convince myself we were yet another step closer to the happy ending.

29

I LEFT ABOUT half an hour later, once I'd stopped hyper-ventilating. They definitely needed some space and I wanted to get back so I could put Pete's financial contribution together with the rest that had been offered and send the parcel off. I sat in the front seat on the top of the bus going back towards Peckham. I held the strip of photos in my hand, so as not to risk bending them. I couldn't help staring at the quadruple image of Tatiana looking up at me. She hadn't managed to not look tense. Her eyes were wide and staring, with a rabbit in headlights expression. Her skin was stretched taut over her cheekbones, her clenched teeth making a hard line of her jaw. The way lots of people look in passport photos, in fact. They would serve their purpose.

I gazed out of the dusty front window of the bus. It was boiling hot. The bus crawled through the traffic in short bursts punctu-ated by long pauses when we remained stationary. It was taking minutes to cover yards. It would have been quicker to get out and walk, but I was in no hurry. I allowed my mind to wander. By the time Pete and Tatiana left for Amsterdam, I should be ensconced in Robin's flat. My flat.

I thought about colour schemes, atmosphere, style . . . I'd never bothered at Boddington Heights, opting for utilitarian and low-maintenance rather than individual expression. The flat opened out onto the garden at the back . . . I'd go for sunflower yellow in the kitchen, I decided. And maybe something dark and sultry for the bedroom, saving calm and relaxing for the front room.

I sank lower in my seat to duck out of the sun's glare grilling me through the window and closed my eyes so I could concentrate better on the rosy vision I was conjuring.

Pete had told me to sell the remaining stock on the stall and keep the takings in lieu of the wages I'd no longer be getting. I could maybe kick-start the jewellery again . . . It might pick up enough to keep the stall going once the candles ran out. Together with the gardening income, I should be able to make enough to live on and still stretch to some paint . . .

The bus lurched forward. I opened my eyes and peered through the window. We ground to a halt after moving about as far as I could spit if my mouth wasn't so dry. I closed my eyes again and put my feet up on the ledge in front.

Gaia was leaving her furniture, so I would inherit the stuff in Robin's flat. This consisted of a mattress on the floor, a battered kitchen table with a splintery bench and some stained floor cushions. But there was also a working cooker and fridge. Mo would have turned green at the sight of the state they were in, but I reckoned I just might be able to get them looking like they weren't harbouring bubonic plague without resorting to a blow torch.

The bus hadn't moved for ages. I sat up and shaded my eyes as I squinted through the front window. From my vantage point I could see through the gridlock to the road works ahead, where the traffic in both directions was being funnelled through a single lane. The sun pounded on the roof of the bus and streamed through the grimy windows. I felt sweat trickle down my back under my T-shirt. I stood up and yanked at the top window, even though it was the first thing I'd done when I'd got on the bus. I was no more successful this time round than the first.

I slumped back down on the seat and threw my head back so my hair hung away from my sticky neck. My gaze fell on the round convex mirror in the corner above me. I stared at my reflection. I looked flushed, my eyes still hooded and bloodshot from Mags's spliff.

I allowed my focus to shift to the rest of the bus behind me. There were only four other people left on the top deck, most having given up ages ago and persuaded the driver to let them off. Two girls were giggling over a magazine. Behind them, an old man shuffled and grunted in irritation at the bus's lack of progress. Halfway down the bus on the same side as me was a lone man. A white guy with dark bushy hair. I realised with a discomforting jolt that he too was looking in the mirror. Our reflected eyes locked. Watching you watching me . . . Strange how a reflection changes things, I mused. Prolonged direct eye contact would have been unthinkable. But in a mirror . . .

I would have lots of mirrors in my flat. There was a guy at the market who made gorgeous ones. He'd give me a good deal . . . I'd seen some with candle holders worked into the frames. That reminded me . . . I made a mental note to sort through Pete's stock and select which candles I wanted to keep for myself . . .

I was still staring in the mirror. So was the man. I heard his mobile ring. He answered it without breaking the eye contact. He barely spoke apart from the occasional grunt. Then, as I watched, he broke into a broad grin. His tongue snaked out and he licked his lips suggestively in a way that was clearly intended for me. I looked away with a grimace of disgust.

I stared out of the side window trying to recover the thread of my thoughts. I felt a presence at my shoulder and jumped as I turned to see the man's leering face as he leaned towards me, one arm on the back of the seat. I could smell garlic and tobacco. I recoiled, shrinking into the corner. He followed and whispered in my ear. I felt the warm rush of his breath on the side of my face.

'Georgi says hello,' he hissed, then stood back laughing at the look of horror on my face.

I leaped to my feet, pushed him aside and bounded down the stairs. I battered my fists on the door of the bus, but it had just started to move.

'You'll have to wait 'til we next stop now, love,' the driver yelled, shaking his head in exasperation.

I turned around wildly. The man stood lounging at the top of the stairs, making no attempt to stop me and sniggering at my panic. How long had he been following me? I knew we'd hung round longer than I'd intended getting the photos, but I couldn't believe we'd been spotted then. That could only mean he must have been with me before.

And that meant I had led him to Tatiana.

The bus ground to a halt again and the doors swung open. The one in front of me stuck. I barged it aside with my shoulder and hit the baking pavement, running back the way I had come.

As I hared along, I fumbled in my rucksack for my mobile. The strip of photos slipped from my fingers and fluttered away, landing face up in the gutter a few yards behind me. I hesitated, wasting precious seconds, torn between going back to pick them up and continuing my headlong dash. In my panic-stricken state, it seemed vital that I make the right choice and I faltered, tortured by indecision. In the end I ran back and retrieved the strip, but refused to be distracted into returning Tatiana's quadruple gaze.

As I stooped in the gutter, I glanced back the way I had come. The man had got off the bus. He was leaning against a wall, watching me with a leer. He was smoking a cigarette. It was obvious he was no longer making any attempt to follow me. I could only think of one possible reason for that. I moaned as I turned, stuffed the photos into my bag and continued my flight back towards the flat.

If the bus had been moving at a normal pace, I would have been close to Peckham by the time I jumped off. As it was, there was only about a mile between me and Pete's flat. A mile of boiling street, poisonous fumes rising in inexorable waves from the stationary traffic. A mile of irritable pedestrians moving slug- gishly through the shimmering heat. A mile of tumbling thoughts and rising panic.

I gripped the mobile and punched in Pete's number, narrowly avoiding falling over a pushchair. I yelled apologies at the irate woman-turned-tiger who shouted abuse at my retreating back. The mobile jigged against my ear as I ran. The only sound in all the world I wanted to hear at that point was Pete's voice. Instead I got the 'unobtainable' drone.

I stifled a cry of despair. Sweat was pouring down my face and body. My heart, pounding out the blood that was pumping too fast round my body, thudded in my ears. I was dimly aware of people at the periphery of my vision moving aside, staring at me with naked curiosity. I punched in the entry for the Nirvana mobile. I recognised Ali's grunt on the third ring.

'Ali!' I screamed. 'They followed me!' I forced the words out, aware of the hysteria in my voice. I was panting so hard, I couldn't even be sure he'd understand.

'They – know – where – she – is!' I gasped.

'On my way,' I heard, before the connection broke.

I wasn't fit enough. It was too hot. I was staggering rather than running now, carried forward by the force of my own momen- tum. The bag thudded against my side. My legs felt boneless as they struggled to lift my cast-iron feet. Every ragged exhalation was accompanied by a moan of horror.

I could hear sirens. Police? Ambulance? Fire? They came from far behind me. They would be stuck in the gridlock, unable to get through.

I had to stop. I had to catch my breath. I staggered to a halt and bent over double, my hands on my knees with my arse against a shop front. I drew in deep shuddering gulps of air, the wheezing preventing enough from reaching my lungs to ease the constriction for several breaths.

It was only after half a dozen chest-expanding moments that the pressure on my rib cage relaxed enough for me to notice something. It was a smell. A familiar smell. One I'd always associated with calm and inner peace. The sweet scent of incense. Usually released into the dullness of the surrounding air by the life-giving properties of fire. A match to a joss stick, or a candle's flickering flame.

But it was strong. Too strong. Sickly sweet and cloying, as though a cocktail of opposing fragrances had exploded into the hot still air.

I looked up the road. A knot of people had gathered by the junction at the turning to Pete's flat. As I watched with mounting despair, I saw more people gravitate towards them, swelling their numbers. I pushed myself off from the wall and forced my jelly legs into a trot. I was about fifty yards away when I heard the first explosion. A cry went up from the crowd, a few people running back in fear. Others in the street, unable to resist the temptation to witness a real-life drama, ran towards the junction. There was smoke in the air now, rising in a vast black cloud over the buildings ahead of me. There was no wind and the smoke rose vertically. Only the sickly incense smell rolled outwards like an invisible shroud.

There was a second explosion, then a third, before I reached the back of the crowd. Each time, the people gasped and swayed. Some had their hands to their faces in horror. One woman guided her sobbing friend out of the frenzy. I pushed my way into Pete's street and through the heaving mass to the front, ignoring the protests. Every person in that seething human stew was gazing in the same direction, with expressions of appalled fascination.

The flames surged from Pete's windows. These were not flames that licked. They rolled out in great furious waves as though they would consume the very air. Choking smoke, ripped by darts of dancing sparks, billowed upwards. You could feel the intensity of the heat, even though we were well over a hundred feet away. The smell of incense pressed down on my wheezing chest with a suffocating weight. There was a small knot of men in front of the building. Two of them kicked down the street door leading up to the flat. There was another smaller explosion. A gasp and a ripple went through the crowd like a collective sigh. Some of the people at the front were getting nervous. There was no one in authority to tell them where to stand. They had made their own decision, based on a balance between personal safety and morbid curiosity. The front row leaned backwards as more people arrived from behind, jostling forwards for a better view.

One of the men in front of the building covered his head and shoulders with his jacket and tried to run through the door and up the stairs to the flat. He reappeared seconds later, doubled over and choking. There was yet another explosion, debris hurling from the window into the street below. The men fell back to the opposite side of the street shaking their heads.

From that point onwards, everything appeared to me to be moving in slow motion with muffled sound, as though I was viewing it all from deep underwater. I could vaguely hear the sirens getting closer. Most of the people in the crowd were silent or talking in subdued murmurs, though some jabbered excitedly, high on the adrenalin, as we watched the fire engulf the roof. I didn't listen to any of them. Their voices, the sirens' wail, the roar of the fire, the cracking of wood and popping of tiles all receded into the distance.

I stood, rooted to the spot, staring mesmerised at the plumes of thick black smoke mushrooming into the sky, turning day to night above Pete's building. Sparks flared out, orange snake trails dancing and fluttering vivid patterns across the darkness, like fireflies on a moonless night. They shot, glimmered and died in a random choreography; fluorescent wiggles of light super-imposed on the impenetrable dark of the smoke. They were like thousands of souls, shining for a brief but glorious instant before expiring into the all-powerful darkness.

I thought it was the most beautiful thing I had ever seen.

30

THE INVESTIGATION CITED a number of factors. Several eye witnesses said they had seen a dark (some said blue, some black, some grey) car (some said a BMW, some a Merc) with blacked-out number plates (they all agreed on that) screeching to a halt outside the building. The driver stayed behind the wheel and kept the engine running as two men jumped out, ignited the rags protruding from the bottles in their hands and hurled them through the open windows of Pete's flat. They leaped back in the car and sped off up the street, after which there were no further reliable sightings. All three were masked.

The whole incident had taken seconds. Crude but effective was how one cop described the attack in the papers next day. The investigating officers said the muslin curtains had been the first to catch. They also said they had rarely seen domestic premises with so much flammable material.

The cops could find no motive for the attack. They also didn't know, as I did, that the assailants would have had no idea how vulnerable their target was to arson and therefore how effective their attack would be. In Georgi's terms, they just struck lucky.

The gas cylinder attached to the camping cooker Pete used for melting wax provided the first and most intense explosion. Paraffin wax melts at forty to seventy-one degrees Fahrenheit. At temperatures greater than that, it becomes as volatile as cooking oil. The almost tropical heat the city had been baking in that day didn't help. Nor did the gridlock that prevented the emergency services arriving within their target time.

Even so, the officers maintained, there should have been enough time to get out of the flat. The two bodies, burned beyond recognition, were found later that evening on the floor of the bedroom, entwined in each other's arms. One was identified as Peter Holloway, an agoraphobic candle maker and owner of the property. The other was a young woman. Which was the sum total of what they knew about her. They tried all the usual methods, but even dental records turned up a blank. In spite of newspaper and TV appeals, no one came forward to give any clues as to her identity.

I was the only person, apart from those who ordered her death, who knew who she was and had the photographic evidence to prove it, but I saw no point in telling the authorities. That strip of photos – taken at a time when she had been filled with both terror and hope – was all I had left of Tatiana. Gaia bought me a carved wooden box lined with red velvet. Inside I kept the photos together with the one of Des I'd salvaged from my flat, along with one of Pete's miniature candles and a lock of my own hair to symbolise my link with them all.

In the weeks following the fire, it became impossible for me not to focus on the scene inside the flat when the bottles flew through the open window and shattered on the floor, spilling their lethal contents. Would they have panicked, ripping down the blazing curtains and trying to smother the flames . . . ? At what point would the wax from the candles begin to melt? Before the cylinder exploded? How much time would they have had, before the smoke and flames had removed any possibility of escape?

I didn't want to think about the state Pete would have been in. I didn't want to, but I had no choice. Had Tatiana tried to persuade him to run out? Into the open, the blinding light, the swarms of people, the massive expanses of uncontained air. Pete wouldn't have been able to do it. But he would have tried to push her out, to force her to run down the stairs, to escape to the outside, to grab yet another chance . . . To choose life.

So why didn't she go? And how hard did she try to persuade him to leave with her? I can only speculate . . . She hadn't lived two decades, yet how much happiness had she known in those years? Brief glimpses, snatched away too soon. Maybe she felt this was just another manifestation of the same pattern. That real happiness, sustained security and contentment, were never going to be for her. Maybe she'd simply had enough and was tired. Maybe the quality of the life she would be fleeing to just wasn't good enough to justify the energy she would have to expend to get to it.

Or maybe she just loved Pete and couldn't bear to leave him. And thought death in his arms beneath the melting wax and heavy incense was the resolution she had sought and finally found.

In the end, everyone traded Tatiana. Just about every person she came into contact with, with the exception of Smokey Pete, used her in exchange for something they needed or desired.

I was no exception. It had never been my intention, of course. But the brutal fact remains that if Tatiana had never come into my life, I would still be living in Boddington Heights. I would still be lonely. I would still be searching for a way to be in this world. I would never have found Nirvana. For the first time in my life, I am part of a community, a family, a support network.

Tatiana gave me that. In exchange for her life, I gained a new one.

I knew it would take the rest of my life to come to terms with that. It's lucky I have close friends.

It's lucky I have Nirvana.

CIRCULATING STOCK

WD121616
23/8/07 WD8/08

21.2.09